X

11-17(3T)

OCT 6 2003

W9-AHQ-843

Sucker Bet

Sucker Bet

James Swain

LARGE PRINT

This large print edition published in 2003 by
RB Large Print
A division of Recorded Books
A Haights Cross Communications Company
270 Skipjack Road
Prince Frederick, MD 20678

First published by The Random House
Ballantine Publishing Group, 2003

Publisher's Cataloging In Publication Data
(Prepared by Donohue Group, Inc.)

Swain, James.
  Sucker bet / James Swain.

    p. ; cm.

  "A Tony Valentine Novel." – Cover.
  ISBN: 1–4025–6386–8

1. Valentine, Tony (Fictitious character)—Fiction. 2. Large type books. 3. Suspense
fiction. I. Title.

PS3569.W225 S83 2003d
813/.54

Typeset by Palimpsest Book Production Limited
Polmont, Stirlingshire, Scotland
Printed in the United States of America
by Bang Printing
3323 Oak Street
Brainerd, Minnesota 56401

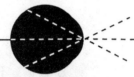

This Large Print Book carries the
Seal of Approval of N.A.V.H.

For Thomas Swain

Special thanks to Deborah Redmond,
Shawn Redmond, and my wife, Laura

It's morally wrong to allow
suckers to keep their money.
CANADA BILL JONES

THE TURN OF A CARD

The mark's name was Nigel Moon.

Jack Lightfoot recognized Moon the moment he stepped into the Micanopy Indian reservation casino. Back in the eighties, Moon had played drums for an English rock band called One-Eyed Pig, his ransacking of hotel rooms as well-publicized as his manic solos. Unlike the other band members, who'd fried their brains on drugs and booze, Moon had opened a chain of popular hamburger joints that now stretched across two continents.

As Moon crossed the casino, Jack eyed the delicious redhead on his arm. She was a plant, or what his partner Rico called a raggle. "The raggle will convince Moon to come to your casino," Rico had explained the day before, "and try his luck at blackjack. She'll bring him to your table. The rest is up to you."

She looked familiar. Jack frequented Fort Lauderdale's many adult clubs and often picked up free magazines filled with ads of local prostitutes. The raggle was a hooker named Candy Hart. Her ad said she was on call twenty-four hours a day, Visa and MasterCard accepted.

"Good evening," Jack said as they sat down at his empty table.

Moon reeked of beer. He was pushing fifty, unshaven, his gray hair pulled back in a pigtail like a matador's *coleta*. He removed a monster wad from his pocket and dropped it on the table. All hundreds.

"Table limit is ten dollars," Jack informed him.

Moon made a face. Candy touched Moon's arm.

"You can't bet more than ten dollars a hand," she said sweetly. "All of the table games have limits."

Moon drew back in his chair. "Ten bloody dollars? What kind of toilet have you brought me to, my dear? I can get a game of dominos with a bunch of old Jews on Miami Beach with higher stakes than that."

Candy dug her fingernails into Moon's arm. "You *promised* me, remember?"

"I did?"

"In the car."

Moon smiled wickedly. "Oh, yes. A moment of weakness, I suppose."

"Shhhh," she said, glancing Jack's way.

Moon patted her hand reassuringly. "A promise is a promise."

Moon slid five hundred dollars Jack's way. Jack cut up his chips. During a stretch in prison, Jack

2

heard One-Eyed Pig's music blasting through the cell block at all hours, and he knew many of the lyrics by heart.

Jack slid the chips across the table. Moon put ten dollars into each of the seven betting circles on the felt. Jack played a two-deck game, handheld. He shuffled the cards and offered them to be cut.

"Count them," Moon said.

"Excuse me?" Jack said.

"I want you to count the cards," Moon demanded.

Jack brought the pit boss over, and Moon repeated himself again.

"Okay," the pit boss said.

Jack started to count the cards onto the table.

"Faceup," Moon barked.

"Excuse me?" Jack said.

"You heard me."

Jack looked to the pit boss for help.

"Okay," the pit boss said.

Jack turned the two decks faceup. Then he counted them on the table.

"What are you doing?" Candy asked.

"Making sure they're all there," Moon said, watching intently. "I ran up against a dealer in Puerto Rico playing with a short deck and lost my bloody shirt."

Jack finished counting. One hundred and four cards. Satisfied, Moon leaned back into his chair.

"A short dick?" Candy said, giggling.

"Short *deck*. It's where the dealer purposely removes a number of high-valued cards. It gives the house an unbeatable edge."

"And you figured that out," she said.

"Yes, my dear, I figured it out."

Jack saw Candy's hand slip beneath the table and into Moon's lap. Moon's face lit up like a lantern. "You're *so smart*," she cooed.

Jack reshuffled the cards. For Moon to have figured out that a dealer was playing with a short deck meant that Moon was an experienced card-counter. Card-counters were instinctively observant, and Jack realized that he was going to have to be especially careful tonight, or risk blowing their scam before it ever got off the ground. He slid the two decks in front of Moon, who cut them with a plastic cut card.

"Good luck," Jack said.

Then he started to deal.

Jack Lightfoot was not your typical card mechanic.

Born on the Navajo Indian reservation in New Mexico, he'd been in trouble almost from the time he'd started walking. At seventeen, he'd gone to federal prison for a string of convenience store robberies and spent the next six years doing hard time.

The prison was filled with gangs. Jack had gravitated to a Mexican gang and hung out in their cell block. The Mexicans were heavy gamblers and often played cards all day long. They liked different games—seven-card stud, Omaha, razzle-dazzle, Texas hold 'em. Each game had its subtleties, but the game Jack fell in love with was blackjack. And whenever it was Jack's turn to deal, blackjack was the game he chose.

Dealing blackjack gave Jack an edge over the other players. He'd worked it out and figured it was slightly less than 2 percent. It was offset by the fact that if he lost a round, he had to pay off the other players, and that could be devastating to his bankroll. But if he won, the other players *had to pay him*. Blackjack was the game with the greatest risk but also the greatest reward.

One night, Jack had lain on his cot, thinking. He'd seen a lot of cheating among the Mexicans. They marked cards with shoe polish or palmed out a pair before a hand began. It occurred to him that if he was going to cheat, wouldn't blackjack be the game to do it in?

He thought about it for months. The Mexicans were suspicious guys, and manipulating the cards was out of the question. But instead of manipulating the cards, why not manipulate the other players into making bad decisions? Guys did it in poker all the time. It was called bluffing.

Why not blackjack?

One night, one of the Mexicans gave Jack a magic mushroom. Jack ate it, then went to bed. When he woke up a few hours later, he was screaming, his body temperature a hundred and six.

While Jack was strapped to a bed in the prison infirmary for two days, his brain turned itself inside out. When he finally came out of it, a single thought filled his head.

With the turn of a single card, he could change the odds at blackjack.

With the turn of a single card, he could force other players into making bad decisions.

With the turn of a single card, he could master a game that had no masters.

One card, that was all it took.

And all Jack had to do was turn it over.

He howled so hard, they kept him strapped to the bed for an extra day.

Nigel Moon's stack of chips soon resembled a small castle. A crowd of gaping tourists had assembled behind the table to watch the carnage. The Brit cast a disparaging look over his shoulder, like he was pissed off by all the attention.

"You've got groupies," Candy said.

Moon's eyes danced behind his sour expression. He sipped his martini, trying to act nonchalant. Candy stared at him dreamily.

"Congratulations, sir," Jack said, his lines committed to memory. "You just broke the house record."

Moon fished the olive out of his martini glass. "And what record is that, my good man?"

"No one has ever won eighty-four hands before," Jack informed him.

The Brit sat up stiffly, basking in the moment. "Is that how many I've won?"

"Eighty-four, yes, sir."

"And no one's ever done that before."

"Not in a row, no, sir."

"So I'm the champ?"

"Yes, sir, you're the champ."

Moon snapped his fingers, and a cocktail waitress came scurrying over.

"Drinks for everyone," he said benevolently.

The crowd gave him a round of applause. Candy brought her mouth up to Moon's ear and whispered something dirty. Moon's eyes danced with possibilities.

Jack gathered up the cards. He'd dealt winning hands to players before, and the transformation was always fun to watch. Weak men turned brave, the shy outspoken. It changed them, and it changed how others saw them. And all because of the *turn of a single card.*

"A question," Moon said.

Jack waited expectantly.

"Is there a limit on tipping?"

"Sir?"

"I know there's a limit on betting," Moon said. "Is there a limit on tipping?"

"Not that I'm aware of," Jack said.

Moon shoved half his winnings Jack's way. Standing, he leaned over the table and breathed his martini onto Jack's face. "Do something wicked tonight. On me."

"Yes, sir," Jack replied.

Jack's shift ended at midnight.

He changed out of his dealer's clothes into jeans and a sports shirt and drifted outside through the back door. Standing in the parking lot were his other dealer buddies. They were planning an excursion to the Cheetah in Fort Lauderdale to gape at naked college girls. Jack told them he had plans and begged off. His buddies got into their cars and left.

Jack lit a cigarette. A full moon had cast a creamy patina across the macadam. The casino backed onto a lake, and across its surface floated a dozen pairs of greenish eyes. The Micanopy reservation was in the Everglades, and alligators were always hanging around, eyeing you like a meal.

He smoked his cigarette down to a stub while thinking about the raggle. She had melted when Moon had started winning, and Jack had watched her leave the casino draped to his side. Was she falling for him? He sure hoped not.

A black limo pulled into the lot. Behind the wheel sat Rico's driver, a spooky Cuban guy named Splinters. The limo pulled up and the back door popped open. Rico Blanco sat in back, jabbering on his cell phone.

Jack got in.

"South Beach," Rico told his driver.

The limo glided out of the lot. Rico was a New Yorker and liked to boast that he was the only member of John Gotti's crime family currently not in jail. Tonight he wore a designer tux with a red bow tie and looked like a million bucks. Rico put his hand over the phone's mouthpiece. "I hear you were a star tonight."

"Who told you that?"

"Candy," Rico said. "She called me a little while ago."

"It went great."

"Let me ask you something. You think she's in love with him?"

Jack nodded.

"Damn hookers," Rico said. "They smell money, their brains melt. Every time I use one, know what I tell them?"

Jack had no idea what Rico told them. But Rico had a line for everybody, and if you hung around him long enough, you got to hear it. Jack opened the minibar and helped himself to a beer. "No, what do you tell them?"

"I tell them, honey, you know it's time to quit the business when you start coming with the customers. Think any of them listen?"

"No," Jack said.

"Fucking-a they don't," Rico said. Taking his hand away from the mouthpiece, he said, "Yeah, Victor, I'm still here. No, Victor, I'm not driving while I'm talking on the phone; I've got someone to drive for me." Rico looked at Jack and rolled his eyes. Victor was the senior partner in the operation and often treated Rico like a kid. "Yeah, Victor.

9

I'll see you tomorrow. Nine sharp. Brunch at the Breakers. Bye." He killed the power. "So where were we?"

"Hookers," Jack said.

"Speaking of which, I've got some girls lined up you're going to love."

"They like Indians?"

"They like who I tell them to like," Rico said. He took a Heineken out of a holder and clinked it against Jack's bottle. "To the best blackjack cheat in the world."

Only one road led back to civilization, and it was long and very dark. The limo jumped into the air as it hit a bump in the road, then bounced hard on the macadam.

"What the hell you doing?" Rico yelled.

"Sorry," Splinters said, not sounding sorry at all.

Jack looked at his shirt. Beer had jumped out of the bottle and soaked it. He swore under his breath. Rico laughed like it was the funniest thing he'd ever seen.

"Jack's all wet," Rico said with mock indignation. "Apologize."

"Sorry," Splinters said.

Jack swallowed hard. "No problem."

"You got a towel up there?" Rico said. "I got some on me, too, for Christ's sake."

A handkerchief flew into the backseat. Rico plucked it out of the air and balled it up. He pressed it against the wet spot on his knee, then leaned forward and pressed the handkerchief against Jack's shirt. Jack pulled back, and Rico's eyes grew wide. Then his hand turned into a rock-hard fist.

"You fucking bastard!" Rico roared.

At seven the next morning, Chief Running Bear, leader of the Micanopy nation, sat in his double-wide trailer a hundred yards behind the casino, staring at a pair of identical TV sets. Two hours earlier, a phone call had awoken him from a deep sleep, and now he rubbed his eyes tiredly while staring at the dueling images.

On one TV, a casino surveillance film showed an employee named Jack Lightfoot dealing blackjack. A player at Lightfoot's table had won eighty-four hands in a row, a feat that Running Bear knew was statistically impossible. The player had never touched the cards, ruling out sleight of hand. There was only one logical explanation: Lightfoot had rigged the game.

On the other TV, a second surveillance film showed Lightfoot standing in the casino parking lot, smoking a cigarette.

Before running the tapes, Running Bear had gone through Lightfoot's personnel file. He was a Navajo and had come to work for the Micanopys with a glowing reference from Bill Higgins, another Navajo, who happened to run the Nevada Gaming Control Board. Indians did not lie to other Indians, and Running Bear could remember Higgins's words as if it were yesterday.

"Jack won't let you down," Higgins had said.

Running Bear shook his head. Jack Lightfoot *had* let him down. He was a cheat, and a damn good one. Bill Higgins had once bragged to Running Bear that he knew every goddamned cheater in the country. So why hadn't he known about this one?

On the second TV a stretch limo appeared. Running Bear leaned forward to stare. The passenger door opened. Sitting in back was an Italian with wavy hair and a mustache. Running Bear found most white men identical, their faces as bland as pudding. Italians were particularly annoying. The men all wore mustaches, or snot-catchers as Indians called them. This one looked like a gangster.

Running Bear stopped the tapes. Sipping his coffee, he listened to the air conditioner outside his window. His casino had been ripped off by a dealer recommended by the most respected gaming official in the country. And that dealer was working with a mobster. *It doesn't get any worse than this*, he thought.

The door opened. The casino's head of security, Harry Smooth Stone, stepped in. He was out of breath.

"More problems," Smooth Stone said.

Running Bear pushed himself out of his chair. Thirty years wrestling alligators had put arthritis in every joint in his body, and he grimaced as his bones sang their painful song. Had he disgraced a dead ancestor recently and not realized it? There had to be some reason for this sudden spate of bad luck.

They drove Smooth Stone's Jeep across the casino parking lot. Jumping a concrete median, they went down a narrow dirt road through thick mangroves that led into the heart of the Everglades. For centuries, the Micanopys had lived in harmony with the alligators, panthers, and bears that called this land home, and had been rewarded in ways that few humans could appreciate.

Ten minutes later, Smooth Stone pulled into a clearing and parked beside a large pool of water. Running Bear knew the spot well; in the spring, alligators came here to mate and, later, raise their young. A half-dozen tribe members with fishing poles stood by the water's edge, looking scared.

Running Bear got out of the Jeep. The men stepped aside, revealing a body lying facedown in the water. It was a man, and he'd been shot once in the head. His left forearm had been chewed off, as had both his feet. Someone had hooked him by the collar. Running Bear said, "Flip him over."

The men obeyed. The dead man was covered with mud, and one of the men filled a bucket out of the lake and dumped it on his face. Running Bear knelt down, just to be sure.

Back in his trailer, Running Bear thumbed through the stack of business cards he kept in his desk. He had decided to dump Jack Lightfoot's body in nearby Broward County—the men in the limo had been white, so let white men deal with the crime—and Smooth Stone was on the phone making arrangements.

"Done," his head of security said, hanging up.

Running Bear found the card he was looking for and handed it to Smooth Stone. "Call this guy and hire him. Tell him everything, except our finding the body."

Smooth Stone stared at the card in his hand.

Grift Sense
International Gaming Consultant
Tony Valentine, President
(727) 591–5115

"He catches people who cheat casinos," Running Bear explained.

"You think he can help us?"

Running Bear heard the suspicion in Smooth Stone's voice. Bringing in an outsider was a risk, but it was a chance he had to take. Jack Lightfoot had cheated them. If word got out that his dealers were crooked, their business would dry up overnight. The casino was the reservation's main revenue source: It paid for health care, education, and a three-thousand-dollar monthly stipend to every adult. If it fell, so did his people.

"I heard him lecture at a gambling seminar," Running Bear said.

"Any good?"

Running Bear nodded. He'd learned more about

cheating listening to Tony Valentine for a few hours than he'd learned running a casino for ten years.

"The best," he said.

CHAPTER 1

"So what did you do before you got into this racket?" the security guard yelled into his ear.

"I was in the consulting business," Tony Valentine said.

"What field?"

"Casinos. I caught crossroaders."

They were standing in the aisle of the Orlando Arena, the seats filled with rabid wrestling fans. Up in the ring, Gladys LaFong was grappling with Valentine's girlfriend, a knockout named Kat Berman. Their stage names were Vixen and Judo Girl, and it was their act the fans had come to see. Valentine was just a prop, not that it particularly bothered him. Kat was going to be a star one day, and he did not mind standing in her shadow.

"Transvestites?" the guard asked.

"Hustlers who rip off casinos. That's what we call them."

"And you caught them?"

"All day long."

The women's choreographed mayhem had whipped the crowd into a frenzy. Gladys was losing and not being a good sport about it. Donny, her husband and manager, climbed through the ropes. Grabbing Kat by her hair, he yanked her clean off the canvas.

Valentine felt a tug on his sleeve. It was Zoe, Kat's smart-mouth twelve-year-old. Her eyes were ringed by black mascara, her lips a menacing brown. Did boys her age really get turned on by fright masks?

"Know what you look like?" Zoe asked.

"No."

"A giant banana."

His clothes were the job's only pitfall. As part of his contract with the promoter, he had to wear a neon yellow suit with padded shoulders that made him look like a comic-book character. Donny's suit was purple and made him look like a grape. Their audiences drank a lot of beer and needed constant reminding of who was who.

"Hey," Zoe said, "you're on!"

Valentine climbed through the ropes into the ring. Donny was bouncing Kat by the hair, and fake blood poured down her chin. After Valentine had lost his wife, he'd wondered if he'd ever be happy again. Then he'd met Kat during a job in Atlantic City. It wasn't a perfect relationship, but she made him feel good, and that was all he cared about these days. He tapped Donny on the shoulder.

"Let her go," he roared into the overhead mike.

"Get lost, old man," Donny roared back.

"*Yeah,*" someone in the crowd yelled, "*get lost, you old geezer!*"

Valentine wasn't getting lost. He twisted Donny's free arm behind his back, and Donny released Kat. She ran across the ring and jumped on Gladys, who'd been standing in the corner, egging the crowd on. The script now called for Valentine to flip Donny over his shoulder. It was a move they'd practiced a thousand times. The big man stomped his foot on the canvas, signaling he was ready to be thrown.

"Go easy, okay?" Donny mumbled.

"You bet," Valentine said.

The promoter was all smiles in the dressing room after the show. His name was Rick Honey, and he was a shaven-headed sanctimonious prick. Rick handed out their checks along with plane tickets to their next gig, a sold-out show in Memphis the following week. As Valentine peeked inside his envelope, Rick cast him a disapproving eye.

"What's the matter, Tony, you don't trust me?"

"You, I trust," Valentine said. "Not your accountant."

Zoe came into the dressing room. "For you," she said, and handed Valentine her mother's cell phone.

He took the call in the hall. Out of principle, he never left his cell phone on, and people were always tracking him down through Kat's.

"It's me," Mabel Struck, his neighbor, said.

Mabel was the other woman in his life. She ran his consulting business when he was out of town, which had been a lot lately. "I got a package earlier from a casino in South Africa. I just read the letter from the head of security and figured I'd better call you."

Valentine glanced at his watch. Tuesday night, nine-thirty, and Mabel was still working. "Can't it wait until tomorrow?"

"He's desperate."

"Mabel—"

"Tony, he sent you a check for five grand!"

"Certified?"

"Yes! I'm sorry, young man, but I grew up knowing the value of a dollar—"

"So did I."

"And I'm not about to let you walk away from a small fortune, so listen up."

Valentine was standing in a tunnel, the manufactured air cool on his face, and he shut his eyes while Mabel read the letter to him. The casino was called Jungle Kingdom, and the head of security spelled out the situation pretty clearly. The casino's blackjack tables were bleeding money, and the casino suspected a high-rolling customer was ripping them off. The problem was, the casino didn't have any proof and couldn't have the man apprehended without fear of a lawsuit.

"We have watched the man play for a hundred hours," Mabel read from the letter. "He plays with different dealers, which rules out collusion. We

19

are also convinced that he is not card-counting. Sometimes, it appears he is reading the backs of the cards. We have examined the cards, and they appear absolutely clean. I have enclosed four decks for your inspection. Your help in this matter is most appreciated. Sincerely, Jacques Dugay."

"Jacques Dugay? He worked in Atlantic City once."

"Were you friends?"

"No, he's a jerk. Go into my study and turn on the black light next to my desk."

"I'm in your study," his neighbor said. "There, the light's on."

"Place one of the decks under the light."

"Okay. Oh, my. The cards lit up like a Christmas tree. Even I can read them, and I can hardly see. All right, how did you know that?"

"I did some work for a casino in South Africa last year. I noticed that they were using playing cards manufactured in the next town. It struck me as really stupid, so I told the management. They said they did it to save money."

"You're saying the cheats went into the playing card factory and marked all the decks that went to the Jungle Kingdom?"

"Yes. The cards are called luminous readers. The cheat marks them in the factory before they're shipped. Cards treated with luminous paint can be read with special glasses or with tinted contact lenses, but not with the naked eye."

"How do you know the cheater isn't marking

20

the cards at home, then having an employee bring them in?"

Mabel had been running his business for two months and already sounded like a pro. He explained how he'd reached his conclusion. "That employee would have to be a dealer or a pit boss. It's a risky play, especially with the eye-in-the-sky. The safest way to get marked cards into a casino is by going to the plant and marking them there."

Valentine felt a tug on his sleeve.

"The cake is melting," Zoe said.

He cupped his hand over the mouthpiece. "You got a cake?"

"Chocolate ice cream. From Carvel."

He took his hand away from the phone. "Mabel, I've got to beat it."

"You still enjoying being a wrestler?" his neighbor asked.

"It's a blast," he said.

Zoe's cake had started to sag, the inscription MEAN GIRLS RULE running down one side. Donny was holding an empty plate, waiting for Valentine to take a slice before going for seconds. Donny's career as a pro football player had been cut short by injury, and he was the humblest guy Valentine had ever known. Kat and Gladys ate their cake leaning against the wall, looking bushed but happy.

Valentine found a chair and dug in. For him, the wrestling had been a welcome relief. He'd opened his consulting business to give himself something to do after Lois had died, having no idea of what he was in for. Back in '78, when he'd started policing Atlantic City's casinos, two states in the country had legalized gambling. Now there were thirty-eight, plus casinos on three hundred Indian reservations. Every one had been ripped off at least once, usually for huge sums. Most never knew it. Those that did, called him.

Which was why he enjoyed the wrestling. No pressure, no worries, his role a minor one. Best described, his life was a breeze, and when the dressing room door opened a minute later, he wasn't ready to have it end. Especially by the handsome guy who waltzed in carrying a bouquet of flowers.

"Daddy!" Zoe yelled.

She rushed across the dressing room and hugged her father. As he tousled her hair, she let out a joyous squeal, and Valentine felt something drop in his stomach. In the six weeks he'd known Zoe, the best he'd done was a lame high five. Donny and Gladys tossed their plates in the trash and left.

"Hey, Ralph," Kat said.

"Hey, beautiful," her ex-husband said. "That was some show."

"Didn't know you liked wrestling."

"No? I think I mentioned in one of my letters that I did."

Valentine blinked. Ralph had deserted Kat and Zoe two years ago. Except for the monthly checks, Kat had said there had been no contact. Ralph crossed the room and handed Kat the flowers.

"Congratulations on your newfound fame."

Zoe was hanging on to both her parents, a smile illuminating her face. It was as happy as a Norman Rockwell painting, and as Valentine pushed himself out of his chair, he caught his reflection in the dressing room mirror. The only thing out of place was the clown in the yellow suit. Kat followed him into the hall.

"I'm sorry I didn't tell you," she said.

"How many?" he asked.

"Four or five. We also talked a few times."

The cop in him wanted to grill her. Had they chatted when Valentine was sleeping, or doing errands with Zoe? "You should have told me," he said.

"I was afraid you'd leave."

"Should I?"

Her lower lip trembled. "Damn it, Tony. Zoe asks about him. If my being nice to Ralph means he'll be nice to Zoe, then I'll do it."

"How nice?" he said without thinking.

Kat slapped his face. Hard. Valentine stepped back, fearful of falling into the chasm that had opened between them.

"You want me to leave?" he asked.

"I want you to stop acting this way," she said.

He took his car keys from his pocket. "You

23

shouldn't have lied to me," he said. Then he walked away.

Ralph was eating the last slice of cake. Kat pulled up a chair, her head spinning. Tony had never been divorced and didn't understand that you could hate someone, yet still care for them deep down. Although their marriage had ended ugly, with Ralph getting loaded and her dialing 911, there had been some bright spots.

Ralph took some quarters from his pocket and handed them to their daughter.

"Go buy your daddy a soda pop, okay?"

Zoe skipped out of the room, her feet barely touching the floor.

"So how do you like selling cars?" Kat asked.

Ralph undid the button on his jacket. His belly fell out, as round as a party balloon. "I quit last week."

"What happened?"

He snorted contemptuously. "A man can't soar with eagles when he has to wallow with pigs."

It was Ralph's favorite line. He'd used it after he'd quit as a bartender, fast-food restaurant manager, real estate salesman, and stockbroker. He removed some legal papers from his jacket and handed them to her. Kat read the first page, then looked up in disbelief. "What the hell is this?"

"I'm cutting off my alimony payments. You're making a good buck, and I'm not. My lawyer said you won't have a snowball's chance in hell if you take me to court." He took out a Bic and handed it to her. "So, if you'll do me the pleasure of signing the last page."

"Is this why you wanted to see me and Zoe?"

"It wasn't the only reason."

"This is so low."

He shrugged. "Happens every day in America."

"What am I going to tell Zoe?"

He shrugged again. "I really don't like the makeup, if you want to know the truth."

Kat felt something inside of her snap. Zoe had appeared in the doorway, a Mountain Dew dangling in her hand. Her mother ushered her into the hallway.

"Go get in the car," Kat said.

Zoe glanced into the dressing room. Her father held a handful of legal-looking papers in one hand, a cheap pen in the other. *Shit*, she thought.

"Is something wrong?"

"Just do as I say," her mother said.

Zoe came out of the underground tunnel to the parking lot behind the Arena just in time to see Tony's '92 Honda Accord pull out of its spot and drive away.

"Hey, Tony!"

She waved to him, hoping he'd stop, only he didn't. God, how she hated Tony's car. It was old and plain and had so many miles on it that the odometer had stopped. Tony had the money to buy something sexy—like a Mercedes or a Lexus—but he wouldn't take the plunge. Zoe hated him for that. She and her mother deserved better than a smelly '92 Honda.

Zoe watched him drive to the lot's exit. His window came down, and he tossed something out. Then the car crossed the street and climbed the ramp to Interstate 4. Tony was a geezer, but he could be a lot of fun sometimes. Especially when hokey magicians were on TV. They never fooled him.

Walking over, she picked up the small box he'd tossed from his car. It was a gift, the wrapping paper bruised and torn. Standing beneath a bright halogen light, she tore away the paper and opened the lid. A cry escaped her lips as she stared at Tony's gift to her mother.

It was so beautiful, she thought.

CHAPTER 2

Palm Harbor sat north of St. Petersburg, on Florida's laid-back west coast. Back when Valentine and his late wife had considered retiring there, there were five thousand residents. Sleepy and small, it had seemed like another world compared to bustling Atlantic City.

Fifteen years later, the residents numbered fifty thousand, the town's quaintness run over by a developer's bulldozer. Every day, the roads got more clogged, the public schools got more over-crowded, and the drinking water tasted a little less like drinking water.

Winter was particularly gruesome. The restaurants were asses-to-elbows with rude northerners, as were the beaches and malls. Valentine had been a rude northerner once, but had shed that skin soon after arriving. Palm Harbor's lazy cadence suited him just fine, and he looked forward to the sweltering summers, when the snowbirds flew home.

He sat on his screened front porch and read the paper. The stock market had been flip-flopping, and he checked his mutual funds. As a cop, he'd never made much money. Now, in retirement, he had more than he knew what to do with.

Mabel came up his front walk, wearing canary yellow slacks and a blue blouse, her hands clutching a Tupperware container. He rose expectantly from his rocker.

"Good morning," he said. "How you doing?"

"Who cares?" she replied.

Florida's elderly took grim delight in discussing their ailments, their deterioration becoming monumental epics of collapse and decay. Mabel was having none of it. *Who cares?* summed up her attitude nicely.

"You up for breakfast?" she asked.

"Sure."

They went inside. Mabel had been bringing him meals since Lois had died, nothing fancy, always hot and good. He set two places at the kitchen table, then fixed a pot of coffee while she stuck the container of scrambled eggs, sausage, and home fries in the microwave. The phone rang and he answered it.

"Go to hell," he said, then hung up.

"Tony, that's rude," Mabel said.

"It was a salesman."

"Salesperson."

"This one was a guy."

"You're being obtuse."

"I'm sick of the intrusions. I don't want to change my long-distance carrier, get my carpets

28

cleaned, or buy penny stocks. If I'm abusive long enough, they'll go away."

Mabel doled out the steaming food. Valentine sprinkled everything with Tabasco sauce and dug in. He was big on sauces, and guessed it came from years of eating crummy diner food.

"You going to tell me about it?" Mabel asked when they were done.

"What's that?"

"What happened between you and Kat. I may be losing my vision, but I'm not *blind*."

He cleaned his plate with a biscuit while giving her the *Reader's Digest* version of the scene in the dressing room. "I drove home realizing what a horse's ass I've been the past two months, dressing up in that ridiculous suit. I'm sorry you had to watch."

Mabel reached across the table and touched his wrist. "Did you call her?"

"I left a message on her cell phone and at her hotel."

"She didn't call back?"

"No."

"What about the diamond pin you bought for her at Avant Gold?"

"What about it?"

"Did you give it to her?"

"I threw it out of the window of my car."

"Oh, Tony . . ."

"Zoe picked it up."

"Do you think she gave it to her mother?"

No, she probably pierced her navel with it, he thought. "I hope so," he said.

"What are you going to do?"

"Get on with my life, I suppose."

They heard a car pull up the driveway, and Mabel went to the front door. She returned with a thick Federal Express envelope. "It's from Jacques. You remember. He sent the five-thousand-dollar check. Luminous readers."

"Right. The jerk from South Africa."

"Tony, that's no way to talk about a client."

"You're right. Open up the envelope. Maybe there's more money."

She did, and to both their surprise, there was. Another check, this one for two grand, his usual fee. Inside the envelope was a leather pouch filled with casino dice and a note. Mabel read aloud. "Dear Tony Valentine. I realize you are a busy man, but I need your help again. We have arrested the gambler for marking the cards, and he gave a full confession. He was once an employee, and has offered to turn in another employee, who he claims is stealing more money than he was.

"The gambler says the scam is happening at our craps tables, but won't say who is involved. Last week, we lost five hundred thousand dollars at craps, so the gambler may be telling the truth. I have sent several dice, in the hopes you will examine them. Sincerely, Jacques Dugay." Mabel looked up. "Wow, a half-million bucks."

"Wow is right."

"You think he got ripped off?"

"You bet. What a dope."

Mabel waved the check in front of his face. "A dope with money."

He heard it in her voice. *Take the job, even if you are in a lousy mood.* Mabel had been raised in the same era as him: tail end of the Depression. Money wasn't their god, but walking away from it was something you just didn't do.

"Okay," he said.

In early 1981, a pewter canister had been found by scavengers in the muddy banks of the Thames near London Bridge. Instead of coins or jewelry, the canister had contained twenty-four ornate dice dating back five hundred years. Close examination of the dice had revealed that eighteen were loaded with quicksilver, while the remaining six were misspotted, and marked only with three numbers on each die.

During the same year, a team of archaeologists on a dig in Pompeii had found similar gaffed dice, only their heritage was several thousand years earlier.

Valentine had heard about both discoveries and hadn't been terribly surprised. While there were hundreds of different ways to cheat at cards, there were only three surefire ways to cheat at dice: loading them, misspotting them, or shaving them.

Sitting at his desk, he used a micrometer to measure the dice Jacques had sent him. Each was a perfect one-inch square. Had one of the sides been short—even by as little as fifteen one-hundredths of an inch—the die would have favored certain combinations and destroyed the house edge.

Then he checked each with a calibrator. In the old days, dice were dropped in a glass of water to see if they were loaded. The calibrator was a little more scientific. He spun each die on its axis. To his surprise, they were clean.

He rolled them across his desk. The fact that they were normal didn't mean that crooked dice weren't being used. The cheater, or cheaters, might be switching crooked dice in and out of the game, without anyone being the wiser.

"So call him up," Mabel said when he returned to the kitchen.

He sat at the kitchen table. "I don't want to."

She split the last of the coffee between two mugs and sat down.

"But he's desperate."

"They usually are when they're losing money."

"Tony . . ."

He sipped his coffee. "The guy's such a jerk."

"How do you know him?"

"He ran one of Trump's joints in Atlantic City for about sixty minutes. Everybody hated his guts."

"Would you like me to call him?"

Mabel was great at finding solutions. It would be fun to let Jacques think that he didn't rate an audience with the boss. "Sure," he said.

Jacques's phone number was in the letter. Mabel dialed it and awoke him from a deep sleep. She stuck her hand over the mouthpiece. "He's cursing in French."

"Tell him French wine tastes like urine and hang up."

She waved him off. To Jacques she said, "We just received your Federal Express package. Tony examined the dice—"

"Zee dice," Valentine corrected.

"—and found nothing wrong with them. He believes the cheater must have switched out the crooked dice for clean ones." Mabel listened for a minute, then stuck her hand over the mouthpiece. "Jacques says that the casino searches its employees before their shift starts and after it's over. That way, the dealers can't bring crooked dice in or take them out."

"Ask Jacques where the craps dealers go on their break."

She asked. "To the employee lounge."

"Are there lockers where they change into their uniforms?"

She asked. "Jacques said yes."

"Tell Jacques one of his dealers is taking normal dice to the lounge and altering them. He needs to search the dealers' lockers and be on the lookout for the following items. Ready?"

"Ready."

"A file, a drill, a vise, a burr for hollowing, celluloid rope, fast-drying cement, ink, a bottle of mercury, some kind of polishing compound, and sandpaper. If any of those items turn up, that's their man."

Mabel relayed it all to Jacques. When she hung up, she was smiling. She wasn't a beautiful woman, but when she found reason to smile, Valentine didn't think there was a prettier face on the planet. "Jacques says you are a genius," she said.

"He's still a pain in the ass," Valentine replied.

He spent the morning sifting through his mail. Over a dozen casino surveillance videotapes of suspected cheaters sat on his desk. Beside them was a stack of mail-order catalogues that had come addressed to U. R. Dead, and he guessed someone he'd put in prison had decided to get creative.

For a while he pushed papers around his desk. Three times the business line on his phone lit up. Mabel was still in the kitchen, and he heard her answer each call. Yesterday he'd been on top of the world. Now, he felt like he'd stepped off a cliff and was falling through space. Going to the kitchen, he found her working on the *St. Petersburg Times* crossword puzzle and pulled up a chair.

"I'm stumped," she said. "The clue reads 'Floored Ali.' The answer is six letters. I was going to write Foreman, only it doesn't fit. George Foreman floored Ali, didn't he?"

"No. Ali floored Foreman."

"Frazier. Joe Frazier floored Ali."

"He sure did. But his name's got seven letters."

34

Mabel frowned. "Then who is it?"

"Wepner," Valentine said.

"I beg your pardon?"

"A strapping can of Ragu named Chuck Wepner. One of the worst fighters to ever grace the heavyweight ranks. He floored Ali."

"Where, in a bar?"

"No, in the ring. Chuck was from Bayonne. Ali fought him because he thought Chuck was a patsy. Chuck was lousy, but he was nobody's water boy. In one of the later rounds, Chuck stepped on Ali's foot. Ali was going backwards and lost his balance. Chuck popped him, and Ali went down. Ali got up and tortured Chuck, opened a million cuts on his face."

"A Jersey boy," Mabel said.

"A Jersey hero," he corrected.

She put the paper aside, then read from a message pad beside the phone. "Your son called from Puerto Rico to say he and Yolanda are loving every minute of their honeymoon. He asked if you were still mad at him, and I said I thought you'd gotten over having to pay for his wedding *and* his honeymoon."

Valentine bristled. "He hit me up for five grand on his wedding night. He knows damn well—"

Mabel touched his wrist. "Tony, stop obsessing over it. You have more money than you know what to do with. Your boy's trying to get his life straightened out."

"That's right. He's *trying*."

"You make that sound like an ugly word."

"He's thirty-five years old. When's he going to start *doing*?"

Mabel had two grown children and had accepted long ago that she couldn't control their lives. She glanced down at her pad. "The second message was from Bill Higgins of the Nevada Gaming Control Board. He said he needed your help on a case."

"I'm not going to Nevada."

"You are in one foul mood, young man."

"Every time a casino gets scammed, I get a distress call. You think these morons would consider having me check their joints out *before* they get ripped off? Fat chance."

"I thought Bill was a friend."

"I'm not going to run every time he calls, friend or not."

There were days when she couldn't win with him. Her eyes returned to her pad. "The third message was from Harry Smooth Stone at the Micanopy Indian reservation casino. He called yesterday, as well. He sounds desperate."

"Too bad," Valentine said.

A person could take just so much abuse. Mabel said goodbye, and Valentine walked her to the sidewalk in front of his house.

"You are such a bear," she said.

"I'm sorry. I don't mean to take it out on you."

"Are you going to sit around, waiting for her to call?"

It sounded pitiful, and he said, "What are you suggesting?"

"Go help Bill Higgins, or Harry Smooth Stone. Take your mind off your problems for a few days."

He didn't want to go to Vegas. Too much time coming and going. The Micanopy reservation casino was in south Florida, and a leisurely four-hour drive. Down today, back tomorrow. Maybe Mabel was right. A change of scenery would do him good.

"I'll think about it," he said.

CHAPTER 3

O n paper, it had seemed like a great idea.
The town of Davie sat fifteen miles due
west of Fort Lauderdale. A carnival had
arrived the day before, and sat in the middle of an
empty cow pasture, the Ferris wheel and brightly
colored tents visible for miles.

Rico's idea was this: Candy would talk Nigel
Moon into taking her to the carnival. Then she'd
get Moon to play a few games, like throw the balls
in the milk can, and cover the spot. Rico knew
these games were rigged and could be juiced to
let the players win or lose. All he had to do was
bribe the carnival owner, and the Moon's "lucky"
streak would be alive and well.

Only Rico hadn't counted on the carnival
owner's stubbornness. He was a Cajun named
Ray Hicks, and he wore suspenders and a porkpie
hat. Rico cornered him outside Hicks's trailer, a
beat-up rig with patched tires and a wheezing air
conditioner, and stuck a C note in the old flattie's
face. Hicks looked at the money, then scoffed.

"Get away from me with that chicken scratch,
boy."

Rico upped his offer. He'd worked with carnival people back in Brooklyn when he was under John Gotti's thumb. The carnival would rent a church parking lot and set up shop. For this privilege, the carnival paid Gotti half the apron, or daily take. Rico's job had been to collect the apron and make sure Gotti didn't get shortchanged.

Hicks spit on the ground. "You're dreamin', boy."

On the other side of the carnival, Moon and Candy were riding the Ferris wheel. Candy wore a flaming red pants suit; Moon, Bermuda shorts and a polo shirt.

"I'm just asking you to let this guy win a couple of stinking Kewpie dolls," Rico said, imagining himself strangling Hicks until his face turned purple. "It will take twenty minutes, tops. Then I'll be out of your hair. Come on, what do you say?"

The sun came out and splashed on Hicks's shoulders. He looked older than Rico had first thought, his face a chiseled road map of the hard life. He hooked his thumbs into his suspenders and snapped them against his chest.

"You wanna talk money, boy?"

Sweat marched down Rico's face. Davie being away from the ocean, the sun was hotter than over on Miami Beach, and he felt himself burning up.

"Sure," he said.

The first thing Rico noticed when he stepped inside Ray Hicks's trailer was the overwhelming stench of shit. Not just any old shit, but animal shit, like at the zoo. The kind of smell that could burn a hole in your head.

The next thing Rico noticed was the big black metal cage sitting behind Hicks's desk. And the chimpanzee in human clothes inside the cage. A big sucker, maybe 150 pounds, his thumbless paws strumming a ukulele.

"Have a seat," Hicks said.

Rico sat in a folding chair directly across from Hicks's desk. Plastered on the walls were black-and-white posters of the musical chimp and his proud owner. NAME ANY POPULAR TUNE, the posters said. THEN WATCH THE FUN!

"Say hello to Mr. Beauregard," Hicks said.

"Hey," Rico said stupidly.

Mr. Beauregard strummed away. The tinny music coming out of his dime-store instrument sounded familiar. *Happy Days Are Here Again.* The chimp made eye contact, and every hair on Rico's body went stiff. Behind the chimp's muddy brown eyes lurked something eerily human. Putting the ukelele down, he took a pack of Lucky Strikes from the floor of his cage and fired one up.

"You let him smoke?"

"Sure."

"Isn't it bad for his health?" Rico said.

"He likes it."

"I get it. He's already got a purple ass, so what's a couple of black lungs."

Hicks's eyes grew into slits. "You're not funny."

Rico disagreed. He happened to think he was fucking hysterical. So had John Gotti, who'd nicknamed him the Mook, which in Italian loosely translated into *big mouth*. He watched Mr. Beauregard crush out his cigarette, then eat it.

"What kind of scam you got going?" Hicks said.

Rico shifted his gaze to his host. "Huh?"

"You heard me. You fleecing this guy?"

"What guy?"

"The bloated Brit with the hooker."

"What I've got going is none of your fucking business."

"Please don't swear in my presence," the carnival owner said.

Rico didn't like the direction the conversation was going. He parted his jacket and exposed the .45 Smith & Wesson strapped to his side. It was his favorite piece, a present from the Teflon Don on Rico's twenty-fifth birthday. Hicks made a face like he'd busted a tooth. Raising his voice, he said, *"Mr. Beauregard, he has a gun!"*

Mr. Beauregard flew out of his cage. It had never occurred to Rico that the cage wasn't locked, and he sat helplessly as the chimp pinned him to his chair and pawed through his linen sports jacket. Mr. Beauregard slid the .45 across the desk along with Rico's wallet.

"Thank you, Mr. Beauregard. You may resume your playing."

Soon strains of *Rocky Mountain High* were

41

competing with the noisy air conditioner. Hicks removed a business card from Rico's wallet and stared at it.

"Club Hedo. That a tittie bar?"

"Yeah," Rico said.

Hicks unloaded the gun and slid it back along with his wallet. "You are scamming the man with the hooker. Correct?"

"Uh-huh."

"And by allowing him to win a few harmless games, you will be able to perpetuate your little charade."

"Right again," Rico said.

"Four thousand two hundred dollars," Hicks said.

"Huh?"

"Four thousand two hundred dollars. That is my price."

Rico screwed up his face. "What kind of number is that?"

Hicks made a clucking sound with his tongue. "Call it a permission fee. Four thousand two hundred dollars is what I pay the town clowns to run my carnival."

"The what?"

"You're not familiar with the term?"

"No."

Hicks turned in his chair. "Town clowns, Mr. Beauregard?"

Mr. Beauregard's crooked fingers froze on the strings of his beloved instrument. He picked up a tin sheriff's badge from the floor of the cage and clipped it to his shirt. Striking a he-man pose, he pounded his chest.

"Thank you, Mr. Beauregard."

The cops. Rico should have known. Organized crime had never gotten a strong foothold in south Florida, and for one simple reason. The local cops were too crooked to be influenced by the mob.

"Forty-two hundred it is," Rico said.

Rico sat in his limo, staring through binoculars at Moon and Candy. They were standing at the Six-Cat booth. Knock three stuffed cats off a shelf, win a prize. It looked easy, only no one ever won. The operator made sure of that. By stepping on a foot break, he moved a loose board behind the cats back a few inches. By widening the shelf, the cats would not fall no matter how hard they were hit.

Rico watched Moon throw the baseballs. One, two, three cats fell in a row. By not touching the foot brake, the operator had given Moon a fair game. Candy squealed as the operator handed her a giant panda bear. She already had a Kewpie doll and a Big Bird, and looked like she'd robbed a toy store. The operator caught Moon's eye and winked.

Rico loved it. Carnival people were great at building up suckers. He folded up his binoculars and put them on the seat.

"Forty-two hundred is too much," Splinters said, sitting behind the wheel.

43

"I got what I wanted," Rico said. "Moon's having a gas."

"Two grand, maybe," Splinters said.

"You think so?"

"Yeah," his Cuban driver said. "Two grand, tops."

"Don't worry about it."

"Fucking guy robbed you."

There it was again: the refusal to let things go. It was starting to get on Rico's nerves. Splinters was not your ordinary Cuban refugee. He was sensitive about things like honor and a man's reputation. Once, in South Beach, Rico had seen him carve up a guy just because he had found Splinters's name funny.

"Fugettaboutit, will you?"

"Ahhh," his driver said.

Splinters just didn't understand how business was done in America. Hicks had given him good value on his dollar. Rico had no gripe with him.

Soon they were speeding south on 1–95, and Splinters was blowing monster clouds of smoke out his window, obviously pissed off. That was the problem with Cubans, Rico had decided. They thought you cared how they felt.

Splinters needed to get over it, or Rico would have to get rid of him.

CHAPTER 4

Valentine ate lunch, then called Smooth Stone and took the job. Smooth Stone sounded relieved. He explained to Valentine how a blackjack dealer named Jack Lightfoot had rigged a game and dealt a player eighty-four winning hands in a row. Smooth Stone wasn't above admitting that he had no idea what had gone down.

"What was he trying to do, get into the *Guinness Book of World Records*?"

"It was damn stupid," Smooth Stone said.

"How much did he take you for?"

"Eight hundred and forty dollars. We have a ten-dollar limit on blackjack."

"You have problems with this Lightfoot character before?"

"No, but he's new."

Valentine found none of this surprising. Indian hustlers had been popping up all over the country. Because Indian casinos were not regulated by government agencies, many of these dealers were exceedingly bold. Valentine had heard plenty of stories, but dealing eighty-four winning hands was a record. The Micanopys needed to address it before another dealer "in the know" tried to rip them off again. He got instructions to the reservation, then set a time to meet Smooth Stone. They agreed on seven that night.

Taking his suitcase to his car, Valentine remembered something. Florida law limited the Micanopys to running Class II games, like bingo and slot machines. Table games like blackjack were forbidden, which meant the Micanopys were breaking the law.

Again.

Eight weeks earlier, Florida's baby-faced governor had sent shotgun-toting federal agents onto the Micanopy reservation with orders to remove a hundred video poker machines. While not a table game, video poker fell into a gray area in terms of classification. "*Video poker must go!*" the governor had declared from the steps of his mansion in Tallahassee.

Eventually, the Micanopys won out, and the federal agents left. Like every other Indian tribe, the Micanopys were a sovereign nation. The governor had violated that sovereignty, and Valentine guessed that had spurred the Micanopys to put in blackjack tables, just to rub his face in it.

He went to Mabel's house to say good-bye. When she wasn't working for him, his neighbor wrote inspired classifieds for the local papers. He found her composing on her front porch and pulled up a chair. She handed him her notepad.

"It's going to run in the Help Wanted section," she said.

Taking out his bifocals, Valentine read the meticulously printed page.

Adult Enhancement Center seeks hostesses to model, massage, and wear Victoria's Secret undergarments. Must be familiar with all aspects of Kama-sutra. English not required. Hours as flexible as you are. Fax résumé and pictures to (727) 981–1405.

"Whose fax number?"

"The police department's," she said. "I figured I'm doing them a favor."

"Mabel, you can't do that."

"This town is filled with sleaze, Tony. Strip joints, lap dances, massage parlors, hookers trolling on Alternate 19, warming their cans in every hotel bar. It's disgusting."

"You still can't print the police department's fax number."

"Spoilsport."

"By the way, I took the job with the Micanopys."

She hesitated. "I guess you didn't hear from Kat."

"No."

Together, they walked down her front path. If his situation had one silver lining, it was that Mabel had shown little resentment toward his romance with Kat. She'd stuck by him, and now that his head had started to clear, he realized how difficult it must have been for her to watch him behave so foolishly. He kissed his neighbor on the cheek, then walked back to his house and climbed into his Honda.

He crossed the Sunshine Skyway forty minutes later, the ocean shimmering like a sea of brand-new coins. Interstate 275 took him to 75, and he headed south and put his foot to the floor. If there was one thing he liked about the folks on Florida's west coast, it was the speed at which they drove, and he did eighty for the next hundred miles.

In Fort Myers he got off and filled the tank. Buying a bottled water, he got behind the wheel and powered up his cell phone. A blinking light indicated the phone's battery was nearly dead. He considered cell phones one of the greatest intrusions in recent memory, and he thought how wonderful it would be to toss it out the window. A great idea, only it wasn't practical. In the casino business, the store never closed. If he wanted his consulting to stay alive, he needed to be able to retrieve messages. He plugged the phone's jack into his cigarette lighter, and the tiny green light came on.

A half hour later, he was sitting in line at a toll booth, waiting to get on Alligator Alley. The Alley bisected the lower half of the Everglades and was one of the last pristine roads in Florida. No strip centers or rows of ugly tract houses; just one rest stop and a gas station for eighty miles. Paying the toll, he slipped a collection of Sinatra's greatest hits into his tape deck and turned on the cruise control.

Singing a duet with Old Blue Eyes, he spotted a tour bus parked on the grassy shoulder and pulled over.

A group of Asians was huddled up to a chain-link fence. He got out and joined them. Down in the swamp, an alligator covered in duckweed was sunning itself. He'd read that Florida was one of the few places in North America where dinosaurs had flourished, and he guessed that alligators were the leftovers.

A tourist said something. Valentine turned, thinking the man wanted him to snap a picture. The man pointed at his car. His cell phone was ringing. Getting in, Valentine looked at the phone's face. It was Bill Higgins, the director of the Nevada Gaming Control Board.

"Hey, Bill," he said.

"Did you get my message?"

"Yeah. Sorry I didn't call you back, but I've been in a bad way."

"That's what the lady who answers your phone said. Feeling any better?"

"A little," Valentine admitted.

"Remember those roulette cheats you helped me

49

bust? They were convicted this morning. They got three years, counting the time they've already done. And they have to give the money back."

"Nice going."

"Couldn't have done it without you."

It had been one of Valentine's better busts. The cheaters, all Venice Beach bodybuilders, had come up with a unique scam. By pressing on the railing of the table on which the roulette wheel sat, they had used their combined strength to bend the table and cause the wheel to become biased. The bodybuilders' girlfriends had then bet a particular group of numbers, called a chevron, and taken the casino for a ride during several visits. Higgins had been unable to make the scam, and had flown Valentine in. He had nailed them by discreetly placing a carpenter's level on the table just as they had started to do their thing.

"I need your help," Higgins said.

"Something wrong?"

"There sure is," his friend said.

Valentine drove to a rest stop and parked his car. Inside, he purchased a soda from a vending machine. Sitting on a picnic bench in the shade, he called Higgins back.

"I'm in a real bind," Higgins said. "A blackjack dealer I recommended for a job at the Micanopy Indian reservation casino has disappeared. I've known this kid a long time, and I'm worried about him."

"And you'd like me to pop down there and see what I can do," Valentine said.

"I sure would."

"What's his name?"

"Jack Lightfoot."

Valentine felt the cold from his drink shoot straight into his head. Harry Smooth Stone hadn't mentioned that Jack Lightfoot was missing. Normally, casinos didn't like it when their personnel went AWOL, and got downright panicky when their dealers started disappearing. Yet Smooth Stone had said nothing.

"You say you know this kid?"

"That's right."

"He involved in anything? You know, like drugs."

"Not that I'm aware of."

"What are the people at the casino saying?"

"Head of security is a guy named Harry Smooth Stone. The Micanopys aren't the most communicative bunch. Harry isn't saying much of anything."

Valentine finished his drink and tossed it into a trash receptacle. Jack Lightfoot didn't sound like the kind of kid who would become a cheater, yet Harry Smooth Stone had said a player at Lightfoot's table had won eighty-four hands in a row. Something wasn't adding up. "Maybe I should pay the Micanopys a visit," he said.

"You don't mind?"

"For you? Never."

Higgins thanked him. He was not prone to dramatics, and Valentine was surprised when Higgins offered to get him a comped suite at the Bellagio the next time he was in Las Vegas.

"Sounds great," Valentine said.

CHAPTER 5

Valentine got back on the Alley. A sign said, MICANOPY CASINO, 20 MILES. He'd told Smooth Stone he'd meet him at seven. Which gave him plenty of time to sniff around the casino unobserved.

The best way to walk around a casino was as a tourist. Tourists were considered suckers by casino people and rarely aroused suspicion. Only, looking like a tourist wasn't easy. People were always pegging him for a cop, which he supposed had something to do with his penchant for black sports jackets and thick-soled shoes. It was his persona, retired or not.

He came to the Alley's only gas station. It contained a small convenience store, and he was soon inspecting a rack of cheap clothes. A gaudy floral shirt and floppy hat set him back fourteen bucks. He changed in a lavatory stall, then appraised himself in a mirror. He looked like a schmuck. Great.

At six he pulled into the Micanopy casino's parking lot. The public's appetite for losing money knew no bounds, and the lot was filled with out-of-state plates. He found a space behind the main building and killed the engine. It bothered him that he still hadn't talked to Kat, and he powered up his cell phone and punched in her number. It rang for a while, and he was about to hang up when a man's voice said, "Yeah?"

"This is Tony. Is Kat there?"

"Kat's busy right now," the voice said.

Valentine could hear Zoe yelling at her father in the background.

"When's a good time for me to get back to her?"

"Never," the voice said.

The line went dead, and for a long minute Valentine stared at the phone clutched in his hand. *It's over*, he thought. *So get over it.*

Parked by the casino's entrance were six orange tour buses. Bingo junkies. It was a time killer for people who'd just about run out of time. Yet more people played bingo than all the state lotteries combined.

Inside, he was hit by a blast of arctic cold air. The casino was rectangular and high-ceilinged, with raised floors that broke up the monotony of the layout. The acoustics were unfriendly, the sounds of people gambling painfully loud. He went to the cage and bought a twenty-dollar bucket of quarters.

Casinos watched everyone who came through the front door, at least for a minute or two. Normally, people immediately started gambling or got a drink. If a person didn't do one of those things, the folks manning the eye-in-the-sky cameras would follow them for a while. He found a slot machine and quickly lost his money.

Then he strolled over to the blackjack pit. The game was two-deck, handheld. That was rare to find in a casino that had only recently introduced blackjack. Usually, the cards were dealt from a shoe, which prevented dealer manipulation.

He studied the various dealers at the twelve tables. They were all men, and they wore loose-fitting blue jeans, denim shirts with wide cuffs, and string ties. In a casino in Las Vegas or Atlantic City, these items of clothing were forbidden. Running table games was different from operating slot machines or a bingo hall, and it was obvious the Micanopys had decided to write their own rules when it came to blackjack. The problem was, they were doing it all wrong.

He switched shirts in the parking lot, then met up with Smooth Stone outside the bingo hall. Smooth Stone was one of those rare individuals who perfectly matched his voice on the phone. Mid-fifties, gaunt, his copper face without cheer. He wore his silver hair in a ponytail, his black shirt buttoned to the neck.

"Running Bear speaks highly of you," Smooth Stone said. "I appreciate your taking the job on such short notice."

Valentine remembered Running Bear from a

seminar he'd given in Las Vegas, the chief sitting in the first row, towering over the other casino owners. An impressive guy, tall and broad-shouldered, with a face you'd put on a statue in a park.

A commotion started inside the bingo hall. Valentine and Smooth Stone stuck their heads in. Up on the stage, Bingo Bob, the caller, was hugging a tiny woman who'd just won a hundred grand. The tiny woman was bawling, Bingo Bob was bawling, and most of the crowd was bawling. Smooth Stone said, "She plays every day. Her daughter needs a kidney transplant."

Sometimes beautiful things happened inside casinos. Not often, but sometimes. Gamblers called it dumb luck. Valentine happened to think it was God's way of putting money into a deserving soul's hands, and he enjoyed being there when it happened.

"So what do you think of our casino?" Smooth Stone asked when things calmed down.

Valentine hesitated. He was going to create an enemy if he didn't handle this right. "If you don't mind, I'm going to answer your question with a question."

"Okay."

"How much did Running Bear tell you about me?"

"He said you helped nab hustlers who rob casinos."

"That's part of what I do."

"What's the other part?"

56

"The other part involves me finding the flaw that allowed you to get ripped off in the first place."

Valentine liked the way his words had come out. Straightforward, yet to the point. Smooth Stone didn't, and his face had turned an angry color.

"You're saying we have problems?"

"Yes."

"And this was why we got ripped off?"

Valentine lowered his voice. "This casino is not being run properly. Any smart hustler would take advantage of you. It's like hanging out a sign."

Smooth Stone looked away. Valentine knew little about Micanopy customs, but he did know Navajo customs through Bill Higgins, and Navajos didn't look you in the eye when they spoke to you. Smooth Stone had been looking him in the eye, and now seemed ready to explode. "And you want to tell Running Bear," he said.

"That's right."

"I could lose my job."

"I'll sugarcoat it."

"Why will you do that?"

"Nobody pays me to assign the blame."

The head of security took a deep breath. He had no choice, and he knew it.

"All right," he said.

They walked out the back exit and across the macadam lot. The casino was a ramshackle structure, with parts tacked on as the business had grown, and in the dark it resembled a winding snake with several meals in its belly. There was a science to the architecture of casinos, a method to the madness of the moron catchers of Las Vegas and Atlantic City. There was no science to the Micanopy casino, yet it still made money.

Running Bear's trailer looked like something you'd find on a construction site, with tacky aluminum siding and a window air conditioner. Walking up the ramp to the front door, Valentine said, "Have you talked to Jack Lightfoot recently?"

"He vanished the day before yesterday."

"Any idea where he went?"

They stood beneath a moth-encrusted light next to the trailer door. Smooth Stone jerked the door open. "I haven't a clue," he said.

The interior had the unadorned clutter of a college dorm, the furniture worn and plain. Running Bear was at his desk, looking older than Valentine remembered. The chief offered his guest a chair, then something to drink.

"A soda would be great," Valentine said.

He watched Running Bear rummage through a minirefrigerator and wondered what he'd gotten himself into. A lot of people were losing sleep over a lousy 840 bucks. The chief placed a soda on the desk along with a plastic cup.

"Tony has some things he wants to tell us," Smooth Stone said.

Valentine took his time pouring his drink. Being tactful had never been a strong suit. He admired the Micanopys for making good with what they had, and didn't see any reason to hurt anyone's feelings.

"A long time ago," he said, "two New York doctors named Hartshorne and May conducted a study of eleven thousand school kids. The goal was to find a way to measure the kids' honesty. They came to a lot of interesting conclusions. There are two you should be aware of. The first was that eighty percent of the kids tried to cheat at least once. That's a high number, but they swore by it. The second was *why*.

"Hartshorne and May said that whether or not kids cheat depends upon the environment you put them into. If you give kids a test, then leave them alone, most will look at another kid's answers. Which means if you let it happen, it will happen."

Running Bear frowned. He glanced at Smooth Stone, who leaned against the wall with his arms folded. "This making any sense to you?"

The head of security nodded. "He's saying that we've created a situation in which cheaters will prosper. He thinks there are more Jack Lightfoots out there. He wants us to change some procedures."

Running Bear stared at Valentine. "More Jack Lightfoots?"

Valentine nodded.

While the chief pondered what that meant, Valentine glanced at Smooth Stone. The head of security dipped his head. Valentine guessed

59

he was saying thanks, and dipped his head in return.

"Okay," Running Bear said, "how do we prevent this from happening again?"

"First," Valentine said, "make your dealers deal out of plastic shoes. Letting them handle the cards during the deal is an invitation for trouble. Second, change the way your dealers are dressed. I realize Western garb is in keeping with your casino's theme—"

"It's Indian garb," Running Bear said stiffly.

"Well, it's all wrong," Valentine said. "Crooked dealers will create spots on their clothing to hide stolen chips. Like behind wide cuffs and down their pants. Your dealers need to start wearing cummerbunds."

"But they look stupid," the chief said.

"Maybe so, but they prevent theft. You ever hear of a pants sub?" Neither man had, so he explained. "The dealer takes two pairs of underwear, puts one inside the other and sews the bottoms together. Stolen chips are dropped behind the waistband and released. They've got nowhere to go but the pants sub. Years ago, a gang of croupiers in Nice got caught using pants subs. They'd stolen fourteen million bucks."

Running Bear frowned. "You getting this down, Harry?"

Smooth Stone picked up a pad and pen off the desk and started scribbling. Valentine suddenly felt warm, and tugged at his collar. There no longer seemed to be enough air in the cramped trailer. Then he realized what was happening.

He was having an epiphany.

He'd been having epiphanies most of his life. Long ago, he had accepted that a part of his brain worked on its own, filtering information. And what this part was telling him was that Jack Lightfoot was dead, and Running Bear and Smooth Stone knew it. If not, they would have been out in the Everglades with bloodhounds searching for him. That was the smart thing to do. In fact, it was the only thing to do.

A man was missing. Find him.

Only, they weren't looking. Instead, they were concentrating on trying to figure out *how* Lightfoot had cheated them. *They knew Jack Lightfoot was dead, but were they his murderers?*

"So what you are saying," Running Bear said, "is that it's a miracle we haven't had more cheating before now."

Valentine blinked awake. Lois had told him he looked like a zombie when he had these episodes. Then he'd hit sixty, and people had stopped commenting about them.

"That's right," he said.

Running Bear opened his desk drawer and removed a videotape. Scotch-taped to it was a check. The chief's long arm reached across the desk. "This is the surveillance video of Jack Lightfoot cheating us. We need to know what he was doing, so we can prevent it from happening again."

Valentine slipped the video under his arm. He planned to overnight the video to Bill Higgins first thing tomorrow. Running Bear and Smooth Stone were either murderers or accomplices to murder, and he wanted nothing to do with them. Standing, he felt a bead of sweat roll down his face. He hoped the men did not see it.

"Call you in a few days," he said.

CHAPTER 6

The first thing Valentine did after he got into his Honda was to tear up Running Bear's check. He was a man of principles. Principle No. 1 said that he didn't work for crooks. It meant turning away business, as certain casinos all over the world routinely swindled their customers. Mabel didn't agree, and felt he should take the money and give it to charity, but Valentine stuck to his guns and felt a hell of a lot better for it.

A gibbous moon gave his car a purple sheen, and he found himself thinking about Donny and his purple suit. Donny wasn't the sharpest knife in the drawer, but he was always entertaining, and Valentine realized how much he missed the big lunk. Then he thought about Vixen and her vegetarian cooking. No meat, no bones, yet most of it had tasted pretty good. Then he thought about Zoe and her barrage of annoying pubescent questions. One day, they would stop, he was sure of it.

And finally, he thought about Kat.

He'd planned to take her out to dinner tonight and give her the diamond pin while telling her how much she meant to him. He wasn't good at expressing himself, so he'd composed a little speech and memorized it. Sitting there in the dark, the words came back to him. *I go to bed at night thinking about you. You make me happy every day. I hope I do the same for you. You've made me look past who I am and try new things.*

He gripped the wheel and stared across the parking lot. The wrestling had been fun, until Kat's ex-husband had shown up. Seeing Ralph and Kat and Zoe together, he'd been reminded of what his own previous life had been like, and how much he still missed it.

He powered up his cell phone and called Mabel.

"You still down in the dumps?" she asked.

"Yeah, but I'll get over it. Anything going on?"

"Our old pal Jacques called earlier."

"What did he want?"

"He searched his employees' lockers like you suggested. Well, you're not going to believe this, but—"

Valentine felt something heavy bump his car. The parking lot backed up onto a swamp, and he was the only living soul out here. "Let me call you back," he said.

He hung up, then heard the noise again, a sharp rustling sound like sandpaper rubbing against a blackboard. A sudden flickering movement caught his eye. Turning his headlights on, he saw an alligator lying beside his car, its tail whacking his door.

"For the love of Christ."

He beeped his horn, and a second gator appeared. It was a monster, and his stomach churned as he saw the bleeding hunk of raw meat between its jaws. He watched the two reptiles fight over dinner.

He thought about starting the car and driving over them, then decided against it. They were just stupid beasts, doing what God created them to do. If he waited a few minutes, they'd probably return to the swamp.

It wasn't unusual for him to get threatened while on a job. Casino personnel stole from their employers at a rate far higher than the national average. When he was called in, the thieves sometimes tried to scare him off. Usually it came in the form of threatening phone calls or a broken windshield. Once, someone had taken a shot at him. But no one had ever used alligators. That was new.

His eyes drifted to the floor of the passenger side of his car. Something was lying there, and he flicked on the interior light. It looked like a steak. Taking out his pocket handkerchief, he picked it up.

It was an inch-thick porterhouse, the meat starting to go bad. He started to toss it out the window when the Honda's folding backseat came down with a loud *bang!* and the alligator hiding in his trunk threw itself between the two front seats and snatched the steak out of his hand.

He heard himself yell, then looked to see if he still had his fingers. All there. The alligator munched on the steak while staring menacingly at him with its giant green eye.

Valentine jammed his elbow into the gator's face, and an electrifying jolt of pain shot through his arm. The gator shook its head, acting more pissed off than hurt. And he thought, *You're out of options*.

Except one. With a strength he didn't know he possessed, he pulled himself through his open window and climbed onto the roof of his car. He'd seen Charles Bronson do this in a movie once and hadn't thought it was possible. He crawled to the roof's center and saw the gator in his car stick its head out the driver's window, looking for him. The other gators circled the car, trapping him.

Valentine lifted his head. Multiple surveillance cameras were perched atop the casino, and he felt certain that whoever was on duty in the casino's surveillance control room had seen him and called for help.

He stared down at the gators, his heart racing out of control. Were they agile enough to climb onto the car? He didn't think so, but didn't want to be surprised, either. He waved at one of the rooftop cameras.

"Hurry!" he yelled.

CHAPTER 7

It had started out as a friendly game of poker, the hands being played for quarters and laugh rights. Then Rico had broken out the booze, and after everyone had a few belts the game had turned serious. With each hand the pots had grown, and now over four thousand dollars in chips was sitting on the table.

"I'm going to shoot the pickle," Rico announced.

The other four men at the table fell silent. To Rico's left sat Barney Swing, a retired New York mobster with kidney stones; next to Barney, another retired hood named Joey Clams; next to him, the ultrasmooth card mechanic Rico had hired from Las Vegas named Sporty. Next to Sporty, in the hot seat, sat Nigel Moon. He'd been knocking back Johnnie Walker straight, and his accent no longer had a nice ring to it.

"Shoot the pickle?" Moon declared loudly. "What in bloody hell does that mean?"

"It means Rico's going to shoot his wad." Sporty explained, having intervened several times when Moon's bad manners had threatened to ruin the evening.

"That's phallic, isn't it," Moon said. "You Americans are filled with the strangest bloody expressions. And all center around sex. All right, Rico, you have everyone's permission—shoot the pickle."

Rico pushed his chips into the center of the table. Rico had spent weeks planning this night, getting the right guys, hiring Sporty to work his magic, and the hardest part, teaching Candy how to talk Moon into playing cards with "some old friends of mine" without making it look as suspicious as hell. She'd done her job, and Moon had come to the Eden Roc Hotel on Miami Beach without a fuss.

Moon called his raise, then turned over his hand. He had a full house, kings over eights.

Rico did his best double take.

"You win," he told the rude Englishman.

Moon raked the pot in. "What you got?"

"Does it matter?"

"To me it does," he said drunkenly.

Rico revealed his hand. He had the straight that Sporty had dealt him off the bottom of the deck. Moon's hand had also come off the bottom. Hustlers called it dealing a plank, and Sporty was the best in the business. An unassuming guy, except for his hands. They were as delicate as butterfly wings, and just as quick.

"Shoot the pickle, my ass," Moon said.

Had it been anyone else, Rico would have shot him.

"I say we take a break," Sporty suggested.

The others agreed and rose from the table.

They went onto the balcony and stared at the glittering lights on the cruise ships anchored off Miami Beach. Down below, girls in string bikinis and muscular boys were playing volleyball under the lights. Rico could remember when no one would have been caught dead in this crummy town. Then the clubs in South Beach had sprung up, and overnight it had become Party Central, with nose candy in every bar and enough gorgeous women to have a heart attack over. He'd come down for a weekend and never left.

He went inside and refreshed everyone's drinks. Moon's he made extra stiff, everyone else's water with a splash of vodka, in case Moon got a whiff. Victor Marks, his mentor, had tipped this little trick. Rico had liked it, but then he'd liked every-thing Victor had taught him. He served his guests.

Barney Swing offered a toast. "Well, boys, here's to not working."

The others said, "Hear, hear," and lifted their glasses. Barney was smiling. He was the only player besides Moon to win any money. Glancing at his watch, Barney said, "I'm flying to Newark tomorrow to see my new granddaughter." He stared directly at Moon. "What do you say we play one more hand, head-to-head?"

Out of anyone else's mouth, the line would have died. But Barney knew how to act. Moon agreed, and they went inside.

Moon and Barney took opposing seats at the card table. Barney picked up the deck and gave it a shuffle. His hands betrayed his advancing years, and cards flew around the table.

"Let me do that," Sporty said. He was sitting to Barney's left. He picked up the scattered cards, squared them, then shuffled.

Standing against the wall, Rico saw what really happened. Sporty had secretly taken another deck out of his jacket and placed it in his lap. This deck was in a prearranged order, what hustlers called a cooler. In the act of shuffling the cards, Sporty tossed them into his lap, then brought the cooler into view.

Moon saw none of it.

Sporty handed the cooler to Barney. Leaning back in his chair, he scooped up the cards in his lap, and hid them in his pocket. Rico was impressed. He had seen some gutsy plays in his life, but nothing like this.

Barney put a thousand in chips on the table.

Moon anted up. "What are we playing?"

"Five-card draw poker."

"Anything wild?"

"Just the dealer."

It was for guys like Barney Swing that the expression *sweet* had been coined. Barney dealt the round, then picked up his cards. Rico saw his hand clearly. Three kings, a jack, and a lowly four.

"Your bet," Barney said.

Moon tossed a grand into the pot.

Barney called, and raised him a grand.

Moon saw his raise and asked for two cards. Barney dealt them off the deck without taking the cards off the table. Moon peeked at his cards. Then his face turned to stone.

The drunk Englishman was holding the eight through queen of hearts, a straight flush. You could play poker your whole life and never get a straight flush. Earlier that evening in the hotel bar, Rico had asked Sporty what the odds were of drawing one.

"Sixty-five thousand to one," Sporty said.

Sporty was practicing as he spoke. The bar was empty, and Sporty was dealing cards into his lap. Only the cards weren't coming off the top. Some came second from the top, others off the bottom, and some from the deck's center. Most card mechanics saw sleight of hand as a means to an end. For Sporty, it was a lifetime passion.

"He gambles a lot," Rico said. "He'll know he's being set up."

"You said he plays BJ," Sporty said, using the pro's term for 21.

"That's right."

"BJ isn't poker. BJ is about playing basic strategy, knowing how to count. Poker is about money. The more a guy wins, the more predatory he gets. And when the cards start to fall his way, he starts believing he's Superman. Get it?"

Rico hadn't believed him until he saw Moon raise Barney two grand. Barney called him, then watched Moon turn over his hand and reveal his straight flush.

"Jesus," Barney whispered, turning over his four kings.

Moon counted the pot. "You owe me five thousand."

Barney dug into his pocket. "Will you take a check?"

Moon hesitated. He wasn't as drunk as he acted, Rico realized.

"Everyone in the room will vouch for me," Barney said defensively.

"All right," Nigel said.

Barney wrote him a check and started to hand it over. Reaching over Barney's shoulder, Rico snatched the check from his hand.

"Barney, this is a *friendly* game, for Christ's sake," Rico said. Folding the check in half, he tore it up and tossed the pieces into an ashtray. "You being on a fixed income and all, I'm sure Nigel will understand."

Moon's mouth dropped open. He looked royally pissed. Rico dropped his hand to his side and opened his fingers, letting Moon see Barney's finger-palmed check. Sporty lit up a cigarette and tossed the match into the ashtray. The fake pieces caught fire.

Moon blinked, slowly understanding.

"Don't you, Nigel?" Rico said.

Rico smiled. Victor called moments like these turning points. It was the thing about being a con man that Rico liked. You got to peel suckers one layer at a time and see how much they could be taken for.

"And a friendly game it will remain," the Englishman said.

Bingo, Rico thought.

Splinters drove Rico and Sporty to Miami International Airport in Rico's limo. The moon was out, a big silver coin waiting for someone to pluck it from the sky, and Rico started to retract the roof. Sporty, who wore his hair in an architecturally complex comb-over, objected. Rico pushed the button in the opposite direction.

"You were great back there. That switch was awesome."

Sporty took the switched deck out of his pocket. "Thanks."

"How long you been handling cards?"

Sporty hesitated. "What's today, Friday?"

"Very funny. Twenty, thirty years?"

"My father gave me a deck when I was five," Sporty said.

The airport was a tomb. Splinters pulled in front of the Delta terminal and threw the limo into park. He had his Walkman on and was clicking his fingers and swaying his head like Stevie Wonder. He was a definite embarrassment, Rico decided.

Rico reached into his jacket to pay the mechanic. A gun appeared in Sporty's left hand. Rico felt his nuts tighten. It was one of those plastic jobs the

Israeli secret police had invented to sneak through airport security systems. He looked toward the front at Splinters. His driver was in la-la land.

"Take your hand out of your jacket," Sporty said.

"With or without your money?"

"Slo-owly."

Rico brought his hand out. Then, carefully, he grabbed his lapel and pulled it back, letting Sporty see the white envelope sticking out of his inside pocket.

Sporty wiggled the gun's barrel. Rico reached in with his left hand and carefully removed the envelope. Sporty took it from his grasp, and said, "Sorry, but your reputation precedes you."

Rico was shocked. What reputation? He'd killed two people in his entire life, which hardly qualified him as some major menace. One to get into John Gotti's gang, one as a favor. Two people and the double-crossing Indian the other night. Make that three people. Among the guys he used to associate with, three scalps didn't qualify for bragging rights. Judging by the way Sporty was clutching the gun, Rico didn't think he'd killed anyone.

Sporty visually counted his money. Satisfied, he said, "Tell me something."

"What?"

"What kind of scam you got going here? I've never been hired to make a sucker win. You setting this chump up for a killing?"

Rico nearly told Sporty the score. He wanted to

tell *someone*, it was such a beautiful thing he and Victor had going. Only if Victor found out, he'd disown him, and Rico didn't want that.

"None of your fucking business," Rico said.

Sporty got out of the limo. The departure area was eerily quiet, the sliding doors to the Delta terminal wide open. He tossed the piece into a receptacle by the door, then glanced over his shoulder as he went inside.

Rico winced. He'd been suckered by a toy gun.

"Hey," Rico yelled at his driver.

Splinters was singing along to his Walkman, his voice better than Rico would have expected, like he'd had lessons or sang in a choir once. An angel's voice trapped inside a lunatic's body. Rico stuck his arm through the window that separated them and tapped his shoulder. Splinters stopped singing and stared at him in the mirror, offended. Finally he disconnected himself and turned around.

Rico punched him in the face.

CHAPTER 8

It was Running Bear who finally came to Valentine's rescue.

The chief sauntered out the back door with a cigarette dangling from his lips. Seeing Valentine's predicament, he charged the alligators lurking around the Honda. For a big guy, he was surprisingly quick, and he grabbed each gator by the tail, dragged it across the lot, and tossed it into the swamp. It was impressive to watch, and Valentine found himself admiring the chief's technique. He'd seen signs for alligator wrestling shows inside the reservation and had assumed it was a hokey stunt, the animals drugged or without teeth.

Done, Running Bear wiped his palms on his blue jeans. Valentine pointed straight down. "You missed one."

Running Bear peeked through the open driver's window. The gator inside nearly bit his head off. The chief staggered backwards, twisting his leg. The gator wiggled through the window and went after him.

Running Bear danced around the gator, then jumped on the animal's back and started to really wrestle. This gator was a lot more aggressive, and soon the chief was gasping for breath. The gator was also getting tired, and its tail no longer banged the ground. Valentine climbed off the roof of the car.

"May I?"

The chief gave him a puzzled look. "May you what?"

"Cut in."

The chief had his arms wrapped around the gator's stomach and was holding the animal vertical to the pavement. "He's still got a lot of fight left in him," he grunted.

"So do I," Valentine said.

They switched places, with Valentine doing the holding. He gently loosened his grip, and the gator started to twist furiously. Using his hips, he body-slammed the animal headfirst to the pavement. The gator stopped twisting and did not move.

"Shit," Running Bear said. "You wrestle?"

"Judo."

"Damn good."

"Thanks. You mind my asking you a question?"

"Not at all."

"Are all the surveillance cameras in this parking lot broken?"

"Broken?" the chief said. "Why do you think they're broken?"

"Because someone stuffed an alligator in the

trunk of my car and your surveillance people didn't do anything about it."

Running Bear took a pack of Lucky Strikes out of his shirt pocket and stuck one in his mouth. Sweat was pouring off his face like he'd just stepped out of a shower. He offered one to Valentine. When it was declined, he lit up and filled his lungs with smoke.

"My boys did this, huh," he said, blowing a giant plume.

"That's right. Probably watching us right now."

Running Bear shot him a glance. "Smooth Stone, you think?"

"That would be my guess."

"Why?"

"You tell me."

Running Bear inhaled deeply and expanded his chest. The gator had awakened, and they watched it disappear in the saw grass and then heard its splash as it entered the water. Running Bear said, "I guess you're not taking the job, huh?"

Valentine nearly said yes, then realized he'd have to return the videotape of Jack Lightfoot, something he had no intention of doing.

"No, I am," he said.

Running Bear looked at him. "You still want to work for us?"

"I need the money," he said.

He got into his car. The seat was covered in reptilian slime. Running Bear stuck his face in the open window.

"I'll deal with Smooth Stone," the chief said.

Valentine understood. Running Bear didn't want him calling the Broward police, who would come onto the reservation if he filed a complaint.

"You do that," he said.

Valentine decided to stay on Miami Beach, the architecture a real time warp for someone of his generation, and was halfway there when he realized he didn't like the way he was feeling. His heart was beating a hundred miles an hour and the opposing traffic was passing by faster than normal. With his cell phone he found the nearest hospital, and walked into its emergency room and was sitting on a doctor's table fifteen minutes later. The doctor was a woman, her manner cool and detached.

"Not a heart attack or a stroke," she informed him when she was done.

He felt himself relax. "Great."

She wrote something on her clipboard. "Everything is fine except your heart rate. Do you mind telling me what you were doing that got you so worked up?"

"Wrestling alligators."

"Seriously," she said.

He showed her the palms of his hands. He'd lost a lot of skin.

"Did you get lost in the swamps?" she asked.

"The gator was in my car," he said.

The doctor excused herself. Valentine went to the door and peeked outside. At the hallway's end,

79

she stood talking to another doctor. Florida had a law called the Baker Act, where people acting strangely could be locked up even if they hadn't broken any laws. Tossing his clothes on, he got out of the emergency room as fast as he could.

Checking into the Fontainebleau hotel, he got a room facing the ocean.

Growing up, he'd known guys who'd bussed tables in Atlantic City in the summer, then went south in the winter to work the Fontainebleau. It had been the only real hotel on Miami Beach, the others simply there to handle the overflow.

He got pretzels from the minibar and went onto the balcony. The beach looked wider than he last remembered, and clusters of mature palm trees surrounded the octopus-shaped swimming pool. Otherwise, the place was still the same.

He was sitting on the bed tugging off his shoes when he remembered Mabel. He'd been talking to her on his cell phone when the gator had nearly taken his arm off, and he'd forgotten to call her back. He picked up the phone on the night table and dialed her number.

"Oh, Tony," she exclaimed. "I was so worried."

"A thousand apologies," he said. Then he told her everything that had happened.

"Thank goodness you're all right," she said when he was done.

He felt like a heel. Mabel had done more good things for him in the past year than anyone on

80

the planet. So why didn't he treat her with more respect? Losing his wife had hardened his heart; he knew that for a fact. But had it also hardened his soul?

CHAPTER 9

C andy Hart had never known love.

It was true. There had been a football player in high school who'd broken her heart, but they'd spent most of their time in the backseat of his car, humping like bunnies. Only fifteen, and already a member of what her Bible-thumping mother called the Itchy Ovary Club. Brad, or was it Burt? She'd known quite a few after him. There was no doubt about it. Candy liked boys.

But none that she'd ever loved with her heart. She'd gone looking plenty of times—in bars, gyms, even in church—and always come back with the bucket half full. It was another of her mother's cockamamie expressions.

At twenty, she had married a carpet salesman named Claude, then run off to Las Vegas when he started beating her. Needing a place to stay, she'd let a slick casino boss talk her into sleeping with a high roller for five hundred bucks. It hadn't seemed like work, and when the casino boss had called a few days later, she'd agreed to do it again.

She knew it was whoring, but she also set rules

for herself. No more than one trick a night. No drugs. And she kept a day job, teaching aerobics at a gym. Her hooker friends thought she was crazy, but Candy knew better.

She'd gone to work for an escort service, then quit after two girls got their throats slit. Scared, she'd called the casino boss who'd gotten her started, and started working exclusively for his hotel.

The casino boss had a cool system. Before he'd send Candy to a room, he did a background check on his computer, making sure her dates were upright citizens when they weren't in Vegas. It made the work easier, and she probably would have hung around if she hadn't let a high roller sweet-talk her into staying longer than the usual one hour. Champagne had followed, and room service. It had been heaven.

The next day, the casino boss had called Candy to his office. His name was Marvin, and he had a face like a bedpan. Candy stood in front of his desk flanked by a pair of security guards.

"Six hours?" he said angrily.

"He fell in love."

"You're not supposed to let that happen."

Candy shrugged. "Tell him that."

"That guy took me for two hundred and fifty grand yesterday. I want him on the tables, giving me my money back, not upstairs doing the horizontal bop until he passes out."

"You want me punching a time clock?"

"I pay you by the hour, right?"

"Yeah."

"So that's what I want. An hour. Get it?"

Candy had stiffened. Last night's Romeo had given her his card and asked her to dinner. Guys had offered this before. Although she'd never accepted, she'd always looked at it as another out. And now Marvin was telling her to forget it. No more dreams.

She was a whore, good for an hour, nothing more.

She hated how it rhymed.

And how it made her feel.

Then she'd done something really stupid. Picking up an ashtray, she'd flipped it across the room like a Frisbee. It had crashed into the floor-to-ceiling window behind Marvin's desk, the glass coming down in a thousand pieces, the desert sand blowing through the open space.

"Fuck you," she'd added for good measure.

And for that, she'd gotten run out of Las Vegas.

South Beach had seemed a natural place to relocate. Great weather, funky people, and lots of tourists with money. Renting a condo two blocks from the ocean, she worked the hotels at night. The concierges were easy to deal with and took a flat 20 percent. During the day, she taught aerobics to plump Cuban women in Coral Gables, and every other weekend went snorkeling in the

Keys. It was as normal as life got, and she'd been happy.

Then she'd met Rico.

A concierge had set them up. She'd gone to his room at the Eden Roc and found him sitting on the balcony, wearing black silk pants and a cream-colored sports jacket. A handsome guy, for a hood. He'd pointed to the empty chair across from his. As she'd sat down, he'd handed her an envelope.

"That's for talking with me," he'd said.

She counted ten hundred-dollar bills.

"So talk," she said.

Rico had a mouth that never quit. He explained how he was a professional con man and needed her to help butter up a sucker. It would require Candy seeing the guy for a week or more. Rico was willing to pay her daily rate, plus expenses. There was only one hitch.

"What's that?" she'd said.

"You can't fall for him."

"You got it backwards," she'd said. "They fall for me."

"He's famous," Rico explained.

"Right."

"Nigel Moon."

Candy had nearly laughed. Fall for one of the world's biggest assholes? She'd seen pictures in *People* magazine of Moon dropping his shorts. All the money in the world couldn't erase that kind of ugly.

"Give me a break," she said.

"He's got a lot of dough."

Nigel Moon was no richer than plenty of guys she'd done in Las Vegas, and she hadn't fallen for any of them. Her body might be for rent, but her soul wasn't.

"I don't care."

Rico had smiled. "That's my girl."

So that was the deal. Candy had been okay with it, until something strange had happened.

After the Davie carnival, they'd gone to Nigel's bungalow at the Delano on South Beach and burned up the sheets. Candy had clutched a stuffed panda the whole time Nigel had screwed her. Then Nigel had ordered room service.

The hotel had a killer restaurant, and they drank champagne and ate lobsters in their bathrobes, the stereo playing a Joshua Redman CD, the music on loud because Nigel's eardrums were shot from his drumming days. Normally, Candy hated loud music, but tonight she hadn't minded, the notes flowing over their overheated bodies like a siren's song.

Still in their robes, they'd ventured outside. The moon hung a few fingers above the horizon, looking ten times its normal size. A hundred yards away, guests ate on the patio. They walked to the edge of the property, away from the noise. Not many stars were visible, and Candy had to search until she found a constellation whose name she knew.

"There," she'd said, pointing.

"Where?" Moon said, straining to see.

"Over there."

"Okay," he'd said after a few moments. "I see it."

"Know which one it is?"

"No."

"The Little Dipper," she said.

"Let's not get personal."

"Huh?" she said.

Turning, he parted his bathrobe and exposed his round English belly and the fleshy little ornament that hung beneath it. Candy had shrieked with laughter.

And that was when the strange thing had happened. Nigel's dick was small, but so were most guys' dicks. Only, most guys lied about their dicks. Yet here was Nigel, telling her he didn't care if *she* didn't care. Making a joke out of his little dick.

Only, it wasn't a joke to Candy. Her whole life, she'd been looking for a guy who would come clean with her. It didn't matter if he was fat or bald or had a little dick, just so long as he was honest about it. All she was asking for was an honest, down-to-earth guy. What her mother had called the full bucket.

And she'd found the full bucket in Nigel Moon.

CHAPTER 10

"You were telling me about Jacques when we got interrupted," Valentine said to Mabel the next morning, trying to get back on track. It was eight-thirty, and his neighbor was at his office, manning the phones.

"He called yesterday in a tizzy," Mabel said. "He checked the employee lockers like you suggested, only he didn't find any of those tools you told him to look for. No sandpaper or drills or fast-drying cement. He thinks you were wrong about one of his employees doctoring the dice on his craps tables."

He'd ordered room service, and a piece of toast hit the plate. "Is that what Jacques told you, that I was wrong? Why that stupid horse's ass—"

"Tony! That's not a nice thing to say."

"All right, he's not stupid."

"Tony!"

"His casino is bleeding money, and he's got the chutzpah to tell you I'm wrong."

"He's just frustrated."

"Call him back, and have him inventory everything in those lockers. One of his employees is doctoring those dice. And I'm going to find out how."

"You're sure about this," she said.

"One hundred percent sure. And you can tell Jacques that if I'm wrong, I'll give him his money back."

His neighbor fell silent. Valentine picked up the toast and bit into it. The end was burned and tasted like soot. He ate it anyway.

"Will you really give him all the money back if you're wrong?"

"*I'm not wrong*. One of his employees is doctoring the dice. That's why his casino lost a half-million bucks."

"Couldn't a player have gotten lucky? It happens, you know."

Had anyone else said that, Valentine would have laughed into the phone. Once in Atlantic City, a computer geek had gotten arrested for scamming a keno game by using a software program to predict the winning numbers. As he was handcuffed, the geek had asked the arresting officer a question. "How did you know I was cheating?"

"Easy," the officer replied. "No one's ever won the Keno jackpot before."

Sometimes players got lucky, and sometimes people got hit by lightning. Not coincidentally, the odds of the two events happening were about the same.

After saying good-bye to his neighbor, Valentine called Bill Higgins.

As director of the Nevada Gaming Control

Board, Bill ran the most powerful gaming enforcement agency in the country. His team of four hundred agents monitored every Nevada casino and gaming establishment. Bill's voice mail picked up, and Valentine remembered that it was three hours earlier on the West Coast, and left a short message.

He decided to go downstairs and take a walk. On his way out, he glanced at the surveillance tape of Jack Lightfoot lying on the chair. It had been bugging him that Lightfoot had helped a player win eighty-four hands in a row. No one was that good.

He skipped the walk and watched Lightfoot on the room's VCR. He was a skinny Indian in his late twenties who handled the cards well. At his table sat an old hippie with a pretty redhead hanging on his arm. Lightfoot dealt the round. The hippie played seven hands and won all seven.

"Huh," Valentine said.

Lightfoot dealt another round. The hippie won every hand. Then he did it *ten more times*. The ten-dollar limit did not diminish the enormity of the feat, and a crowd gathered, clapping and cheering. The redhead acted like she was going to screw the hippie on the table—there was that much electricity in the room.

Valentine grabbed a Diet Coke from the minibar, a six-ounce bottle for three bucks. His one great addiction was Diet Coke. He rewound the tape and watched it from the beginning. By the time it was over, his drink was gone, and he was scratching his head.

Jack Lightfoot had him stumped.

The Fontainebleau had a fancy gift shop in the promenade. Valentine placed two *I Love Miami* decks of playing cards on the counter. A female cashier with a layer-cake haircut rang up the sale.

"Fifteen dollars and ninety-eight cents, please."

"How much are they?"

"Seven-fifty apiece, plus tax."

"That's highway robbery," he said.

She stuck a hand on her hip. "So just buy one."

"But I need two."

"Fifteen dollars and ninety-eight cents, *please.*"

He was fuming when he got back to his room. He hated getting ripped off, especially in a joint as pricey as this. Why not just have a giant at the front door who picked you up by the ankles and shook until your money fell out of your pockets?

Sitting cross-legged on the floor, he turned on the TV. Lightfoot's face filled the screen. He had seen plenty of blackjack cheats over the years, and none were capable of dealing eighty-four winning hands in a row. The random order of a shuffled deck of cards simply didn't allow it. Which meant Lightfoot was using a cooler.

Two-deck coolers were hard to bring into a game, but it happened. Most likely, a confederate wearing an arm sling had sat down at

Jack's table. The confederate had switched the casino's cards for the cooler residing in his sling. To shade the move, a third member of the gang had "turned" the pit boss by asking him a question.

For the cooler to work, Lightfoot needed to false shuffle. Mechanics used one of three false shuffles to get the money: the push-through, strip-out, and Zarrow. Each created a convincing illusion of the cards being mixed. But each also had a tell that a trained eye could detect.

Staring at the TV, Valentine mimicked Lightfoot's shuffling with the cards he'd bought in the gift shop.

Lightfoot's shuffles were slow and deliberate, the way they taught in dealer's school. After a few minutes, it became apparent that when he telescoped the cards together, they were being honestly mixed. Which meant Valentine still didn't know what Lightfoot was doing. And had wasted fifteen dollars and ninety-eight cents.

He killed the TV. The screen faded to black, a tiny white dot pulsating in its center. The elbow he'd used to crack the alligator had started to throb. He'd dreamed about that alligator last night and had a feeling he'd dream about him again. A real keeper.

The phone on the night table rang. He let voice mail pick up, then retrieved his message. It was Bill Higgins.

"Did you find Jack Lightfoot?" Bill asked when he called back.

"No," Valentine said.

"Any idea where he went?"

Valentine hesitated. Pieces to this puzzle were missing, and he felt certain Bill was holding a couple of them. "I think he ran."

"From what?"

"Jack Lightfoot was cheating the Micanopys at blackjack."

Bill breathed heavily into the phone. "You're sure about this."

"Positive."

Valentine's leg had fallen asleep from sitting on the floor. Standing, he jerked open the sliding glass door and went onto the balcony. The sun was spitting a thousand flecks of gold off the ocean. He stretched and felt the feeling return to his leg.

"Did the Micanopys let you talk to any of his friends?" Bill asked.

"I'm not a cop anymore, Bill."

A prop plane passed over the hotel, and Valentine clapped his hand over his cell phone. Tied to the plane's tail was a red and white banner: CLUB HEDO—SOUTH BEACH'S PREMIER MEN'S CLUB. When the plane was gone, he took his hand away.

"You're sure he was cheating," Bill said.

Valentine heard a loud racket on Bill's end. It sounded like someone vacuuming the carpet. Then the noise disappeared.

Going to the edge of the balcony, he leaned over

the railing. The prop plane had passed the last hotel on the beach and was heading toward Key Biscayne. He sucked in his breath, the deception hitting him like a punch in the stomach.

Bill was on Miami Beach.

CHAPTER 11

Valentine pulled back from the railing, still staring at the prop plane. As a rule, people in law enforcement did not lie to each other the way they lied to practically everyone else. What made it was worse was that Bill had been doing it for days. Walking inside, he shut the sliding glass door, then told Bill he needed to run.

"Thanks for the help," his friend said.

Valentine hung up, then dialed his house.

"Grift Sense," his neighbor answered.

"Do you sell wrapping paper?"

"That's the first time I've heard that today."

"I need you to help me find someone," he said. "You near the computer?"

"I'm looking at the big blue screen at this very moment."

"I need to find a guy staying at a hotel on Miami Beach. I realize that's a tall order, but I know two things that should make it easier. The hotel is south of the Fontainebleau, which puts it in South Beach. It's big, and not one of your boutique joints."

"Define big."

"Over five stories."

Mabel typed away. A minute later she cleared her throat. "I'm on a South Beach Web site on Yahoo. There's a section with a map of hotels. By clicking the mouse on a hotel, a page comes up with pictures and information and the hotel's phone number. What did you say your friend's name was?"

"Bill Higgins." Then he remembered something. Bill had visited Atlantic City once, and Valentine had been unable to locate him. Later Bill had told him that he checked into hotels under an alias, just in case someone in the lobby recognized him and had a score to settle. Out of curiosity Valentine had asked Bill his alias, then stored it away.

"Or Jason Black," he added.

"This all sounds very mysterious," Mabel said. "Would you like me to call these hotels and find Higgins or Black?"

"You're a mind reader," he said.

Thirty minutes later, Mabel hit pay dirt.

"Your friend is staying at the Loews under Jason Black," she said. "I would have called you sooner, but Jacques called. He finished doing the inventory of his employees' lockers like you suggested."

"Did he tell you what he found?"

"Yes."

A notepad and pen were next to the phone. Valentine picked up both. "Go ahead."

96

"Shoe polish, hair gel, combs, brushes, a mustache trimmer, mouthwash, breath mints, aftershave, hair tonic, toothpaste, deodorant, a clothes iron, a small sewing kit, a newspaper, a picture of a dealer's girlfriend in the buff, and a chocolate bar."

"That's it?"

"Yes. Jacques didn't think any of it was significant. I told him you'd be the judge of that, and he got a little testy. So I said, 'If Tony can't figure out how you're being cheated, you'll get your money back.' Jacques said, 'I will hold you to that,' and hung up. Well, did I feel terrible. You were grumpy this morning when we spoke. I should never have told Jacques what you said."

"Mabel."

"Yes, Tony."

"I'm not wrong about this."

"But what if you can't figure out how the employee is cheating?"

"Then I'll take up shuffleboard and start complaining about my hemorrhoids."

She giggled into the phone. "Sorry, boss."

He started to say good-bye, then remembered his manners.

"Thanks for chasing my friend down."

"You think I could be a bona fide detective one day?"

"I sure do," he said.

Mable hung up feeling giddy. Tony didn't toss

out compliments very often. And he hadn't even scolded her for telling Jacques he'd give the money back. So it was working. He was getting out of his bad mood. Finally.

How she detested Kat! Couldn't Kat see that Tony's heart hadn't mended from losing his wife? As a result, he fought with his son, said nasty things to strangers on the phone, and told off clients when it suited him. He was depressed, and didn't need a big-breasted woman in leotards in his life. What he needed was someone who could look after him and run his business and get into his head when it was necessary. He needed a friend, and Mabel considered herself the prime prospect for the job.

She heard the doorbell ring and walked into the living room expecting to see the blue and white FedEx truck parked in the driveway. Only, it was a hot-pink Mustang that took up the spot. Mabel put on her best brave face and opened the door.

"Mabel," Zoe yelled.

The twelve-year-old hugged her. She looked different, and Mabel realized Zoe had washed the hideous black dye from her hair. Kat followed her in and kissed Mabel on the cheek. She wore stonewashed jeans and a tight sweater. Mabel gritted her teeth. Did every piece of clothing have to cling?

"Boy, is it good to see you," Kat said.

Mabel swallowed hard. "Where have you been?"

"It's a long story. Is Tony here?"

"He left yesterday."

"I'll bet he's mad at me for not calling." Kat put her arm around Zoe's shoulders and rubbed her head affectionately. "They gave me only one phone call, and I used it to call my lawyer."

"One phone call? What do you mean?"

Kat continued to hug her daughter and took a deep breath.

"I was in the Orange County jail," she said.

Kat had driven straight from jail, and neither she nor Zoe had eaten. Mable brewed a pot of coffee, then got out eggs and bread and made French toast, all the while feeling like a shit. She'd once spent a couple of days in jail because of a classified ad she'd run, and had found it the most degrading experience of her entire life.

Kat sat at the kitchen table, staring into the depths of her cup. She did not open up until they heard Zoe turn on the TV. "Ralph, my ex, came by after the show and tried to serve me with papers so he could stop paying alimony. I sort of snapped." The TV had gone mute, and Kat glared at the wall. "Zoe! You know the rules. No channel surfing." The volume came back on and Kat relaxed. "Where was I? Oh, yeah, beating up Ralph."

Mabel turned from the stove. "Did you really?"

"Yeah. I got him in a hammerlock and started pulling out his hair. He had these implants put in, looks like tiny cornrows. No more!"

It was a delicious image, and Mabel took a plate

into the next room for Zoe, then returned to the kitchen and slid a second plate Kat's way.

"You're an angel," Kat said, smothering the food with maple syrup and digging in. "Ralph had me arrested for battery. Thank God for Zoe."

"What did she do?"

"She saved my ass," Kat replied, the syrup dripping off her chin. "Ralph got custody of her while I was in jail. He made her wash her hair out, then threw away all her clothes and bought new stuff at Kmart. Just to get back at me, I guess.

"Zoe's always been a little snoop, and she looked around Ralph's apartment and found a batch of summonses in a drawer. Seems Ralph's bounced checks up and down the East Coast since leaving me. Zoe realized her dad was on the lam, so she called me in jail. I told my lawyer, and this morning, Ralph got hauled in front of the judge."

"A happy ending," Mabel said.

Kat wiped her mouth with a napkin. "Not yet."

"How so?"

"I've got to find Tony. We've got a show in Memphis next week."

Mabel picked up Kat's plate and took it to the sink, rinsing away the remains with warm water. The words that came out of her mouth did so without any conscious thought.

"He's on a cruise."

"To . . . where?"

Mabel turned, showing her best game face. "He didn't say."

"Do you know which line?"

"He told me he was driving to Miami and was going to book himself on the next cruise he could find. I don't think he had a destination in mind. He just wanted to—"

"Climb into a hole?" Kat's face was flushed, yet her voice did not change. "I wish you'd told me sooner, Mabel. I've had enough surprises the past few days."

Kat's gaze had turned cold and unfriendly. Mabel stood her ground. *May God strike me dead for lying,* she thought. She loved Tony in a way this woman could not understand—loved his principles and his values and his big, wonderful heart—and was not going to let Kat hurt him again.

"I'm sorry," Mabel said.

The uniformed valet at the Loews was a pissant Cuban who acted like he'd never seen a car with a hundred sixty thousand miles. Valentine tossed him the keys, hitting him squarely in the chest. The valet's face puffed up in a confrontational snarl.

"You speak English?" Valentine asked.

The valet's look turned homicidal. Valentine's question was obviously not politically correct in this corner of the world.

"You a cop?" the valet asked.

"Show me your green card, and I'll show you my badge."

The valet jumped into the Honda and gunned it. Valentine laughed for the first time that day, and it made him feel good. He went inside.

The Loews was a mammoth hotel and as cold as a meat locker. It was stupid. Up and down the beach, they were building monoliths, with fancy carpeting and fine paintings, instead of what Miami needed, which was beachfront joints with bamboo furniture and cool tile floors. That was what Miami Beach used to be, and it had been great. This wasn't.

He stopped at the hotel's restaurant. He was always hungry when he was working, and he read the menu on the door. Sixteen bucks for a dozen shrimp buried in cocktail sauce. With tax and tip, twenty bucks easy. He'd starve first, and went searching for the house phones.

They were by the elevators. He dialed zero and an operator came on.

"Room of Jason Black, please."

"My pleasure, sir."

It sounded like something a coolie would say. It wasn't her pleasure at all. It was her fricking job. The call rang through and Bill picked up.

"Guess who," Valentine said.

"Tony?"

Valentine thought about playing Bill along, seeing how many more lies he could trick him into saying. Only, Bill was a friend, and he wanted to give him another chance to keep their friendship alive. "Very good," he said.

102

Bill's voice changed. "How did you know I was here?"

"I was a detective for thirty years, remember?"

"Are you nearby?"

"In the lobby," Valentine said.

Bill's suite looked lived-in. Chinese take-out cartons on the table, empty bottles, the muted TV turned to CNN. Like he was on a stakeout. They shook hands a little too formally. Valentine sat on the couch, Bill in the room's only chair.

Bill hadn't changed much over the years. Full head of black hair, his body lean. Facially, he wore an expression that Valentine likened to that of a cigar-store Indian, but had never said so, fearful of offending him. That expression was now gone, replaced by one of apprehension and worry.

"I've done something really bad," Bill said.

"Can it be fixed?"

Bill clasped his hands together. "I don't know. Probably not."

"You gonna tell me what happened, or do we have to arm wrestle?"

Bill flashed a rare smile. From the minibar he removed two Diet Cokes, pouring one for Valentine without asking. "I got a call from the Justice Department a month ago," he said, "asking me to help them investigate the mob's infiltration of Florida's Indian casinos. Specifically, they wanted me to look at the Micanopys."

"Why you?"

"Five years ago, I went undercover for Justice and infiltrated the Indian casinos in northern California, then wrote a report citing where I thought organized crime was operating."

"So you have a history with them."

"Right. When they called this time, I said sure."

"What happened?"

"I stepped onto a land mine. I didn't know that Florida's governor and Running Bear squared off two months ago, and the governor got his nose bloodied. Well, the governor wants revenge. He had the state's attorney general start a rumor that the Micanopys had mob ties. The rumor reached Washington, and Justice called me. I was brought in believing the Micanopys were crooks. I just had to find the evidence."

"A witch-hunt."

"Exactly."

"How does Jack Lightfoot figure into this?"

"Jack was working for me."

"You're kidding me."

Bill stared at the bubbles in his soda. "I saw Jack dealing blackjack at an Indian casino in northern California. He won so many hands, I knew he had to be cheating. I ran a check on him and found he was on parole. I cornered him and told him he could either return to prison, or work for me.

"I used Jack to infiltrate a number of Indian casinos, then a joint in Vegas. Jack was the best undercover man I've ever had. Because he'd been in jail and was a hustler, other hustlers instantly trusted him."

"What did he find at the Micanopys'?"

"Nothing."

"Why didn't you pull up stakes?"

"I was going to," Bill said. "Then Jack calls, says he got approached by a hood named Rico Blanco. I pull up Rico's rap sheet, see he's a member of the Gotti crime family. I get Jack to wear a wire, and start taping their conversations. It seems Rico is now working with a con man named Victor Marks. Rumor has it he scammed that TV show, *Who Wants to Be Rich?*"

"And Rico's his partner."

"Right. I tell my superiors in Justice, and they tell me to find out what Rico is up to."

Valentine smelled a rat. "Go on."

"Seems Rico is buttering up a sucker named Nigel Moon. The plan is to have Nigel come to the casino so Jack can deal him eighty-four winning hands. It goes perfect, and Jack meets up with Rico later. Somehow, Rico found out Jack was wearing a wire, and killed him."

"And you have it on tape."

"Had it," Bill replied. "Justice took the tapes and pulled me off the case."

"Why?"

"They want to build a case against the Micanopys. Look at the evidence I gave them. Jack has a record. And he was tied up with a known mafioso. And they were scamming the casino.

All Justice has to do is edit out the parts they don't want."

"You're saying the tribe is screwed."

Bill nodded. "And I caused it."

Bill's shoulders sagged. He looked defeated, his face drawn and tired. He rose from his chair, and they went out onto the balcony.

It was a sun-kissed day, the sea a shimmering cobalt mass. Coming off the Atlantic was a smell that was pure south Florida, the salt and mildew and oysters choking on sand blending together in an intoxicating scent. Valentine put his hand on Bill's shoulder.

"What are you going to do?" he asked his friend.

Bill turned and looked him square in the eye.

"Want to know the truth?"

"Yes."

"Stick a gun in my mouth," he said.

"Seriously," Valentine said.

"Seriously," he replied.

CHAPTER 12

"She's lying," Zoe declared.

Kat was lost. She ripped off the sunglasses that gave everything a velvety look of a dying sunset, and tried to get her bearings. Mabel had given her instructions to the Tampa airport, and like a dope Kat hadn't written them down. Had she gone the wrong way on 60? Up ahead she saw the beach. She had.

"Who's lying, honey?"

"Mabel."

"Her name's Mrs. Struck, honey."

"Okay, Mrs. Struck. She's lying."

There was no place to make a U-turn. That was one of the infuriating things about Florida. For a state with a trillion tourists, the roads were hardly marked. The people who really suffered were the Europeans. They came so far, only to spend half their time lost.

Traffic was bumper to bumper, and Kat threw the Mustang into park, then glanced at her daughter. Zoe had crossed her arms and was giving her the Little Miss Ugly pout that was part of the Berman genetic code.

"You're not listening to me," Zoe said.

"I'm listening to you and driving the car."

"So what did I just say?"

"You said Mrs. Struck was lying."

"That's right. I heard what she told you, that Tony had gone on a cruise. That was bullshit the moment it came out of her mouth."

"Zoe!"

"Tony hates cruises. I heard him tell Donny that once. So before we left, I did a little snooping." Reaching into her pocket, her daughter removed a square of paper and unfolded it. "I found this next to the phone in Tony's study. It's a phone number where he's staying. See for yourself."

Kat snatched the paper out of her daughter's hand. Tony's name was written on it, and the name of the Fontainebleau hotel, and a phone number.

"Your face is doing that funny thing," her daughter warned.

Kat stared at herself in the mirror. She had thin bluish skin that flushed salmon pink whenever her blood pressure rose. Traffic inched forward, and she threw the car into drive.

"You shouldn't have done this," she told her daughter.

Zoe stared resolutely ahead.

"Are you listening to me?"

"Say thank you, Mom."

"Excuse me?"

"Say thank you."

"Now you listen to me, young lady—"

"You wanted to find Tony, right? I mean, it's why we drove all the way over here, isn't it? Well, I found Tony. So, say thank you."

They had come to the roundabout on Clearwater Beach. It was not for the timid, and Kat punched the accelerator and merged into the maddening swirl of vehicles. To drive around it, she needed to change lanes, only none of the cars were willing to let her in. Zoe hit the horn, and a space appeared. Moments later, they were finally going in the right direction on 60.

"Thank you, Zoe," she said.

Valentine did not like talking about suicide while standing on a hotel balcony, so he took Bill Higgins out for coffee. One block south of the Loews, they got sucked into the South Beach parade of freaks and model types, and ducked into an eatery where people were sitting on futons and the servers were guys with boa constrictors wrapped around their necks. They beat a hasty retreat and found a restaurant where the chairs had four legs and you were allowed to sit in them.

"Black," Valentine told the waitress taking their order.

She Rollerbladed away, leaving them in their quiet corner. Bill lit up a cigarette and offered him one.

"I've been clean for two months," Valentine said.

"Want me to put this out?"

"I can take it. So tell me why you want to blow your brains out. I mean, you've got a couple of more good years left."

Bill cracked the thinnest of smiles. "You think so?" Plumes of purple smoke escaped each nostril. The waitress Rollerbladed back with two steaming cups, then sprinted away. "Look, Tony, this is going to ruin me, and not just in terms of my job. Once this comes out, Running Bear will know I set him up, and he'll let every tribe in the country know. I'll be an outcast among my own people."

"He's got that much clout?"

"Yes. You know anything about him?"

"I know he wrestles alligators pretty well."

Bill blew the steam off his cup. "Running Bear is a half-breed, only one in his tribe. His daddy was a white marine who ran off after he got Running Bear's mother pregnant. The day Running Bear was born, his mother took him down to the creek to be drowned—"

"She did what?"

"You heard me. That's the Micanopy tradition, been going on for centuries."

"Why?"

"It keeps them pure. The Micanopys are the last pure tribe of Indians in North America. No outsiders have ever been let in. A true sovereign nation. If any tribe rightfully deserves to have a casino, it's them. So where was I?"

"Running Bear's mother was about to drown him."

"Right. So she's dunking him in the water, and one of the tribe's elders holds up his hand. He takes the baby from her and looks at him. And says, 'This one was meant to help us.' So Running Bear was spared. A few years later, his mother dies. Running Bear gets passed around the tribe. He becomes a delinquent. The police start chasing him, and he hides in the swamps, living with the alligators.

"Eventually, he grows up. He enlists in the army. He becomes a ranger and ends up going to South Vietnam as the head of a long-range reconnaissance unit. He goes back and forth into enemy territory, creating havoc. I guess compared to the Everglades, the rice paddies in the Mekong Delta were a cakewalk.

"In '68 he came home on leave. Somehow the Viet Cong found out, and they set a trap for his unit and executed his men. Running Bear was devastated. He got discharged, drifted around for a while, then got arrested.

"While in prison, he started going to the library. He'd heard about the Cabazon Indians in California operating a poker room, and how the white man shut it down. The Cabazons sued, and eventually the case made its way to federal court. Running Bear followed the case closely. When the Cabazons won, he took the court's majority opinion and taped it on the wall of his cell."

The white man. All the years they'd known each

other, Bill had never used that expression. It had come out of his mouth sounding ugly, the product of an open wound hidden somewhere in his psyche. It bothered Valentine to think that was how Bill viewed him.

"The gist of the court's opinion was that the Cabazons could run poker games without having to adhere to local laws. This was their right as a sovereign nation. What Running Bear figured out was that this right applied to all Indian tribes, not just the Cabazons.

"In 1981, the chief of the Micanopys stepped down, and an election was held. Running Bear ran as a dark horse and promised to build a casino. At the time, the only industry on the reservation was running rodeos. They were so rinky-dink run that the tribe would use their pickup trucks to light the ring.

"Running Bear won the election. Two years later, Micanopy bingo was born. Within a year, every tribal member was receiving a monthly stipend. And Running Bear built a school and a hospital. All around the country, tribes were watching. You ever been on a reservation?"

"Only to work for a casino," Valentine said.

"Many have no running water or electricity. When the Rural Electrification Act was passed by FDR in 1936, it didn't apply to the Indians. There's also chronic unemployment and the suicide rate is sky-high. And the kids who are problems, you know what happens to them?"

"No."

"They get sent off to reform schools where they're not allowed to speak in their native tongue or send letters to their parents. They're cut off from their world and trained not to be Indians. It's barbaric."

Valentine could hear it in Bill's voice, but had to ask anyway.

"You one of those kids?"

"Haskell Institute, class of '64."

Valentine's coffee had gone ice-cold. Through the restaurant window a conga line of tattooed bodies was passing, South Beach's revelry kicking into high gear. Bill's face had turned to stone. The check came and Valentine picked it up. Eleven bucks for two lousy cups of coffee. He paid and they went out.

The geeks and freaks parted like the Red Sea, and Valentine and Bill walked back to the Loews. Next door was the original hotel, an unassuming three-story structure. Bill's vibes were nothing but hostile, and Valentine suggested they go outside to the verandah.

They took a table in the shade and said nothing for a while, Valentine wondering how to get things back on track. "What's eating you?" he finally asked.

"You pissed me off."

"I did?"

Bill stared at him, then shifted his gaze toward

the water. "I asked you what you thought of Running Bear. You told me he's a guy who wrestles alligators pretty well."

"That pissed you off?"

"He's a savior."

"As in Jesus?"

Bill looked back at him. "As in Jesus. You have a problem with that?"

Valentine didn't know what to say, so he kept his mouth shut.

"You're Catholic, right? In your religion, Jesus was born to a virgin mother, and heaven is a celestial vacation spot where souls sprout wings and become angels. Indians see Creation differently. The earth is our God. It is all things good, and all things bad. Our saviors are products of this earth. Running Bear broke the cycle of poverty for his tribe and set the example for other tribes. Do you have any idea how many other tribes now have casinos? Three hundred."

Valentine sipped his soda. Running Bear swore and smoked cigarettes and ran a casino. It didn't sound like any savior he'd ever read about. But Bill believed it, and when it came to religion, that was all that really mattered.

"You know," Valentine said, "you're really pathetic when you're sulking."

"Is that your idea of a joke?"

"I've never known you to cave in like this. There's got to be a solution."

"Name one."

The sun caught Valentine in the face, and he used his hand to shield his eyes. "You need to dig up evidence linking Rico and Jack Lightfoot to Victor Marks. Something that shows the three of them working this scam. A nice tidy package that you can hand over to the Broward County police."

"That's a tall order," Bill said.

"I'll help you."

"How?"

"I'm doing a job for the Micanopys. Smooth Stone called me the same day you did."

Bill's stony gaze melted. "Why didn't you tell me?"

"I just did. Any evidence you can share with me?"

"I've got a tape of Rico and Victor Marks that Justice didn't get," Bill said. "They're talking in some kind of code."

"How long until Justice closes the Micanopys down?"

"The governor of Florida is in Spain. He doesn't get back until next week. I'm sure he'll want to be here for the fun."

Valentine stood up from the table. "Not if I can help it."

"I really appreciate this, Tony."

It was as close to an apology as he was going to get out of Bill. Leaning across the table, Valentine smacked him on the arm. A group of ladies at a nearby table looked up in alarm.

"What are friends for?" Valentine said.

CHAPTER 13

Running Bear had decided to pay a visit to Harry Smooth Stone's trailer.

Smooth Stone's shift had ended at noon. Through a surveillance camera, Running Bear had watched him leave the reservation. Then he'd called Smooth Stone at home, just to make sure that was where he was. Harry had answered, already half-asleep.

Running Bear tried the door and found it locked. The trailer was identical to the one he worked in. Someday, they would all be housed in a gleaming steel and glass building, but that day was years off. First a water treatment plant needed to be built, then a hospice. Nice digs for the casino people would come later. The tribe's elders had decided this, and their word was law.

He put his shoulder to the door. The hinges gave way. He went in and flicked on the overhead light. The air reeked of cigarettes. A desk, two file cabinets, a TV, and a VCR made up the furnishings. He got behind the desk and tried the top drawer. Locked. Again he put his muscles to work.

The lock popped, and he pulled the drawer out.

A black ledger book practically jumped into his hands. He opened it to the first page. Smooth Stone's handwriting was primitive and easy to recognize. Like Running Bear, he'd dropped out of high school and had finished his education later on.

The page was dated and contained the names of five blackjack dealers. Next to each name was an equation that derived a percentage. The percentages were totaled at the bottom of the page and used to determine another percentage. That percentage was circled: *44%*.

Running Bear leafed through the other pages in the ledger. They were nearly identical to the first, except the dates and percentages changed. Some days, the percentage was in the thirties, while others it was in the fifties. He looked at the names of the dealers again. Two of them worked the day shift, two the evening shift, and one the graveyard shift. His eyes locked on the last name on the page.

"God damn," the chief said.

It was Jack Lightfoot's.

Taking a ruler off the desk, he placed it against the edge of the page. The page came out cleanly, and he folded it into a neat square and tucked it into his shirt pocket. Then he put the ledger back in the drawer. The trailer had grown hot, and he was sweating profusely, a sensation he did not find uncomfortable. He flicked off the light and stepped outside.

★　　★　　★

Smooth Stone was waiting for him in the parking lot. With him were four of the dealers whose names had been in the ledger. All were large men. They stood beside Running Bear's Jeep, looking agitated.

"Find what you're looking for?" Smooth Stone asked.

Running Bear shrugged and walked down the trailer steps. He walked with his palms pointing toward the sky, letting them see he wasn't armed. "Not really," he said, then kicked Smooth Stone in the groin when he got close enough, just to see what the others would do. As he'd expected, the men took a universal step backwards. Had they known anything about combat, they would have jumped him, their combined weight enough to beat the best fighter in the world.

Running Bear punched the closest dealer in the face. Hit him hard, and sent the man flying over the hood of the Jeep and onto the ground in a sprawling heap.

That left three dealers. A porker named Joe Little Owl stepped forward and threw a haymaker. Running Bear ducked the punch. Little Owl was still coming forward when their skulls met.

One of the two dealers still standing looked Running Bear squarely in the eye, then took off down the road at a dead run.

That left Karl Blackhorn, a Choctaw with a bad attitude. Recently, Running Bear had reprimanded him for being rude to customers, and he saw

Blackhorn draw a knife from a sheath on his belt, its long blade dancing in the sun.

"Kill him," Smooth Stone said, writhing on the ground.

With his heels, Running Bear felt for a soft spot in the road. Blackhorn inched forward, grinning wickedly. "Payback time," he said.

Kneeling, Running Bear picked up a handful of dirt and tossed it into Blackhorn's face. Blackhorn stepped back, swiping desperately at his eyes. Running Bear kicked the knife out of his hand. It flew through the air and disappeared in the mangroves.

Blackhorn fell onto Running Bear's Jeep. Blinking wildly, he jammed his hand down into his jeans and tried to pull a gun. Running Bear stepped forward and grabbed his wrist.

"Don't be a fool," Running Bear said.

Then the gun went off.

Valentine got his Honda from the Loews valet. Alligator slime had penetrated the cloth seats and floor mats, and he drove to the Fontainebleau trying not to gag.

Back in his room, he took Bill's tape and slipped it into the cassette player next to his bed. It was easy to tell which man was Rico Blanco and which was Victor Marks. Rico sounded Sicilian, either first-generation or maybe a native who'd come over as a kid, and used words like *gotta* and *outta*. Victor Marks used a voice-alteration machine and sounded like Al Pacino with a head cold. Valentine strained to understand what they were saying.

Victor: "You've got to play the C for that old pappy."

Rico: "I can do that."

Victor: "You know the difference between a payoff and the payoff against the wall?"

Rico: "Yeah."

Victor: "Listen, kid. I'm talking about playing this apple without a store, boosters, or props. If you're good, you can take off this touch without help, but it's going to come hot."

Rico: "Hot I can handle."

Victor: "What if he tries to run? What are you going to do then?"

Rico: "I gotta raggle."

Victor: "The raggle doesn't always work. What if he blows?"

Rico: "I'll put the mug on him."

Victor: "Sounds like you got all the bases covered."

Rico: "You bet."

The conversation ended, and Valentine killed the tape. Hustlers and crossroaders had a special language, and over the years he'd gotten pretty good at deciphering it. Paint meant marked cards, a mitt man someone who switched cards during a game. There were hundreds of expressions, only Rico and Victor Marks weren't using any of them. A raggle? Play the C for that old pappy? Put the mug on? He was clueless.

His stomach growled. It was lunchtime. Only too many things were bothering him to think about food. Like how Jack Lightfoot was cheating, and Bill's situation, and Jacques's dice cheater, and this damn tape. Too many puzzles to keep straight.

His stomach growled again. His body was telling him something, and he grabbed his jacket and headed out the door.

He decided to take a drive and got his car from the valet.

Traffic crawled, then stopped, then crawled some more. A kid on a moped scooted between lanes, making them all look stupid. He pulled into the entrance for the Castaway Hotel. Down the road, he could see the Fontainebleau. It had taken him ten minutes and a gallon of gas to go a lousy half mile.

The Castaway was one of those old Miami Beach dumps that he could identify with, the flowery wall coverings and mushy carpet a throwback to his youth. Behind the hotel was a poolside restaurant, and a greeter-seater showed him to a table with an umbrella. Next to the pool, a trio was playing jazz, the music battling with screaming kids and their parents screaming at them. He ordered a hamburger and coffee.

Ten minutes later his lunch came. The waiter said, "We're changing shifts. Mind cashing out?"

Valentine paid the bill. It was seven bucks, so far the best deal he'd found. He watched the new shift come in. Several of the waiters were in street clothes and carried their uniforms in see-through dry-cleaning bags. He stared at the uniforms, then removed from his wallet the list of items that Jacques had told Mabel he'd found inside the dealers' lockers, and read them again.

shoe polish
hair gel
combs/brushes
mustache trimmer
mouthwash/breath mints
aftershave
hair tonic
toothpaste
deodorant
clothes iron
sewing kit
newspaper
nude picture
candy bar

Smiling, he powered up his cell phone and called Mabel.

"Grift Sense."

"Do you do psychic readings?"

"Very funny," his neighbor said. "I've been trying to call you. Don't you ever leave your cell phone on?"

No, he never did. He hated hearing cell phones ring in public places and private ones, as well.

He ignored the question, and said, "I solved the mystery of Jacques's dice cheater."

"You did! Jacques called twenty minutes ago. He's so irritating!"

"Tell Jacques the craps dealer who has the clothes iron in his locker is the cheater."

"The clothes iron?"

"That's right. I'm surprised I didn't figure it out sooner."

"Figure what out?"

"I've known a lot of craps dealers over the years," he said, "and none iron their shirts. They have them dry-cleaned. Jacques's cheater is using the iron to shrink the dice. You put a die up to a red-hot iron and hold it against the metal for a split second. The iron shrinks the circumference of the die. That causes the die to be biased, and certain combinations will come up more than others. The neat part is once the die cools off, it returns to its original size. All the evidence disappears."

Mabel laughed with delight. "That's wonderful. Now we get to keep the money."

"After you call Jacques back, I've got two more things for you to do."

"Fire away," she said.

"First, I need you to call Detective Eddie Davis in Atlantic City and ask him to run a check on a guy named Rico Blanco."

"The same Rico Blanco who ripped off your son?"

Valentine nearly slapped himself in the head. Two months ago, a hoodlum named Rico Blanco had stolen fifty grand from Gerry by getting him to bet on a videotape of a college football game. It had to be the same guy.

"You're a genius," he said.

"Thank you. Then what?"

"Turn on my computer—"

"Done."

"—and boot up Creep File. Pull up the file on Victor Marks."

Creep File was a database of over five thousand hustlers, crossroaders, and con men that he'd crossed paths with during his years policing Atlantic City's casinos. It was a veritable Who's Who of Sleaze.

"Here he is," Mabel said. "Victor Marks. Professional con artist. Came to Atlantic City in 1982. Doesn't read like he stayed long. No picture."

Valentine closed his eyes and tried to remember him. He drew a blank.

"There's no physical description," Mabel added, "so I guess he got away. Ah, here's something. He had a partner who you arrested. Saul Hyman."

Valentine smiled thinly. Saul he did remember. An old-time scuffler, one of those guys who couldn't stop stealing if his life depended on it.

"Pull up his file, will you?"

Mabel's fingers tapped away. "Saul Hyman, aka the Coney Island Kid. Your notes are several pages long. Did he really do all these things?"

124

"That's the tip of the iceberg. See if the file has his last known address."

Mabel laughed out loud when she found it. "You're not going to believe this."

"What's that?"

"He lives on Miami Beach."

Saul Hyman lived in a retirement village in north Miami called Sunny Isles. He had to be pushing eighty, and Valentine imagined him doing what most old guys in Florida did: going to doctors, going to the track, and ogling the pretty girls who dotted the landscape like palm trees.

"Would you like his phone number?" Mabel asked.

"How did you get that?" Valentine asked.

"I typed his name into a search engine called whitepages.com."

Valentine scribbled the number down. "While you're at it, give me Gerry's number in Puerto Rico."

Mabel gave him the hotel's number, and Valentine wrote it beneath Saul's. His son was honeymooning at the Ritz-Carlton with his pregnant bride. Nothing but the best for his boy, especially when his old man was paying. "Listen," he said, "have you ever watched that TV show, *Who Wants to Be Rich?*"

"Once in a while."

"Victor Marks scammed it. I'd like to figure out how."

"As in cheated it? I don't think that's possible."

"Why not?"

"I read in *TV Guide* that the security on the show is like Fort Knox."

"Talk to you later," he said.

CHAPTER 14

Gerry Valentine's father had been yelling at him since he was a kid.

It had started when Gerry had gotten caught selling marijuana in the sixth grade, and had continued until a week ago, when he'd hit his father up to pay for his honeymoon. Twenty-three years of yelling, and always over the same thing: Gerry didn't listen.

Gerry didn't deny it. He marched to the beat of his own drummer, always had, always would. Take the night before in the hotel casino. For years, his old man had told him not to gamble in the islands. "The regulation stinks," his father liked to say, "and there's no one to gripe to if something seems fishy."

Only, Gerry hadn't listened. Yolanda had gone to bed early, leaving him with the evening to kill. Taking the last of the money his father had lent him, he'd gone downstairs to give Lady Luck a whirl.

The hotel's casino was small and European in flavor. Gerry knew enough to avoid playing roulette, the Big Wheel, and Caribbean stud

127

poker—which were games for suckers—and he also steered clear of the craps table, which gave a player decent odds if you knew what you were doing. The only other game that gave you a chance was blackjack, and he found a vacant seat at a table with a hundred-dollar minimum.

Having grown up in Atlantic City, he knew a thing or two about the game. The only smart way to play had been published in a book by Edward Thorp called *Beat the Dealer*. Thorp had doped out a system that he called Basic Strategy. It was as exact a science as algebra.

Sitting beside Gerry was a cruise-ship drunk. The drunk wore an ugly parrot shirt dotted with catsup and a green avocado-like substance. Belching into his hand, he said, "You Puerto Rican?"

"Italian. What's it to you?"

"Sorry. With that tan, you look Puerto Rican."

"You got something against Puerto Ricans?"

"Puerto Ricans aren't allowed to play in the casino," the drunk said defensively.

"Says who?"

"Says the government. They just want us tourists playing." The drunk lowered his voice. "If you ask me, I think it's because they're too stupid to understand the rules."

Yolanda was Puerto Rican. Had he been on his home turf, Gerry would have smacked the guy in the head. He glanced at the dealer. He was an effeminate Puerto Rican with olive skin and wavy hair. He didn't say much, but in his eyes a fire was burning. *He heard the drunk*, Gerry thought.

His father had told him to never play with a pissed-off dealer. But what could the dealer do? A pit boss was watching, and the cards were dealt out of a plastic shoe. Deciding to go against his old man's advice, Gerry had stayed put.

That had been his first mistake.

The dealer had cleaned out everyone at the table. Because Basic Strategy required intense concentration, Gerry had noticed the inordinate number of small cards being dealt. Small cards—two, three, four, five, six—favored the house, while big cards—ten, jack, queen, king, and ace—favored the players. Not enough big cards were coming out of the shoe, which meant something fishy was going on. He'd decided to call the dealer on it.

That had been his second mistake.

"How do you know the dealer was cheating?" Yolanda asked the next day, applying a fresh ice pack to Gerry's eye. For his imprudence he'd been asked to step outside, where a security guard had punched him.

"Because I figured out what the dealer was doing."

"You did?"

"He was keeping a slug of high cards out of play. My old man told me about it. It isn't very hard, once you understand the basics. I should have done what my father said."

"Which is?"

"If you think you're getting cheated, leave."

"Why didn't you?"

"Because I'm a dope," he said.

His beautiful bride kissed him on the cheek. "No, you're not."

There was a knock on the door. Yolanda ushered in a waiter with the meal she'd ordered from room service. She was loving every minute of their honeymoon, and Gerry struggled with how to tell her that he no could longer pay for their room, or her treatments at the spa, or the lavish meals, or all the other bills they'd rung up. The phone rang and she answered it.

"Hi, Dad," she said cheerfully.

Gerry groaned. She spoke to her own father in Spanish. Which meant it was *his* father, the last person on earth he wanted to talk to. He made a move for the bathroom.

"He's right here," Yolanda said.

"No, I'm not," Gerry whispered. "Tell him I'm in the crapper."

"*Talk to your father,*" she whispered back, handing him the phone.

Gerry held the receiver in his outstretched hand. He could already hear his old man yelling at him, and he hadn't even told him what he'd done. He stared at his wife's protruding belly. Was he *really* ready to be a parent?

"Hi," he said.

There was a time in every man's life when he had to admit his mistakes, and Gerry realized now was that time, even if it meant his father might explode and Yolanda might kill him. But before the words could come out of his mouth, his father stopped him dead in his tracks.

"I don't know how to ask you this," his father said.

"What's that?"

There was a brief silence. Then his old man let him have it.

"I need your help," he said.

CHAPTER 15

Rico knew something was wrong the moment he laid eyes on Candy Hart.

It was lunchtime, and they were sitting in the Delano's patio restaurant. The tables were filled with pasty-skinned young women and their coke-sniffing boyfriends, the waiters balancing monster trays as they darted between tables. Candy had called him an hour ago. Nigel had gone to play eighteen holes on the Blue Monster, and she wanted to talk.

It was the clothes, Rico realized. She was wearing a yellow sundress that made her look like a Sunday school teacher. That was okay—she couldn't be a hooker twenty-four/seven—but her hair was different, and she wore less makeup. No more bedroom eyes, he thought.

"I want out," she said.

"Out?"

"Out."

"Now?"

"Uh-huh."

Rico tapped his fingertips on the table. Too many people were around for him to raise his voice. So he just frowned, working it out in his head. Candy's leaving he could handle; he could always find another pretty hooker. But Candy wasn't leaving, she was staying right here at the Delano, shacked up in Nigel's bungalow. Removing his wallet, he dropped two thousand dollars on the table and slid it her way. Her eyes locked on the money, then met his face.

"What's that for?"

"Your last payment. I don't want anyone ever saying Rico Blanco stiffed them."

"You sure?"

"It's yours."

She started to pick up the money. Rico brought his hand down forcefully on the bills. In a harsh whisper he said, "Do you really think it's gonna last with this guy? He's slept with more women than I've had bowel movements. You'll wake up one morning and he'll be gone. For good." He saw her eyes well up and went for the kill. "You know why I'm scamming him? Because he's got it coming. Nigel Moon is a fake."

The waiter brought their drinks, and Rico drew his hand away. Candy picked up the money and stared at him. Rico looked at his beer. It was an Amstel Light. He hated light beer. The waiter had brought the wrong drink.

"What do you mean, he's a fake?"

"You want the gory details?"

Candy's cute mouth twisted into something harsh and unfriendly. "No."

"Well, for starters—"

"I said *no*. Shut up."

"I'll pay you five grand to stay in."

"Is that what I'm worth to you, Rico? Five grand?"

"That's on top of what I've already paid you," Rico said.

Candy picked up the money and threw it into Rico's face. In a loud voice she said, "Stick it up your ass, you crummy piece of shit," and stormed down the path toward the hotel's bungalows. Rico sipped his beer, trying to act nonchalant. People were staring at him, and his money was scattered all over the floor.

He glanced at the glass door that led from the patio into the hotel. His driver was standing behind it, his face pressed to the glass. Rico motioned to him with one finger. Splinters came out and picked up his money.

Five minutes later, driving north on Collins Avenue, Splinters lowered the window that separated him from his boss. "I can't believe she did that to you."

Rico opened a real beer from his private stash and chugged it. "Me neither."

"She cursed you in front of all those people."

"Don't remind me."

"And threw your money on the floor."

"Shut up, will you?" It was strange, but the worst part had been the taste the Amstel Light had left in his mouth. It tasted exactly like beer wasn't supposed to taste. The Eden Roc came into view. Splinters put his indicator on and parked by the front entrance.

A uniformed doorman opened Rico's door, and he got out. He was halfway to the elevators when he had an idea. He retraced his steps.

Splinters was still in the limo, playing with the radio. He'd told Rico that in Cuba there was nothing good on the radio. Rico went around to the driver's side and tapped on the window. It lowered automatically.

"I need you to do a job for me," Rico told him.

"Sure," Splinters said, his fingers clicking to the music blaring out of the speakers.

"Kill her," Rico said.

Gerry didn't know what to make of the way his father was acting.

First his old man had wired him money to pay for his hotel *and* for Yolanda to stay a few more days *and* for Gerry to fly to Miami that afternoon. Then his old man had met him at the airport, all smiles and hugs, and helped him rent a car, which he'd put on his credit card. And not just any car, but a BMW 540 from Hertz, a hundred bucks a day.

Driving over the Causeway to Miami Beach, Gerry had found himself whistling to a song on the radio. It all seemed too good to be true. Then he'd spotted the flashing lights of the police cruiser in his rearview mirror.

"I'll take care of it," his father said when

Gerry showed him the speeding ticket at the Fontainebleau. They were drinking sodas by the pool with scores of pretty girls all around them. Gerry felt his father's eyes burning his face.

"Cut it out," his father said.

"What?"

"You're a married man."

"Just because I'm on a diet doesn't mean I can't read the menu."

His old man leaned across the table, grabbed Gerry's ear, and gave it a twist. "Listen to me. First your eyes wander, then your dick wanders. And because your dick has only one eye, it sees only half the picture. So cut it out, okay?"

Gerry grunted in the affirmative, and his father let him go. This felt a lot more like his old man. A bikini-clad girl strolled by their table and gave him a wink.

"How you doing," he said without thinking.

She stopped to chat, leaning over the table so they got the full picture.

"Did you see those lungs?" Gerry said when she was gone.

"She nearly poked my eye out," Valentine said. "Besides, they're not real."

"They were beautiful," his son said.

"You like fake titties?" his father asked.

Gerry grinned. There was a word you didn't hear very often: *titties*. Used exclusively by old geezers of his father's generation.

"Come on," his father said, "answer me."

"Yolanda's thinking of getting them after she has the baby."

"That's the stupidest thing I've ever heard," Valentine said. "Talk her out of it."

"But Pop—"

"You want a woman who's got her brights on all the time?"

The grin faded from Gerry's face. "No."

"Then do as I say. You'll thank me later on." Valentine had finished his soda and wiped his mouth with a paper napkin. "I need to talk to you about something that can't leave this table."

"What's that?"

"Rico Blanco."

Gerry sat up straight in his chair. Two months ago, Rico had scammed him out of fifty thousand dollars, then sent some thugs called the Mollo Brothers to collect. Not having the dough, Gerry had given them his bar in Brooklyn. There had only been one hitch. The bar belonged to his father.

"What about him?" Gerry said.

"He's running a strip joint on South Beach. I want you to talk to him, see what he's up to."

"Rico isn't going to talk to me."

"I thought you were friends."

"He scammed me, pop."

"You got the bar back, didn't you?"

"Yeah."

"So, talk to him. Even if it's just on the phone. Whatever you can get out of him will be helpful."

Gerry shifted uneasily in his seat. In some ways,

the conversation they were having was worse than being yelled at. He was having to be honest with his father, something he wasn't used to doing. He put his elbows on the table and saw his father do the same.

"Look, Pop, I'm going to tell you something that won't make you happy, but you'd better know anyway."

"What's that?"

"When I first opened the bar, Rico tried to shake me down. I showed him the liquor license. It's in your name. I told him you were a cop and that you were connected. He left me alone after that."

His father pulled back in his chair, staring at him like he'd grown horns.

"You told him I was dirty."

"Yeah."

"Damn it, Gerry."

Gerry found himself missing the yelling. "There's more," he said.

"How can there be more?"

"Go back in time a few months. I gave the Mollo brothers the bar to pay off Rico. A few days later, the Mollos get blown up in a car. Rico thinks it was you."

"Did you tell him that, too?"

Gerry buried his head in his hands. "Yeah."

"So Rico thinks I'm also a murderer."

"Yeah," his son repeated.

"If you called Rico, and told him I wanted to meet him, do you think he'd agree?"

Gerry lifted his eyes and met his father's gaze. He hadn't even raised his voice. "Probably. You're not mad at me?"

His father shrugged, then reached across the table and gave Gerry's arm a squeeze.

"I'll get over it," he said.

CHAPTER 16

Running Bear had forgotten how much he hated being in jail. A day had passed since he'd shot Karl Blackhorn. Blackhorn had gone to meet his ancestors on the way to the hospital, and Running Bear, Smooth Stone, and the other three dealers had been arrested by tribal police and thrown into the reservation jail.

He stood at the bars in his cell. They were rubbed smooth where other inmates had instinctively held them at chest height. Smooth Stone and the others were a stone's throw away, whispering frantically. Like mice knowing they were about to be eaten by a cat, he thought. He sat on his cot, leaned against the concrete wall, and shut his eyes.

The last time he'd been incarcerated—over twenty-five years ago—he'd had a vision. In it, he'd seen his people living in nice homes and having enough food to eat and good health care, and all the other things they didn't have when he was growing up. He'd seen a future where there was no future. And it had changed him.

When he opened his eyes, a Micanopy woman in a business suit was standing in his cell. In her left hand was a briefcase; in her right, a plastic chair. Running Bear motioned for her to sit. "So, Gladys Soft Wings, how are you?"

"I wasn't sure if you'd remember me," she said.

"You went to Stetson and got a law degree," he said. "And now you're here to represent me before the elders."

"Yes, and to the Broward police, if you'd like me to."

Running Bear considered it. It would be up to the tribe's elders to decide which story to present to the police when they reported the shooting—his, or Smooth Stone's. The elders were old men set in their ways, and Running Bear had clashed with them many times over how he marketed the casino.

"One thing at a time," he said.

She did not seem offended. Opening her briefcase, she removed several sheets of paper, then read aloud Smooth Stone's and the other dealers' accounts of what had happened. In their story, Running Bear had vandalized Smooth Stone's trailer, then attacked them when confronted. Running Bear laughed softly when she was done.

"You find this funny?"

"I find their reasoning funny," he said. "It was five against one. Blackhorn had a knife and a gun. I was unarmed."

"Blackhorn is dead. And you're a martial arts expert."

"They attacked me."

"So it was self-defense. But why were you in the trailer?"

"I hired a consultant to do a job. This consultant is an expert in catching cheaters. Someone put an alligator in his car. I suspected Smooth Stone, so I went to his trailer. I found a ledger in Smooth Stone's desk that implicated the men who attacked me."

Gladys opened her briefcase again and handed him a sheet of paper. It was a list of the items the tribal police had found in Smooth Stone's trailer after they'd searched it.

"The tribal police didn't find a ledger," she said.

Running Bear removed from his shirt pocket the page he'd torn out of the ledger. Unfolding it, he handed it to her. "I took this as a memento."

Gladys studied the page. Running Bear could vividly remember her as a child. Shoeless, dirty most of the time, hardly ever spoke. And now here she was, wearing nice clothes and talking for a living. He saw Gladys shake her head.

"I don't know what any of this means," she said.

"Neither do I," Running Bear said. "But I know someone who does."

"Your consultant?"

"Yes," he said. "My consultant."

Saul Hyman's condo was on the fourth floor of a

dumpy high-rise in north Miami. Valentine had called and caught Saul riding his stationary bike. Hearing his voice, Saul had acted like he was a long-lost brother and not someone who'd once busted him.

"Of course you can come on over," Saul said. "Provided it's a social call."

"I'm retired," Valentine had replied.

"How many years has it been?" Saul asked an hour later, ushering Valentine in. He was small and wiry, maybe one-fifty soaking wet, and sported a debonair little mustache, which he dyed along with his hair. Normally, Valentine didn't like dye jobs. But Saul's looked okay.

"Twenty."

"Miss me?"

"Not for a minute."

"You were my favorite cop."

"Why's that?"

"That partner of yours wanted to beat the daylights out of me. You stopped him."

Valentine vaguely remembered the incident. Atlantic City had been a candy store in the early days, and cheaters were often pummeled before reaching the station house. Saul led him into the living room. It was small and had a view of two apartment buildings across the street. Between them, he could see a tiny sliver of ocean.

"Nice view."

"Thanks," Saul said, pointing at a chair as he took the couch. "So when did you retire?"

"Last year. I opened a consulting business. I help casinos nail cheats."

"I hope you're charging them through the nose."

"You bet."

Saul smiled, and the sunlight reflected brightly off his teeth. They'd been artificially whitened and looked like piano keys. "Good for you," he said.

"Because I went out on my own?"

"Because you're making money off the fucking casinos." He slapped his hands on his knees. "So, how about a drink? I can offer you soda or fruit juice. I've got this Indian doctor, Deep Pockets Chokya, who made me swear off the hard stuff."

"That's his real name?"

"That's what I call him. Every time I see him, I leave a little lighter."

"Diet Coke, if you have it."

"Diet Coke I can do."

Saul sprang off the couch and disappeared. While he waited, Valentine appraised Saul's digs. It wasn't a great place, but it wasn't a trailer park, either. Saul's philosophy toward cheating had obviously paid off. "It's better to gamble with someone else's money than your own," he'd said after Valentine had arrested him. "Much better."

It had happened at the old Resorts International in Atlantic City. The casino had just opened, and security was a shambles. But the owners had done a smart thing. In the basement was a computer that did daily financial analysis of the different games. And the computer said something was

144

wrong at their roulette table. Resorts' security had called the police. Valentine had been given the assignment, and set up shop in Resorts' surveillance control room.

Sitting in front of a video monitor, he'd watched the roulette table through an eye-in-the-sky camera called a pan/tilt/zoom. Roulette tended to attract an eccentric mix of people, and it took a while before he'd spotted Saul and sensed that something was not right.

Saul gambled every day. Like most gamblers, he was superstitious and followed a set routine each time he entered the casino. First he went to the coffee shop and smoked a cigarette. Then he went into the casino and played roulette. He would always place even-money bets—red, black, odd-even—and usually leave after fifteen minutes to play craps or blackjack. He was a smart gambler and sometimes won big. But just as often, he lost his stake.

What Valentine hadn't liked was the sameness of Saul's routine. It felt rehearsed, so he decided to videotape Saul for a week, then compare the tapes. After reviewing them, he wrote down the four things Saul did every single day.

(1) He always smoked.
(2) He always bet a hundred-dollar black chip.
(3) He always tossed his hundred-dollar chip on the table and asked a stickman to place his bet for him.
(4) He always asked the same stickman.

Valentine had pulled up the stickman's record. In the past year, he'd filed several grievances with the casino's human resources department, unhappy with his vacation time, his hours, and his level of pay. He was one angry individual.

The next day, Valentine had parked himself on a chair at a shoe-shine stand in the casino. In his lap he'd put a newspaper. Underneath the newspaper was a pair of binoculars. He'd talked baseball with the shoe-shine man until Saul had come in.

Saul had followed his usual routine. Valentine had watched with his binoculars, and what he'd seen was a thing of real beauty.

Approaching the roulette table, Saul said hello to the stickman, then tossed a black hundred-dollar chip on the table and asked the stickman to make his bet. Only Saul's chip never hit the table. It was attached to a piece of monofilament and flew up his sleeve. At the same time, the stickman dropped a black chip that was palmed in his hand onto the table. To help disguise the switch, Saul blew smoke on the table.

Saul and the stickman did their thing three times. The stickman was stealing chips off the table and palming them, letting Saul play with the house's money.

But what Saul had done next was even better. Instead of leaving with his winnings, he went and played blackjack. He was giving Resorts a chance to win its money back. More than 50 percent of the time, Resorts would. But the rest of the time, Saul would walk away a winner. And he wasn't risking a dime.

Saul returned with a tray. He served his guest and made the couch sag as he sat down. "So what brings you to Miami?"

"I'm doing a job for the Micanopy casino," Valentine said, deciding to get to the point. "A friend of yours is a suspect in a murder case."

Saul put his drink down. Hustlers were a lot of things, but few were murderers. His voice turned serious. "Who?"

"Victor Marks."

Saul blinked, and then blinked again. "Victor Marks is the gentlest guy I've ever known. You know what his nickname was? The Butterfly."

"You talk to Victor recently?"

"We haven't spoken in years. You sure Victor's involved?"

Valentine nodded. "He's working with a hood named Rico Blanco. The police fingered Rico in a murder at the Micanopy casino."

Saul drew back in his seat. Valentine sensed that Saul was wrestling with his conscience. Every hustler had one, only it tended to follow a more convoluted path than most. Valentine lowered his voice.

"The victim was running a scam with Rico Blanco. Something went wrong, and Rico killed him. I don't want the same thing to happen to Victor Marks."

Valentine heard Saul mumble under his breath. Mabel did that a lot, and Valentine guessed he would one day, too. You grow old, lose your friends, you need someone to talk to. Saul's filmy eyes rested on Valentine's face.

"Neither do I," the elderly con man said.

Valentine played the tape of Rico Blanco and Victor Marks on Saul Hyman's stereo.

"They're talking about conning a sucker out of a lot of money," Saul said when the tape ended. "The raggle is a pretty girl who's part of the scam. Playing an apple without a store, booster, or props means that Rico is running solo. The rest of it is Victor asking Rico if he's got the moxie to pull it off. That's the hard part."

Valentine ejected the tape from the cassette player. "Why's that?"

"It's like fishing for marlin," Saul said. "Anyone can throw a line in the water and snag one. But then you've got to fight the fish and reel it in. That's the challenge."

"Why does Victor use a voice-alteration machine?"

"Victor's always been careful," Saul said. "I'm probably the only person in the world who's got a photograph of him."

"Can I see it?"

There was no hesitation in Saul's voice. "Yeah, sure."

A minute later the two men were sitting on the couch leafing through a dusty photo album. Saul had spent his entire life on the wrong side of the law. In the 1930s, he'd worked on Coney Island as a spiritualist and worn a turban and walnut stain on his face. He'd graduated to being a three-card monte man, then a racetrack tout. Later, he'd moved to Palm Springs and played the sophisticate, and sold fake oil stock and rubber plantations.

"Here we go," Saul said, finding the picture.

Valentine stared at two couples at a table in a nightclub. Saul with a pretty lady, Victor Marks with a frowning woman. Marks had his hand in front of his face. There wasn't much to see except a thick head of hair and bushy eyebrows.

"That's Vic and his date, and me and Sadie at the Copacabana in New York," Saul said. "We were there to see Count Basie. Vic nearly punched the photographer for taking a photo. I paid the guy and made him destroy the negative." Saul stared longingly at the photograph. His finger touched the picture and drew an outline around Sadie's head.

"Your wife?"

"Yeah. Died last January."

Valentine felt a fist tighten in his chest. Lois had died in her sleep two years ago January. "I'm sorry," he mumbled.

"Me, too," Saul said, swiping at his eyes. "I didn't get where I am by sitting on my ass. Sadie was always there supporting me. When I was in the slammer, she came every week and brought me pies and cookies." He spread his arms to indicate the

149

room's modest furnishings. "This was my way of paying her back."

Loss. It was supposed to mean something was missing. But it was really a monster, ready at any moment to leap out of the shadows and snatch someone away. And when it did, nothing on this earth could replace the loss.

"And now it doesn't mean shit," the elderly con man said.

CHAPTER 17

C andy Hart was taking a bubble bath when the phone rang. She ignored it, preferring to lie in the tub with her head partially submerged, blowing bubbles through her nose. It was a little kid's trick and, like her collection of stuffed animals, something she never wanted to let go of.

The phone rang again while she was toweling off. She glanced at her watch on the sink. Nearly two. Nigel was a poor golfer, and she imagined him on the ninth hole of the Blue Monster, staring at a dozen balls in the drink. Picking up the receiver, she said, "Hi."

"Ms. Hart?"

"Yes?"

"This is Carlos at the front desk. I've got a limo driver here who says Mr. Moon called his company and asked that you be picked up."

"Did he say why?"

"I'll ask him." Candy heard Carlos say something to the driver, then come back on the line. "Mr. Moon says he wants you to meet him someplace special."

151

Candy smiled. "Tell him to wait."

Twenty minutes later she walked out of the hotel. The Delano was in a downtrodden neighborhood, and the owners had erected an impenetrable evergreen hedge around the front entrance. Next to the hedge, smoking a cigarette, was a skinny Cuban in a black driver's uniform. He smiled, revealing a mouthful of gold, then opened the limo's back door. It was filled with dozens of red roses. Candy got in and stuck her face in the flowers. The scent was intoxicating, and she felt the car pull away.

Leaving Saul Hyman's condo, Valentine called Bill Higgins on his cell phone. Ten minutes later, they were sitting in a corner of the Loews restaurant, sharing a pot of coffee. Valentine spelled out what Saul had told him, then said, "I think Saul knows more than he's letting on. I want you to tail him for a few days. You still remember what he looks like?"

"I sure do," Bill said. "I arrested him after he fleeced a Texas oil tycoon in a bridge game. The Texan was a world-class player, too."

"Let me guess," Valentine said. "Saul had inside help."

Bill nodded. "Saul played the Texan at a table by the hotel pool. At the next table was Saul's plant. The plant was reading a newspaper with a slit in it. He looked at the Texan's cards, and by breathing through his nose, he signaled to Saul how to bet."

"The whiff," Valentine said.

152

"You've heard of it?"

Valentine said yes. He'd seen his grandmother and one of her friends do it at a card game in the Catskills over fifty years ago.

"I didn't have enough evidence for a conviction," Bill said. "But I took what I had to the state gaming board, and they barred Saul from ever returning to Nevada." He picked up the pot and refilled their mugs. "So, why do you think he's involved?"

The coffee was unusually good, maybe the best cup Valentine had tasted in Miami. He'd be back here again. "I'm pretty good at knowing when people are lying to me. I didn't think Saul was, but then I got to thinking. Saul says he hasn't seen Victor Marks in years. That's bull. He and Victor were friends for forty years. You ever have a buddy like that?"

"Sure," Bill said.

"I bet you talk to him every few weeks."

"At least."

"So Saul's lying. He should have said, 'I haven't heard from him since Thanksgiving.' That I would have bought. But not in years."

Valentine wrote down Saul's address on a napkin, then described the condo building right down to the height of the hedges. "There's a wall around the property. If Saul tries to leave, he'll have to go out through the front entrance. I saw his car keys sitting on a table. He drives a Toyota."

Bill paid for the coffee, and they rose from

the table. Everything had seemed fine until that moment, then the facade on Bill's face cracked and the deep worry lines broke through. Valentine said, "Something wrong?"

"I got a call from the Broward police. A body was found in a Fort Lauderdale Dumpster. They think it's Jack Lightfoot. They want me at the morgue to make an ID."

Valentine could tell that Bill was hurting inside. That was where they were different. He hardly ever felt bad for crooks. They walked outside to the valet stand.

"You want company?" Valentine asked.

"If you're up to it," his friend said.

Whoever had dumped Jack Lightfoot's body was not very smart. He had seaweed in his hair and swamp water in his lungs, and both arms and one of his legs had been chewed off. It was obvious that he'd died in a swamp.

Enough of his face remained to make a positive identification, and Bill's hand had shaken as he signed the coroner's statement. An hour later, Valentine dropped him off at the Loews, then went back to his hotel. He felt dog-tired, and the king-size bed in his room was calling to him. Walking into the Fontainebleau's lobby, he spotted an Indian woman in a dark business suit by the elevators. Late twenties, short black hair, flat face, a little stocky. She approached him with an expectant look on her face.

"Mr. Valentine?"

He nodded, and she handed him her card. Gladys Soft Wings. Her title was legal representative for the Micanopy nation. It was a deceiving name. There didn't appear to be anything soft about her.

"I'm here on behalf of my client, Chief Running Bear."

"Your client?"

"The chief was involved in an altercation with five other tribe members. One of them died."

"I hope it was Harry Smooth Stone."

"Excuse me?"

"He put an alligator in my car. Nearly bit my hand off."

Gladys took a square of paper from her pocket. Unfolding it, she handed it to him. "This is the only evidence I have against Smooth Stone. Running Bear found it in his trailer."

Valentine studied the equations written on the ledger paper, then handed it back to her. "The equations are the hold for five blackjack dealers at your casino."

"What's that?"

"The hold is the equation a casino uses to determine how much money it's making at its games. If these numbers are accurate, these dealers are cheating."

"How can you be certain?"

"The average hold for a blackjack table is twenty percent. Your dealers are showing a hold of forty-four percent. They're pocketing twenty-four percent and letting the casino keep the other twenty."

Gladys looked relieved. "Running Bear said you would know. Now I need to ask you a favor."

"You want me to explain it to the police?"

She seemed taken aback. "Actually, to the elders of my tribe. How did you know?"

"It's what I do for a living," he said.

The elders of the Micanopy nation were five pewter-haired men whose median age Valentine guessed to be seventy-five. They sat behind a long table wearing equally long faces. Each wore a dungaree jacket and a denim shirt, their faces road maps of the lives they'd lived. Valentine remembered reading how Micanopy warriors had prevented the white man from settling in Florida until the early 1900s. These men's fathers and grandfathers, he guessed.

To the elders' right sat Running Bear and Gladys Soft Wings. To their left, Smooth Stone and his three accomplices and their attorney, a pointy-headed Indian kid in a cheap suit. Behind them stood six tribal policemen armed with Mossberg shotguns.

Both attorneys presented their clients' version of the story. Unlike a court of law, no one was asked to swear on a Bible, and a blindfolded statue called Justice did not look down on them.

Then it was Valentine's turn. He gave his credentials, then removed the piece of ledger paper that was Running Bear's only evidence and laid it on the table. The elders collectively lowered their heads.

"This piece of paper was found in a ledger of Harry Smooth Stone's."

"Objection," the pointy-headed lawyer said, jumping to his feet. "We don't know if that came from a ledger of Harry's or not."

"It's his handwriting," the lead elder said. "Sit down."

The lawyer swallowed hard. "You sure?"

"I taught him to write," the elder barked. "Sit down."

The lawyer returned to his seat. The lead elder shot him a look that said he wouldn't tolerate another interruption. Valentine pointed at the equations on the paper and continued. "This is classic evidence of cheating—something I've seen in dozens of cases. The head of the gang keeps a ledger to assure the rest of the gang that no one's getting shortchanged. It's the only way everyone can get along."

The lead elder made a face. "Are you saying *all* of these men were cheating?"

"That's right."

"Why didn't our security people spot it?"

That was a good question. Clearing his throat, Valentine said, "Your security people probably did."

The lead elder frowned. So did his colleagues.

"Please explain."

"I need to ask you a few questions."

The lead elder considered it. "All right."

"How many people live on the reservation?"

"Twenty-five hundred."

"How many are related?"

"Nearly everyone," he said stiffly.

"How many people work in the casino's security department?"

The elder looked to Running Bear, who said, "Forty-six."

"All related?"

Running Bear had to think. "Yes."

"Which means your security people are watching their cousins, aunts, and grandparents, which is the worst possible thing you could have in this business."

The lead elder stuck his jaw out. "Why is that?"

"In most casinos, security people are ex-cops and detectives. They never fraternize with anyone on the casino floor, nor do any socializing. This dis-association allows them to be objective observers. If you compare that to what's going on in your casino—"

"Excuse me," the pointy-headed lawyer said. "But is anyone going to offer up a shred of evidence here? Or are we going to let this man run off at the mouth? My clients have rights."

The elders collectively frowned. They impressed Valentine as smart men who knew the truth when they heard it. What the lawyer was asking them to do was go backwards. It was the only thing the legal profession was really good at.

"Do you have any more proof?" the lead elder asked.

"Give me the surveillance tapes of these men dealing blackjack, and I'll give you loads of proof," Valentine said.

"You can do this right away?"

"I'll need a day or two," Valentine said.

The elders went into a huddle, then took a vote.

"Done," the lead elder said.

Before Valentine could say another word, the elders had filed out of the room, followed by Running Bear and the other accused men. He'd taken this job because he wanted to escape from his problems. It wasn't working out that way, and he found himself wishing that he'd stayed home.

"Nice job," Gladys said as they left the trailer.

CHAPTER 18

He followed Gladys into the casino through a back door, then into a stairwell marked EMPLOYEES ONLY. On the second floor they stopped at a door with a surveillance camera hanging over it. Gladys knocked once, then looked into the camera.

"Come on," she said under her breath.

A lantern-jawed Indian wearing a blue blazer opened the door. His name was Billy Tiger, and he was running surveillance while Harry Smooth Stone cooled his heels in jail. He ushered them in.

The heart and soul of every casino's security was its surveillance control room. These rooms were generally darkened spaces filled with expensive monitoring equipment used to detect and videotape suspected cheaters. The air was kept a chilly sixty-five degrees so the equipment would not malfunction. It also kept the personnel from turning into zombies as they stared at black-and-white images on their monitors for eight hours a day. Tiger led them to a corner office and shut the door.

"I figured you'd want some privacy," he said.

Valentine was missing something. How did Tiger know what they wanted? As if reading his thoughts, Tiger said, "I got a call from the elders. All five of them. They said you needed to see some tapes."

"All five of them?" Gladys said.

Tiger wore the slightly bemused expression of someone who woke up every day with a smile on his face. "Yeah. It was pretty funny. They can't make a decision without taking a vote. I'd hate to see them ordering takeout."

From his shirt pocket, Valentine removed the piece of paper that Running Bear had taken from Smooth Stone's ledger. "I need to see a recent surveillance tape of each of these dealers, except Jack Lightfoot."

Tiger read the list. "That shouldn't be too hard."

"And their personnel files."

"I'll get right on it."

Tiger started to leave the room. Valentine had an idea and stopped him.

"Which of these dealers has the least experience dealing blackjack?"

Tiger took the paper and looked at it. "Karl Blackhorn. He was pretty new."

"How new is that?"

"Four, five months."

"Let's start with him," Valentine said.

★   ★   ★

161

Soon, Valentine and Gladys were watching a tape of Blackhorn. He was easily the sloppiest blackjack dealer Valentine had ever seen.

"How did this guy ever get a job?" Valentine asked.

"Running Bear," Gladys explained. "When the casino has openings it can't fill, he hires Indians from other tribes. If they have families, they can live on the reservation and go to school without cost. Other tribes around the country have adopted similar policies."

Valentine watched Blackhorn deal a round. Each player at the table was dealt two cards. As Blackhorn came to himself, he hesitated. Standard casino procedure called for him to use his second card to flip his first card faceup. Then he was supposed to slip his second card underneath his first.

Only Blackhorn didn't do this.

Instead, he glanced at the players' hands. Then he awkwardly turned his *second* card faceup onto his first. Valentine stared at the screen. Had Blackhorn forgotten the rules and flipped over the wrong card? It happened sometimes and, as far as he knew, made no difference to the game's outcome.

The piece of paper from Smooth Stone's ledger lay on the desk. Picking it up, he stared at the numbers beside Blackhorn's name.

DROP: 12,104 WINNINGS: 5,812
HOLD: 42%

Blackhorn had kept 42 percent of the bets wagered at his table. The best blackjack dealers in the world kept 20 percent. These dealers were considered A dealers and assigned to work the tables when "whales" came to town. And here was a wet-behind-the-ears kid winning *twice* as much money.

"Let me see his file," Valentine said.

Gladys handed him a Pendaflex folder. Valentine read it, then said, "Blackhorn was in prison for armed robbery. Your casino did a background check and turned it up. Yet you still hired him."

"That's right."

"Let me guess. This was Running Bear's doing."

"Yes. Running Bear spent time in prison. So do a lot of boys on the reservation. It's a by-product of high unemployment and poor schooling."

So what, Valentine nearly said. No legitimate casino would allow a person with a criminal record to work for them. It was too damn tempting, the money flowing back and forth, night after night. Running Bear had a vision and thought he could change people by treating them well. Only, it didn't work that way with criminals.

"I'd like to see another tape of this guy," Valentine said.

They found Billy Tiger standing in front of a curved wall of video monitors, watching the action in the casino. Without taking his eyes away, he said, "You done?"

"We want to see another tape of Blackhorn," Gladys said.

Tiger peeled his eyes away. And hesitated.

Gladys said, "Is that a problem?"

His bemused expression had faded. "Not at all," he said.

While Gladys and Tiger went looking for the tape, Valentine returned to the office. He suddenly felt exhausted. Maybe wrestling alligators had something to do with it. Or the sheer physical exertion of having to be nice with his son. His eyes started to droop, and he stared at the TV on the desk. It contained live feeds of the casino's hot zones and included the parking lot. A black limousine was parked by the entrance. Beside it stood a redhead smoking a cigarette. He put his face so close to the screen that his nose touched it. One thing that hadn't slowed down as he'd gotten older was his memory. He'd seen this woman before.

She tossed her cigarette. Then said something to the skinny Hispanic driver and pointed at her watch. The driver made a conciliatory gesture with his hands. The tape of Jack Lightfoot, Valentine thought. The redhead was the raggle.

She got into the limo. So did the driver. Reaching down, the driver removed a handgun from a pocket on the door and slipped it into his lap. Then he shut the door and drove away.

Valentine ran out of the room, looking for Gladys Soft Wings.

CHAPTER 19

Splinters had always considered casinos filthy places. In Havana, he'd gone to school in a building that had housed a casino during the Batista regime. Castro had closed the casino after the revolution, along with whorehouses and sex shows, and replaced them with schools and hospitals. Every schoolkid knew the story by heart. Even the bad ones.

"You're sure Nigel Moon said he'd meet me outside the Micanopy casino," Candy said from the backseat.

Splinters was driving on the twisting, single-lane road that eventually returned to the turnpike, and his eyes searched for the break in the mangroves where he and Rico had dumped Jack Lightfoot's body. "Yes, ma'am. That's what he said."

In his mirror, Candy had a cell phone against her ear. They were in a dead zone, and she could not get a connection. She tossed the phone into her bag.

"I'm going to kill him. Why are you driving so slow, anyway?"

On the shoulder of the road Splinters saw a sleek

black racer. It looked dead until it sprang to life and slithered away.

"Kill who?" he asked.

"Nigel fucking Moon, the bozo who hired you."

Splinters didn't like that. Did she have a gun? That could be a problem.

"How?" he asked.

"How what?" she said indignantly.

Splinters looked in the mirror. The hooker's face was flushed and had turned hot pink. With the hair it almost made her look like she was on fire. He'd watched her from afar a couple of times and had memorized the contours of her body. More than once he'd imagined her naked, and him inside of her, and what her reaction would be.

"You're going to kill him," he said.

"With my bare hands."

He felt himself relax. The break in the road appeared. He tapped the brakes and tucked the gun in his lap behind his belt. "Damn," he said loudly. "I got a flat tire." He pulled off the road and parked beside the trail. It was well-worn, and he looked down it but saw no hikers or fishermen. He got out and opened Candy's door. She gave him a look that suggested her patience had run out.

"I'm not getting out in this fucking swamp."

"But—"

"You heard me."

Her face was still a hot pink. The effect it had on him was remarkable, and he hid behind the door, not wanting her to see the erection in his trousers. He imagined screwing her, and her fighting with him like a wild animal. "Tire's flat," he explained. "I gotta change the tire." She wasn't budging, so he said, "It's dangerous for you to stay in the car."

She got out and brushed past him. He saw her walk toward the front of the car and pulled the gun from behind his waistband. Coming up from behind her, he shoved the barrel into the small of her back. "Know what this is?"

She froze, her head tilting slightly back. "Your dick?"

He started grinning. He hadn't known many whores with a sense of humor. He took the purse from her outstretched hand and tossed it into a stand of mangroves. "It's a gun. Would you rather see my dick?"

Candy looked over her shoulder into his eyes. She was scared.

"Okay," she said.

"You want to fuck me?"

"It crossed my mind."

"Oh, yeah?"

"Yes."

"I wanna hear you say it."

"I want your big Cuban prick inside of me."

Splinters made her turn around and say it again. Then he made her undress herself. She wore a red lace bra, one of those garments that cost hundreds of dollars. She slipped out of it without being asked. Heaven. Pointing at the trail, he said, "You first."

"Speed up, will you?" Valentine said.

Gladys Soft Wings's hands gripped the wheel of her Volvo. Valentine had run out of Billy Tiger's office, grabbed her by the arm, and dragged her to the parking lot. Now he was insisting she speed down tribal roads, something she was loath to do.

"Someone's life is at stake."

She hit the gas. The roads twisted like a corkscrew, and the tires screeched on every curve. She'd bought the car to drive on I-95, south Florida's crazy drivers more frightening than anything she'd ever known. Rounding a curve, she saw a black limo on the side of the road and slammed on the brakes.

Valentine hit the windshield. He saw stars, then pulled himself off the dashboard, the warm sensation of blood creeping down his face. He touched his nostril and swore.

"Sorry. Why aren't you wearing your belt?"

"Because I'm a dope." He pulled out a handkerchief and pressed it against his nose. "Do you have a gun by any chance?"

"No. Don't you think we should—"

"Call the tribal police? No." He climbed out of the car, then stuck his head back in before shutting the door. "I want you to drive up the road a hundred yards and wait. If someone besides me comes out of that trail, beat it. Understand?"

"Are you going to tell me what's going on?"

"No," he said.

The Volvo pulled away. Valentine walked down the trail until he was in the thick of the swamp. It was like being in a forest, only the ground was gooey soft. He heard voices. Peering around a cypress tree, he saw two figures standing on a grassy knoll next to a pond. He put on his bifocals. It was the redhead and the limo driver. The redhead was naked. The driver was stripping out of his uniform while holding a gun on her, the act made more complicated by the big boy distorting his trousers.

Valentine weighed his options. Making a run at them was out of the question. The distance was too great, and he'd given up wind sprints years ago. The other option was sneaking up on them and disarming the driver, which wouldn't be terribly hard once they started going at it. He stepped off the trail into a thicket of mangroves.

As he approached, he listened to the redhead talking to the driver. Her voice was soothing, like she knew she was about to get raped and didn't want to do anything to make it worse. The driver told her to get on her knees.

Valentine parted a bush and had another look. The redhead was on all fours. The driver was behind her, poised to make his statement. She was still talking, the fear absent from her voice. Leaning forward, he felt his shoe catch an exposed root and fell into a disgustingly soft belly of muck.

His head came out of the water just in time to hear the redhead scream. Rising, he stared into the clearing. The redhead had tried to run, and the driver was holding her underwater. Her legs were thrashing as air bubbles burst the water's surface. The kicking grew faint, then stopped altogether. Valentine broke through the mangroves.

"Let her go."

The driver's eyes went wide. He had the gun in his left hand, the girl's head in his right. He looked *scared*. Like he'd seen a ghost. And Valentine supposed he probably did look like a ghost, his wet hair in his face, the blood from his nose flowing down his chin. Or a dead man risen from a swampy grave.

"*Who are you?*" the driver said.

"Jack Lightfoot," he growled.

Valentine saw the redhead sink beneath the water's surface. "I deal blackjack," he said. "Remember?"

The driver was out of the pond and picking up his clothes, the gun still pointed in Valentine's direction. He was going to run, and Valentine stepped back into the mangroves and ducked out of sight. Barefoot, the driver raced past moments later, swearing in Spanish.

Valentine pulled the redhead out of the pond and gave her CPR. Her face had turned blue, and he didn't think there was much hope. In between breaths, he wiped at the blood on his face, hoping not to get any on her. Stupid, but he did it anyway.

She was a natural redhead, and it was hard not to look at her privates. That had always been the hard part of police work. Every day, he'd be confronted by things that he knew were wrong but wanted to do anyway. Like staring at naked corpses.

He heard something like a frog trying to climb out of her stomach. An eruption in the making. He leaned backwards, but not in time. She puked on him.

"Oh, my God," she gasped. "Oh, my God."

She lay on her back, fighting for breath. Valentine lay down next to her. The world was spinning, and his head was starting to throb. She reached out and found his arm.

"Who are you?"

"Tony Valentine."

"I'm Candy. Where's—"

"The guy trying to kill you? I scared him off. Look, try not to talk."

She found his hand and squeezed it. "I owe you, Tony."

Gladys Soft Wings entered the clearing. She was visibly frightened and stared at them lying in the grass, holding hands.

"I hope I'm not interrupting something," she said.

CHAPTER 20

Splinters pulled off 595 at the first exit. Parking behind a Shell station, he threw his driver's uniform back on while muttering to himself. He hadn't gotten laid, the hooker had nearly escaped, and he'd seen a fucking ghost. Someone had put a curse on him, and he hadn't even known it.

Back in the limo, doing eighty, he started to feel really bad. Rico had told him to do one thing, and he'd gone and done another. Rico wouldn't like that if he found out. He would kill Splinters for something like that. The exit sign for Davie loomed in his windshield.

He slowed down. Off to his left, striped carnival tents filled a cow field. He'd been fuming for days over the outrageous bribe Rico had paid the carny owner. *Four thousand two hundred dollars.* And for what?

He put his indicator on. An idea was percolating in his head. He would get the money back—all of it—and show Rico his loyalty. He changed lanes and nearly ran another vehicle off the road.

Black limousines were symbols of power, and

he circled the carnival's perimeter without anyone stopping him. Parking beside the owner's trailer, he hopped out and looked around. Peals of laughter floated down from the carnival Ferris wheel. It was Friday afternoon, and the grounds were teeming with teenage kids.

He walked up the trailer ramp and rapped loudly on the door. When no one came out, he pushed the door open and stuck his head in. The shit smell that greeted him was like a punch in the face, and his eyes settled on the caged chimpanzee. Rico hadn't mentioned anything about a fucking ape.

Splinters stepped inside and shut the door. The chimp was strumming a miniature guitar, his head swinging back and forth. The tinny sounds of Madonna's *Like a Virgin* sent an icy chill running down Splinters's spine. First a ghost in the swamp, now a chimp playing his favorite song.

"Play something else," he said.

The chimp broke into Prince's *Purple Rain*, another favorite. Splinters decided he was hallucinating, the music really nothing more than random chords he was mistaking for these songs. He got behind the desk and started opening drawers. Suddenly, the chimp started hissing at him like a cat.

Splinters drew his gun. He didn't want to shoot the chimp, but if the chimp started making noise, Splinters wasn't going to have a choice. The chimp stared at the gun, then flopped on his back and played dead, his feet twitching comically.

Splinters jerked open the top drawer of the desk. Inside lay a stack of hundred-dollar bills. He counted out forty-two hundred dollars and was stuffing the money into his pockets when the chimp came flying out of the cage.

"You want to hear a cool scam?" Zoe asked.

They were sitting on a couch in the Fontaine-bleau's lobby, Kat watching the front doors. She'd checked into the Castaway the night before, then started trying to reach Tony. No answer in his hotel room or on his cell phone. She didn't want to leave a message and sound desperate, so she'd parked herself in his hotel. It would be better to see him in person, she'd decided, and get things back on track.

"Tony taught it to me," her daughter said. "A world-famous poker player showed it to him. He doped out the math for me and everything. It's really cool."

"It's mathematical?"

"Yeah, sort of. You want to hear it?"

From where she sat, Kat had a bird's-eye view of the hotel valet stand. A black Volvo pulled up, and a muddy Tony and an Indian woman got out. With them was a woman with red hair whose clothes were also muddy. She was glued to Tony's side, and Kat felt her stomach do a slow churn.

"Sure," she said.

"It's called the birthday bet. You go into a room where there's thirty people, and you bet someone a dollar that two or more of the people in the room share the same birthday. No shills."

"Shills?" Kat asked, watching the trio cross the lobby floor. Tony had a funny look on his face. Was he dazed, or smitten?

"No stooges. You don't have to know anybody in the room. Now, you tell the person you're betting with that the odds are twelve-to-one in his favor, because thirty people divided into three hundred and sixty-five birthdays is 12.17. The sucker usually takes the bet, and you win!"

"Really," Kat said, watching them wait for an elevator. The redhead was hanging on Tony like he'd just saved her life and she just *had* to show her appreciation.

"I'll tell you how it's done," Zoe said. "It's based on a principle called progressive calculation. You're not betting on two people sharing one particular birthday. You're betting that two people will share *any* birthday. The chances are fifty-fifty with twenty-two people in the room. Every additional person increases the odds in your favor. With thirty people in the room, the odds are four-to-one against your opponent. You will almost always win. Pretty cool, huh?"

Kat watched them get into an elevator and the doors shut. In the six weeks she'd known Tony, she'd seen a lot of different women try to glom on to him. He was honest and caring, things you didn't find often in men. The funny part was, he was always slow to catch on. She glanced at her daughter, who was writing the calculations onto a napkin. A hundred and forty IQ, so why was she pulling Ds in school?

Zoe showed her the math. "See how it works? If you're in a room with fifty people, the odds are over thirty-to-one in your favor."

Kat rose from the couch. She missed Tony, and she wanted to get him away from these two women and get on with their lives, only what she had in mind wouldn't work with her twelve-year-old daughter clinging to her side.

"Let's go," she said.

"Excuse me, but I think I have a right to know what's going on," Gladys Soft Wings demanded when Candy was in Valentine's bathroom, taking a shower.

Valentine shook his head. He sat on the bed, eating Cracker Jacks from the minibar. Because he was covered in puke, he had showered first, then changed into clean clothes.

"You're not going to tell me who this woman is?"

"No," he said.

"Why not?"

"Because it won't help Running Bear's case," he said, opening a soda and taking a swig. "Right now, that's all you should care about. I'll explain later."

"Is that a promise?"

"What the hell kind of question is that? You ask me to be an expert witness for your client, but you don't trust me when I tell you I'll do something?"

Gladys acted hurt. "Hey. I'm sorry."

He held up the bag of Cracker Jacks. Gladys took a handful and shoved them in her mouth. They munched away until the bag was empty.

"I need to talk to this woman alone," he said. "Go back to the casino and get another tape of Blackhorn dealing blackjack. While you're at it, search his locker."

"I'll need the elders' permission to do that."

"Get it. Tell them it's important. Write down everything you find. Then call me."

Gladys Soft Wings crossed her arms and looked at him defiantly. He tried to imagine her arguing a case in court and guessed she'd be about as tenacious as a pit bull with a bone.

"Are you always so demanding?" she asked.

"Usually," he said.

Gladys left, and Candy came out of the bathroom. Instead of putting her clothes back on, she was wearing a fluffy hotel bathrobe. She'd blown out her hair and put on some makeup, and was as pretty as a high school beauty queen. Valentine blinked, then it registered. She was going to thank him for saving her life. He went to the TV and hit power. The screen came to life, Jack Lightfoot dealing blackjack to Candy and her date.

"Where did you get that?" she asked.

"Go put some clothes on and I'll tell you," he said.

Ten minutes later, they were sitting on Valentine's balcony, the sound of kids roughhousing in the hotel pool filling the air. "I'm an ex-cop," he said. "The Micanopys hired me to figure out how Jack Lightfoot was ripping them off. I saw you standing in the parking lot and remembered you from the tape."

"You said ex-cop," she said.

"That's right. You don't like cops?"

"I'm a hooker," she said.

He let an appropriate amount of time pass. Before casinos had come to Atlantic City, he'd worked vice and known plenty of hookers. Some had been decent women who'd gotten on the wrong track; the rest hard-nosed criminals who'd rip off their own brother. Candy, he guessed, fell somewhere in the middle.

"You don't dress like a hooker," he said, seeing where it would get him.

She gave him a sad smile. Then her face melted and reflex tears welled up in her eyes. *That's good,* he thought. *She still knows how to cry.*

"I'm trying to get out," she said.

"Going to school?"

Her eyes shifted down to the pool. "I teach aerobics."

"Good for you." Her face softened. Valentine decided to take a stab in the dark. "Why is Rico Blanco trying to kill you?"

"I told Rico I wanted out," she said.

"Of the scam?"

She nodded. Valentine pointed inside the room at the TV. "Who's your date?"

"Nigel Moon."

"Should I know him?"

"He's a famous rock-and-roll drummer. Rico hired me to butter him up."

"You fall for him?"

"Yes."

Her eyes seemed hypnotized by something or someone in the pool that he wasn't seeing. He'd known a couple of hookers who had fallen for johns. The relationships had lasted a little while, then run aground when reality set in.

"You realize you're in a lot of trouble," he said.

"I haven't broken any laws."

"Rico murdered the blackjack dealer. When Rico gets caught, he'll drag down everything in sight. Including you."

"And you can stop that from happening," she said.

"Yes."

"How?"

"I'll tell the cops the truth. Rico's a con man. He hired you to lead Nigel around by the nose. There would be no reason for you to know anything else about the scam. If the cops decide to prosecute you anyway, I'll go to court as your witness."

"Provided I help you out."

"That's right."

Still looking at the pool, she said, "And if I don't?"

"Then you're on your own, sweetheart."

Candy blew out her cheeks. The sun was giving her skin a lobster complexion. She brought herself back from a long way and stared into his eyes.

"Rico is planning to rip off a bookie named Bobby Jewel," she said.

"How is Nigel involved?"

"Rico is going to use Nigel's money. Rico's been planning it for a long time."

"How much money are we talking about?"

"He said millions."

"When?"

"The next couple of days."

"What else?"

"That's all I know." She looked deep into his eyes. "You still going to hold up your end of the bargain?"

"I gave you my word, didn't I?"

Her chair made a harsh scraping sound on the concrete balcony. Valentine walked her out of his room to the elevator. She pressed the button, then threw her arms around him, and gave him a kiss that Valentine didn't think he'd ever forget.

"Thanks for the save," she said.

CHAPTER 21

Hey, rube!

The words made Ray Hicks's head snap. Carny slang for trouble. He was helping out at the cotton candy stand. The sun was low in the sky, the carnival starting to empty out. An employee hurtled past, then another. Hicks caught the second man's arm.

"Talk to me."

"Shooting," the man said breathlessly.

Hicks looked up and down his carnival. Everything looked fine. "Where?"

"By the trailers."

A line of dirty-faced kids was waiting to buy cotton candy. The man who dispensed the candy had run out of change, so Hicks was standing there with a pocketful of coins, helping out. The man who dispensed the candy knew damn well that Hicks was not going to give him his money to hold. In a whisper, he asked Hicks, "Should I shut down?"

Hicks looked at the kids' expectant faces. He'd been swindling people for years, but he was not in the business of disappointing them. "Give them free candy."

"Free candy?"

"You heard me." Hicks hitched up his trousers and hurried across the lot. If there had been a shooting, it would mean a visit from the town clowns, and another fat bribe to keep everyone happy. Some days, it just wasn't worth getting out of bed.

The trailers were behind the concession stands, and he came around the corner to see a dozen employees running around like headless chickens. Pushing his way through the crowd, he found a ticket-taker named Smitty who had more brains than all of them combined.

"It looks bad," Smitty told him.

"How bad is that?" Hicks said.

"He might die."

Hicks twirled the plastic toothpick that had resided in his mouth since breakfast. "Who we talking about here? A customer?"

Smitty's eyes went wide. "You don't know?"

"Spit it out, boy."

"Mr. Beauregard got shot by a robber."

Hicks nearly knocked Smitty down as he barreled up the ramp to his trailer. Inside, a gang of employees was clustered around the desk. Mr. Beauregard lay with his eyes shut while a Mexican fortune-teller named Princess Fatima pressed a blood-stained towel to his forehead. Kneeling, he said, "Mr. Beauregard, it's me. Mr. Beauregard, look at me."

The chimp's eyes did not open. Hicks thought of

all the times Mr. Beauregard had feigned playing dead, just to get a rise out of him. From the cage he removed the ukulele and plucked a few chords. Mr. Beauregard's eyelids fluttered. Princess Fatima caressed his brow and silently cried, knowing all too well what the future held.

An ambulance came, accompanied by two police cruisers. Hicks knew the best thing to tell the police was nothing at all, and he climbed into the back after Mr. Beauregard was wheeled in on a gurney. The EMT person was a bottled blond with a kind face. As the ambulance pulled out of the carnival grounds, she said, "We're going to take him to a good animal hospital over in Fort Lauderdale. They deal with the circus animals when they come to town."

"No," Hicks said.

"Excuse me?"

"I want you to take him to a people hospital."

"But, sir . . ."

"Please do as I say. I'll pay you. Cash."

The EMT woman discussed it with the driver. Hicks laid his hand on Mr. Beauregard's forehead and tuned them out. Ten years ago, he'd found Mr. Beauregard in a strip shopping center in Louisiana, huddled in a cage. He'd bought him for a hundred dollars and moved him into a cage in his trailer, hoping to train Mr. Beauregard to do some simple tricks. But Mr. Beauregard had already been to school. Play a tune on the radio, and he would duplicate it on his ukulele. Tell him the name of a city, and he'd find it on a map. He could think, and add numbers, and he also *knew* things, just as people knew things—like hate and fear and jealousy and betrayal—and it had all sunk home for Hicks one day when Mr. Beauregard kicked a carnival worker in the balls for calling him a "dirty monkey." That was when Hicks had realized that Mr. Beauregard wasn't just a clever animal, but an evolutionary marvel. He heard the EMT woman talking to him and looked into her kind face.

"I said, we're going to take your friend here to a regular hospital. Okay?"

Mr. Beauregard's forehead had grown cold, and Hicks took his hand away.

"Thank you, ma'am," he said.

Opening a topless joint on South Beach had been Victor Marks's idea.

"A man needs a place to do business," Victor had told Rico. "It should be a strip club, too. No one knows how much money a strip club is supposed to make."

Rico hadn't understood Victor's reasoning.

"You need a way to launder your money in case the IRS comes calling," Victor explained. "That's how your old boss, John Gotti, screwed up. He put on his tax return he sold kitchen fixtures for a living. And look at what happened to him."

So Rico had opened Club Hedo. A former Arthur Murray Dance Studio, it sat a block removed from the beach. Every day, guys strolled in wearing flip-flops and sand stuck between their toes, paid a stripper twenty bucks to give them a lap dance, then went back to their families and their beach chairs. Weekends saw a lot of Europeans, but mostly it was the beer and T-shirt set.

It was Friday night, and the club was packed. Rico was in his office in back. Through a one-way mirror, he kept one eye on the action while watching basketball on TV.

Miami College, who he had money on, was getting slaughtered. They were a brand-new team and they stunk. The starters were freshmen, and the pressure had done a number on their heads. They hadn't won a game all season.

His phone rang. It was big Bobby Jewel.

"You sweating through your underwear yet?" Jewel asked.

"It ain't over till it's over," Rico said.

"I know who said that," the bookie said.

"Hundred bucks says you don't."

"Yogi Bear."

"It was Yogi Berra, you idiot. Yogi Bear was a cartoon character. You owe me a hundred." Through the mirror he saw Splinters enter the club. He said good-bye to the bookie, expecting Splinters to come back and tell him how things had gone with Candy. Only, Splinters didn't do that. Bellying up to the bar, he ordered a rum and coke and clicked his fingers to the music. The DJ liked disco, and Splinters sang along to an old Donna Summers song, having the time of his fucking life.

Rico picked up the phone and called the bar—"Send that asshole back here"—and looked at the TV. Fifty seconds left in the game, and Miami College was down by six. Splinters sauntered in. His starched white shirt was covered in tiny red dots.

"What did you do, cut her fucking head off?"

"I drowned her," his driver said.

"In the ocean?"

"In the swamps, where we dumped the blackjack dealer."

"So what's with the shirt? You cut yourself shaving?"

Splinters glanced at the TV. He knew a little bit of what was going on, and how important Miami College was to the scheme of things. He removed two stacks of hundred-dollar bills from his jacket and dropped them on the desk.

"Where did you get that?"

The phone rang. Rico answered it.

"You've got a visitor," his bartender said.

Rico stared into the mirror. Goofy Gerry Valentine from Brooklyn was sitting at his bar, nursing a Budweiser. *What the hell did he want?*

"Tell him I'm not here."

"He says his father's in town, wants to set up a meeting."

"*His father?*"

"That's what he said."

An alarm went off in Rico's head. Gerry's old man had blown up the Mollo brothers in Atlantic

City and was not someone to take lightly. "Tell him to come back tomorrow morning."

The bartender relayed the message. Through the mirror, Rico watched Gerry leave. Splinters started to walk out.

"Tell me where you got the money," Rico demanded.

"You don't know?" his driver said.

Rico leaned back in his chair. That was the crazy thing about Cubans; they never answered you directly. "You shot the carny owner," he guessed.

"His chimp."

"You shot his chimp?"

"Fucker attacked me."

Rico massaged his brow with his fingertips. The night before, he'd dreamed he was five years old and visiting the Bronx Zoo with his parents. They'd gotten separated, and Ray Hicks's chimp had walked out of a cage, taken Rico by the hand, and led him to his mom and dad. Everyone had been smiling, and then Rico woke up.

Through the wall, Rico heard hooting and hollering, the strippers taking turns spinning naked on a barber pole. He removed a leather bag from beneath his desk and tossed Ray Hicks's money into it. Standing, he shoved the satchel into Splinters's hands.

"I did good, huh," his driver said.

Rico looked at the TV. A Miami College player was at the free throw line. He missed both shots.

The buzzer sounded, ending the game. In one swift motion. Rico drew his .45 Smith & Wesson and shoved the barrel into the satchel's folds.

"Not really," he said, pulling the trigger.

CHAPTER 22

Leaving the Fontainebleau, Candy walked around South Beach for several hours, thinking about how close she'd come to dying that afternoon. With each passing minute she reminded herself of all the things she wanted to do with her life.

It was dark when she returned to the Delano. The Alice in Wonderland lobby was filled with strung-out party people. Standing beneath a billowing white curtain, she called Nigel's bungalow on a house phone, got no answer, then walked down to the Rose Bar and didn't find him there. Going outside, she spotted him at a table in the patio restaurant, still in his golf clothes. With him, inhaling a shrimp cocktail, was Rico.

Payback time, Candy thought.

She sat down next to her boyfriend. He kissed her and said, "Where you been hiding?"

Rico stared at her. Then he started to cough.

"Shopping," she said. "Hey, Rico, how's it going?"

"Spend a lot of money?" Nigel asked.

189

"Window-shopping," she said. "Cat got your tongue, Rico?"

"Rico was just telling me how we're going to fleece a local bookie," Nigel said, laughing like someone who'd been drinking all afternoon.

"Wow," Candy said.

Rico's face was turning blue, and he was smacking the table with his hand. An attentive waiter brought a glass of ice water. He downed it.

"Damn cocktail sauce," he gasped. He composed himself, then glanced furtively around the restaurant. "Nigel, this isn't exactly legal what we're talking about, you know?"

"Is there anything fun that *is* legal?" Nigel asked.

"How much are we fleecing his bookie for?" Candy asked innocently.

Rico started choking again. His water glass was refilled, and he asked for the check. Two plump German girls approached the table and in halting English asked Nigel to autograph the restaurant's paper menus. Nigel obliged, smiling when one kissed his cheek. Candy excused herself to the ladies' room.

Only, she didn't go in. Instead, she waited off the lobby until Rico walked past, and followed him outside to the hotel's valet stand. Rico handed his stub to the attendant, who then disappeared through a thick stand of hedges.

"I want you to get lost," she said to his back.

He spun around, an unlit cigarette dangling from his lips. "There you are."

"Don't even think about it."

"What?"

"Sweet-talking me, you bastard."

"It was my driver's idea," he said. "I told him to scare you off."

"Go to hell."

The valet brought up Rico's limo. Rico tipped him, then waited until the valet was behind his stand. Popping the trunk, Rico said, "I want to show you something."

"No."

"Give me a chance."

Candy walked around the vehicle. And nearly screamed. Inside the trunk was Rico's Cuban driver wrapped in a plastic sheet. His shirt was soaked in blood, and his pink tongue hung out of his mouth like a dog's. Rico slammed the trunk hard. Candy's legs had turned to rubber, and he grabbed her arm and held her up.

"Work with me, will you?"

She tried to pull away. "*No.*"

"Don't fall in love with Nigel Moon," he said under his breath. "He'll screw you for a couple of weeks, then get rid of you like a case of the clap. He's bad news. That's why I'm scamming him."

She swallowed hard. "What are you talking about?"

"There's a concert promoter in New York named Santo Bruno. He books all the big acts.

Two years ago, Santo offered One-Eyed Pig fifty million dollars to do a reunion tour. I'm talking ten shows, Candy. Guess what happened?"

"What?"

"Nigel said no, and the deal fell apart."

Candy vaguely remembered seeing it on the news. "Why did he do that?"

Rico flipped on his shades. "Why don't you ask him?" he said.

CHAPTER 23

The afternoon had turned into evening, and still no sign of Gerry.

Valentine sat on his balcony, growing worried. Gerry's cell phone was in Puerto Rico with Yolanda, and there was no way to reach him. What if something had happened during his meeting with Rico? The phone in the room rang. Valentine ran inside and snatched it up.

"Where have you been?"

"Right where I've always been," Mabel replied. "Someday, Tony, I'm going to convince you to keep your damn cell phone on."

It was the first time Valentine had ever heard his neighbor swear. He swallowed the snappy retort about to trip off his tongue. Taking his cell phone out, he hit power.

"You just did," he said.

"Oh, my," she said. "Did you actually just turn your cell phone on for my benefit?"

"Yup."

"I'm touched. I left a message for you earlier. Rather than repeat it, why don't you just pick it up, and hear what I had to say?"

The line went dead. His cell phone beeped, a message waiting in voice mail. He retrieved it and heard Mabel's voice. "Tony, it's me. I've been trying to reach you. Now, you may not like this, but I made an executive decision an hour ago."

"Uh-oh," he said.

"Jacques called. He said the craps dealer admitted to shrinking the casino's dice. The craps dealer told Jacques he wanted to cut a deal. He said another gang of cheaters was ripping the casino off for a thousand bucks a night at roulette. Jacques had the roulette wheel tested and also watched surveillance tapes of the table, but he didn't see anything wrong. He wants you to look at the tapes.

"First I said no," his neighbor said, "knowing how busy you are. But Jacques insisted and said he'd wired your fee to a nearby Western Union office. I called the office, and, yup, the money's there, so I caved in and said yes. I mean, he *has* been a good customer."

"And a jerk," Valentine said into the phone.

"So here's what I had Jacques do," Mabel said. "He sent an E-mail to your hotel that contains a copy of the surveillance tape of the roulette wheel. Go to the front desk and ask for Jodisue. She'll retrieve the E-mail from her computer, and you can have a look. And, Tony . . ."

"Yes, Mabel," he said.

"Start leaving your cell phone on!"

★　　★　　★

Jodisue was the night manager, a gal his age who'd migrated down from Boston. As she led him back to her office, Valentine spied a half-finished letter on her computer screen and the remains of a club sandwich in a cardboard box on her desk. With eyes in the back of her head, she said, "You hungry?"

"Yeah. How did you know?"

"Intuition."

She pointed at an empty chair. As he sat, a bag of potato chips landed in his lap. Opening it, he shoved a handful in his mouth.

Closing out of her document, Jodisue went into E-mail and pulled up Jacques's missive. There was a note and an attachment.

> Dear Tony Valentine,
>   Here is the tape. I see nothing, but I am not you. Thanking you in advance, I remain,
>
> > Jacques Dugay

She double-clicked her mouse on the attachment. "You a cop or something?"

"I'm a consultant," he said, staring at the static blue screen. "I catch people who cheat casinos."

"I thought it was the other way around."

"It's pretty serious crime. About a hundred million a year alone in Las Vegas, and that's just the cheating they know about."

"Don't you have to be there and actually see it?"

"The surveillance films are usually enough."

Windows Media Player appeared on her computer screen. Jacques's film was taking its time downloading. They bantered for several minutes, and Valentine felt like he was dancing. The film began to play. It was of good resolution, and showed a game of roulette with over a dozen players placing bets. Right away, Valentine saw something he didn't like, and pointed at the screen.

"This guy bothers me," he said.

The man in question was an employee. His job was to change the players' cash into chips, which was called the buy-in.

"How come?" Jodisue asked.

"His body language is wrong."

"Maybe he's upset about something," she suggested.

"He wouldn't bring it with him to work."

"How can you know that?"

"Casinos are strange places," he said. "There's constant energy flowing back and forth. It's impossible not to get caught up in it. Now, look at the guy. He's detached himself from the action. He's on the outside, looking in."

Jodisue stared at the screen. "You're very perceptive."

Valentine thought back to what Jacques had told Mabel. If the cheats were stealing a grand a night, it was probably going out in dribs and drabs, and not in one big killing, where it might be picked up by the cameras.

The film ended. Without being asked, Jodisue

196

moved the cursor over the screen and hit replay. The film started over. This time, Valentine watched the change man to the exclusion of everyone else at the table.

Part of the change man's job was to deposit the players' money into a locked drop box. Twice the bills got stuck, and he had to jiggle the plunger to get them down the chute. Valentine leaned back in his chair, convinced he'd made the scam.

"You mind my asking you a question?" Jodisue said.

"Go ahead."

"The lady who works for you . . ."

"Mabel?"

She nodded. "She your wife?"

Jodisue's fingers wore no rings, and the framed pictures on her desk contained nothing but panting canines. Another time, another place, he would have taken her out for a milk shake, if for no other reason than to say thanks.

"Yes," he said.

"That's what I figured," Jodisue said.

Back in his room, Valentine lay on the bed and called Mabel. "You still steamed at me?" he asked.

"A little. You know, Tony, you need to think about people besides yourself every once in a while."

The truth be known, he *did* think about other people *all* the time—Gerry, Kat, Bill Higgins—but

197

what his neighbor was saying was, he needed to start thinking about *her* more, especially if she was going to run his business.

"I will," he promised. "Scout's honor."

"Good. Did you watch Jacques's film?"

"Yes. The cheater is the change man at the table. He's using a double drop box."

"What's that?"

"The box has a second box hidden in one of its walls. He uses a plunger to push the money down a chute into the box. By pushing the plunger sideways, the money goes into the hidden box. It's based on an old magic principle. Tell Jacques the man who empties the drop box is also involved in the scam."

"He'll be so happy," she said.

"I know it's late, but I need you to go on the Internet."

"I'm in your study," his neighbor said. "Give me a minute."

Riding up in the elevator, he'd thought about the surveillance tape of Karl Blackhorn he'd watched earlier. Blackhorn was cheating, yet nothing on the tape looked suspicious, except for the one time he'd turned over the wrong card in his hand.

"Ready," she said.

"Type in this address: www.blackjackedge.com."

"Done. It says I need a password."

"Griftsense," he said.

"How clever. Is this a site for people who cheat at blackjack?"

Valentine acknowledged that it was. The site's members were card-counters, mathematicians, and some of the smartest BJ hustlers in the world. "I want you to post a message for the discussion group."

"Go ahead."

He shut his eyes. "Dear group. I have a question regarding the change in house advantage on a two-deck game of blackjack when the following occurs. During the deal, the dealer's cards are dealt facedown. Normally, the dealer would turn over his first card and expose it to the players at the table. Instead, the dealer turns over his second card. Does this switch alter the house advantage, assuming the players are using Basic Strategy? Thanks for your help."

"What's Basic Strategy?"

"It's the best way to play blackjack without cheating. A mathematician named Thorp developed it. It shrinks the house edge."

Mabel read the message back to him. It sounded fine, and he told her to send it, then heard a knock on the door. Putting the phone down, he crossed the room and put his eye to the peephole. Kat stood in the hallway, dressed in a leather miniskirt and a red silk blouse. Attached to the blouse was the diamond pin he'd planned to give her. His heart did a little pitter-pat.

Picking up the phone, he said, "I need to run."

Up until Kat, he'd slept with only two women in

199

his life, and the effect she had on him as they sat on the bed was remarkable. His heart started to race, and his eyes started to see things better than they had in years. Even his voice sounded different.

"I missed you," she said, then explained the whole sorry episode with Ralph. When she was done, she said, "Zoe's downstairs playing video games near the pool. I slipped a lifeguard ten bucks to keep an eye on her."

"You're not mad at me?"

"No," she said.

Her lips parted ever so slightly, and Valentine realized she wanted him to kiss her. Traveling with Zoe, they'd gotten good at finding moments to slip away, the sex always better on the sly. The clothes started to come off, then Valentine felt a stab of pain in his arm and pulled back.

"What's wrong?"

"I banged up my elbow the other night wrestling an alligator," he explained.

"Jesus. Wait till I tell Donny."

Pain, he'd learned from judo, was good at clearing a person's head, and he took her hands and squeezed them gently. "I'm sorry about everything that happened in Orlando. But if I've learned anything in life, it's that things happen for a reason."

"They do?" she said.

"Yeah, they do. I needed to leave you for a while and help out a friend of mine."

"Is that why you're here?" she said.

"Yes."

"What about our show in Memphis next week?"

"I won't be there."

"This job?"

"I've decided to hang up the banana suit and retire the hair gel."

"Why . . ."

"Three days ago in Orlando, I looked in the mirror and didn't like what I saw."

"Which was what?"

"A sixty-two-year-old guy dressing up like a cartoon character so he could impress a woman twenty years his junior."

Valentine heard the scraping sound of a plastic key being put into the door. Kat jumped off the bed and buttoned her blouse. Gerry came in with a greasy bag of Chinese takeout clutched to his chest. He looked at Kat, then his father, said "Whoa," and started to back out the door. Kat said, "I was just leaving," and brushed past him with Valentine following her down the hall with his shirt hanging out of his pants.

At the elevator she said, "And I thought we had something wonderful between us."

A tray of food sat outside one of the rooms. The meal looked the same way he was starting to feel—devoured but not finished.

"We did," he admitted.

"Then why are you doing this?"

Because I wasn't put on this earth to play the fool,

201

he thought. The elevator doors parted and she got in, then stood with her arms crossed.

"It's Memphis or forget it," she told him.

Then she was gone.

CHAPTER 24

Saturday morning found Billy Tiger sitting on an upturned orange crate in Harry Smooth Stone's cell. Smooth Stone, Tiger's uncle on his mother's side, sat on a metal cot, his back to the concrete wall. In the room's muted light he looked a hundred years old, the bars' shadows forming a checkerboard on his sunken chest.

"This isn't good," Smooth Stone said.

Tiger had just come from the employee lounge. Gladys Soft Wings had obtained the elders' permission to clean out the lockers of the four dealers accused of cheating. Tiger had seen what was in the lockers, and didn't think there was anything that could incriminate the dealers. Then again, he didn't know how the men were cheating.

"It's not?" he said.

"If Valentine sees what's in the lockers, we're screwed."

Tiger cursed. He knew that Smooth Stone had been rigging the casino's game for a long time. The slot machines shorted players on jackpots ("Who ever counts the coins?" Smooth Stone said), while others didn't pay out at all, the EPROM chips that generated the machine's random numbers having been gaffed. At bingo, when the jackpots got too large, stooges in the crowd sometimes won.

Tiger had known it all along, but he'd never said anything. Smooth Stone had a reason for what he did.

It had all started three years ago, when a group of Las Vegas gamblers had swindled the tribe. Somehow, these gamblers had learned that a particular make of video poker machine had an overlay in its computer. Anyone who played one of these machines continuously for an hour would win seventy-five dollars. It had been the Micanopys' misfortune to have fifty of these machines in their casino.

The gamblers had hired retired people to work for them. For eight hours a day, the retired people would play these machines. One of the gamblers would sub whenever someone wanted to eat or hit the john.

The scam had lasted a month, then was spotted by the casino's auditor. Smooth Stone had gone to the Broward County police, convinced the gamblers had ties to the game's manufacturer in Nevada. When the cops had refused to help, he'd gone to the state's attorney general, then the FBI. And gotten nowhere.

The injustice had eaten a hole in Smooth Stone. Had the gamblers ripped off a casino in Las Vegas or Atlantic City or Biloxi, the authorities would have thrown them in jail and let them explain their way out. That was how it worked in the white man's casinos.

Smooth Stone slapped the cot with his hand.

"What?" Tiger said.

"Sit next to me," Smooth Stone said.

Tiger made the cot sag. When Tiger was a child, Smooth Stone had bounced him on his knee and told him stories. Smooth Stone cupped his hand next to Tiger's ear.

"I got something I want you to do," Smooth Stone whispered.

Tiger stared at the scuffed concrete floor. He had come to Smooth Stone out of a sense of loyalty, but now suddenly felt afraid. "What's that?"

"The key is Valentine. Without him, there isn't a case."

"Okay . . ."

"We need to scare him off."

Tiger gave him a look that said *I don't think so.* He'd been in the surveillance control room when Smooth Stone's gang had stuffed the alligator into the trunk of Valentine's car, and he'd seen Valentine take the alligator and smash it headfirst on the pavement.

"You're crazy," he whispered.

"He has an old woman who works for him," Smooth Stone said. "We'll do it through her."

Tiger buried his head in his hands. Now they were going after old ladies. He wanted to argue, but it was too late for that. He was an accessory to everything that had happened, including murder.

If Smooth Stone and the other dealers went to jail, so would he. He stared up into Smooth Stone's face.

"I hate this," the younger man said.

CHAPTER 25

Saul Hyman did not want trouble.

He'd started the day with a luxurious hot shower, then fixed breakfast and gone onto his balcony. Munching on a bagel, he'd stared through the apartment buildings across the street at the sliver of blue that was the mighty Atlantic. It was a razor-sharp day, the kind that made all the nonsense of living in Miami worthwhile.

And now it had been spoiled by the car parked across the street.

The car was a navy Altima. What had caught his eye was that it was in a no-parking zone. A bicycle cop had pulled up and chatted with the driver. The bicycle cop had left, and the Altima had stayed. Had to be another cop, Saul decided.

Going inside, he found the binoculars Sadie had given him for girl-watching. *Whatever turns you on,* she'd been fond of saying. Back on the balcony, he quickly found the car. The driver was reading the paper. Saul got in tight on his profile. He looked just like a cigar-store Indian, and Saul's blood pressure began to rise. The man in the car was Bill Higgins, director of the Nevada Gaming Control

Board, one of the most powerful law enforcement agents in the country. What was he doing here?

Looking for me, Saul thought.

He paced the condo, looking out his window at Higgins every few minutes. Saul hadn't worked Las Vegas in ten years. The last time he'd tried, Higgins had intercepted him at McCarran airport, and Saul had flown out the same day.

So why was he here?

Only one reason came to mind. This Victor Marks thing.

Saul kicked the furniture. Upon retiring, he'd promised Sadie he would never get involved with Victor again. Now he'd broken that promise, and look what had happened.

"Stupid, stupid, stupid," he said aloud.

He needed to get out of the condo, to take a walk and think things out. Going into the bedroom, he turned on the light in Sadie's closet. He'd kept all of her things, and he pulled out a floral dress he'd always liked. Stripping, he slipped it on, then opened a drawer and rummaged through her wigs. He'd always been partial to Sadie as a blond.

He made his mustache invisible with pancake, then appraised himself in the vanity. Saul Hyman, ancient drag queen. A straw hat and a pair of sunglasses lessened the pain, but only a little.

He didn't want to risk seeing a neighbor, so he took the stairwell to the lobby. At the bottom he opened the fire exit and stuck his head out. Empty. He walked to the front doors and ventured outside.

The fresh salt air invigorated him. He walked down the condo's driveway toward the sidewalk. Plenty of people were out. He'd blend right in.

He glanced across the street at Higgins in his car. The bastard was staring at him. Higgins's face, normally as animated as granite, had broken into a sickening sneer.

Saul started to sweat. Known cheaters put on elaborate disguises and tried to steal money from casinos every day. And guys like Bill Higgins saw right through them.

"Oh, no," he groaned.

Higgins got out of the car and started to cross the street. Did he want to talk about the good old days, or did he want to talk about Victor? Saul beat a trail back to his building and spied Stan and Lizzie, his neighbors, sidling down the drive.

"Saul?" Lizzie asked.

Damn, damn, damn. Saul walked with his eyes downcast.

"Saul, is that you?"

"Morning," he muttered under his breath.

"Oh, my," Stan said. They were regulars at the Wednesday night poolside barbecue, and Saul could imagine next week's banter. *Guess what. What? Hyman on four is a little light in the loafers. You don't say?*

The lobby's crisp air-conditioning hit him like a slap in the face. Sadie's dress was clinging to his legs. He tried to disengage himself and felt the fabric tear. It had been one of his late wife's favorites.

The elevator came. He started to board it, then glanced outside. Higgins was gone. So was the Altima. A stupid cop trick, designed to scare the daylights out of him.

It had worked.

Pretending to be asleep, Gerry watched his father do his morning exercises. Jumping jacks, push-ups, deep knee bends, and a crazy judo exercise where he stood on his head in the corner. He did twenty minutes every day, no matter how he felt. Gerry had tried it for a week, and decided he liked being out of shape.

Finished, his father sat on the edge of the sofa bed, and said, "Hey."

Gerry opened his eyes. "How did you know I wasn't sleeping?"

"You stopped snoring. You hungry?"

Gerry sat up. "Yeah. You mind my asking you something?"

"Depends what it is."

"It's about Kat." He followed his father to the bathroom and stood in the doorway as his father lathered up to shave. "I realize it's none of my business, but how come you busted up with her? She seems okay."

"She is okay," his father said, running the razor beneath the hot water. "I just couldn't be the person she wanted me to be."

"I thought you liked the wrestling."

"I did. I also like Halloween. But not all the time."

"You told me yourself, the change was doing you good."

Valentine shaved, then wiped his face with a washcloth. "I had this case once, a guy who disappeared. He lived in New Jersey, ran an accounting firm. He was a heavy gambler, and he had lines of credit at every casino. One day, he cleaned out his bank accounts and bolted. Left his wife, his kids, even his dog. Boom, gone.

"I got handed the case. I put a professional skip tracer on him, then went on to other things. There were so many places he could have gone, I didn't see the point of killing myself trying to find him.

"Two years later, the skip tracer calls me, says, 'You won't believe this.' Turns out the guy has reappeared. He's living in New Jersey, about fifty miles from where he lived before. He belongs to a country club and is married to a woman a lot like his first wife. His life is almost identical to the one he had before. The local cops arrest him, and I arrange to meet with the guy. I was curious, you know?"

"Sure," Gerry said.

"His name was Stanley. So I say, 'Stanley, why didn't you run?' And Stanley gives me a funny smile, and says, "There was nothing to run to."

"I thought about that remark for a while. And

211

what I figured out was this. Once you reach a certain age, the patterns of your life are set. You may think otherwise, but you're just lying to yourself. Stanley came back to New Jersey because it was the only life he had. There was nowhere else for him to go.

"I got involved with Kat because I thought I could change who I was. My life was like a suit of clothes that I'd gotten sick of wearing. So I started wearing a different suit. Turns out, it didn't fit."

"Can't stop being a cop, huh?" his son asked.

Valentine shook his head. "Not if my life depended on it."

CHAPTER 26

Saturday mornings were meant for tending to the garden or sleeping in, not for coming to Tony's house and picking up messages left by panicked casino bosses. Mabel did it for only one reason, and that was because Tony asked her to.

Tony's voice mail was empty. Booting up his PC, she checked for E-mail. He had one message, the sender someone named mathwizard, its subject matter "Your Problem." She clicked the mouse on it, and the message filled the screen.

Hey Griftsense,
Interesting BJ problem.
There is no difference between which card is turned over by the dealer, provided the dealer does not know the identity of his cards before he turns them over.

But if the dealer did know the cards' identities, he could alter the game's outcome by choosing one card over another. Here is how the players' odds would be affected.

213

Card Shown by Dealer	Player's Advantage (+) or Disadvantage (-)
Deuce	+10
Three	+14
Four	+18
Five	+24
Six	+24
Seven	+14
Eight	+5
Nine	-4
Any ten, jack, queen, king	-17
Ace	-36

The strategy, which I call Big Rock/Little Rock, has an enormous impact on the game's outcome. When a dealer chooses to expose a Big Rock (any ten, jack, queen, king, or ace), instead of a Little Rock (deuce through seven), he'll win most of the time.

Off to Geneva for a lecture. Take it easy.

Mabel printed the message on the laser printer. Tony corresponded with many world-class black-jack hustlers who held down legitimate jobs, like movie producers and college professors. They cheated for the thrill more than the money itself, and she guessed mathwizard belonged to this strange group.

She called the Fontainebleau, asked for the front desk, and got the hotel's fax number. Then she made up a cover page with Tony's name on it.

She was glad she'd talked him into going to south Florida and taking the job. He sounded so much more alive when he was working on a case.

Moments later, the fax went through the machine.

Growing up, there were a lot of things that Gerry hadn't done with his father. Like going to baseball games or the movies, or just hanging out and doing father-and-son stuff. It had a lot to do with his father's long hours as a cop, and also Gerry's unhappiness at his father *being* a cop. They didn't know each other very well, which was why taking his father to Club Hedo on Saturday morning was no treat.

Disco music rocked the club. Up on the stage, three girls in G-strings were playing with hula hoops. One of them was a cutie, and Gerry could not help but stare. Knowing a sucker when she saw one, the girl motioned him over. Embarrassed, Gerry bellied up to the bar.

"Tell Rico the Valentines are here to see him," he told the bartender, then ordered a couple of sodas.

"You dated a topless dancer, didn't you?" his father said.

"A couple of them. Why?"

"I was wondering what you saw in them."

"They were fun in bed," he admitted.

"I bet you had an exit line before you started taking them out," his father said.

Gerry felt his neck burn. It was the truth, although why it shamed him now, he had no idea. In the back bar mirror he saw the cute dancer standing on the edge of the stage, waiting for him to come over. *That's it*, he thought. *Shame me in front of my old man.* The bartender returned with their drinks.

"Rico will be right out," he said.

Gerry sipped his drink. In the mirror he saw the stripper sticking her tongue out at him. "So how do you want me to handle this?" he asked his father.

"Handle what?"

"What should I do when Rico comes out?"

"Introduce us."

His neck burned some more. "And then what?"

"Watch the fun."

Rico strolled out of his office. He'd replaced his New York hoodlum attire with a pair of pleated pants, a silk shirt, and a thick gold chain. A million-dollar suntan rounded out the reformation. He came over and slapped Gerry's shoulder.

"Gerry-o, how's it hanging?"

"Same as you left it," Gerry said.

"So this must be your famous father. I've heard a lot about you, Mr. Valentine."

"Same here," Valentine said.

Rico pointed to a corner table in the back, and they crossed the room in a blinding snowstorm of strobe lights. Rico pulled back two chairs, showing some manners. Valentine cased the room, then sat down. Rico sat next to him, then got in his face.

"So, Mr. Valentine, or should I call you Tony?"

"Call me Mr. Valentine," Valentine said.

Rico cleared his throat. "Okay, Mr. Valentine. You and I have a little bit of a history, but I'm willing to consider that water under the bridge."

"Same here."

"Gerry tells me you're connected in Atlantic City."

Valentine felt his son kick him beneath the table.

"That's right," he said.

"Matter of fact, Gerry says you're *the* most connected guy in AC."

Another kick.

"So what if I am?" Valentine said.

Rico leaned back in his chair and gave him a hard look. From his jacket he removed a deck of playing cards. They hit Valentine squarely in the chest.

"Prove it," Rico said.

Valentine squinted at the cards in the crummy bar light. They were from the Riverboat Casino in Atlantic City. Every hood from Maine to Miami had heard about the scam going on there. A gang of Riverboat employees was getting marked decks onto the blackjack tables. They weren't stealing a lot of money, but a computer analysis done by the casino had picked up the fluctuation. The problem was, no one could figure out how the scam was working. Valentine had a theory, which was that someone with juice—maybe a pit boss—had found a weak link in the system.

Because the scam had been going on for so long, it had grown into the stuff of legend, with the Riverboat's losses reputed to be in the millions, and the thieves actually a group of well-connected insiders that included local politicians, the police, and the casino's flamboyant owner.

The cute stripper appeared and sat in Gerry's lap. Her blond dye job, fake tits, and rhinestone G-string clashed with her schoolgirl innocence. Nibbling on Gerry's ear, she said, "Give me some money."

Stone-faced, Gerry shook his head. "We're here on business."

Valentine tossed the Riverboat's cards back to Rico. "How long you had these?"

"About a year," Rico replied.

"And you couldn't find the marks?"

Rico shook his head.

"Shuffle them."

Rico took the deck out of the box. He gave the cards a riffle shuffle. Valentine took them, shuffled, then held the top card away from the deck with his forefinger and thumb.

"Nine of clubs," he said.

Rico snatched the card out of his hand and turned it over. "Do it again."

Valentine did it three more times. The playing card's logo was the paddlewheel to a riverboat, and he pointed at the spokes on the wheel, and said, "It's called juice. It's a combination of clear nail polish and ink. When it dries, it's invisible to the naked eye. But if you train yourself to throw your eye out, you can just see it."

"That's how it works?" Rico said.

No, it wasn't, but Valentine took pleasure in imagining Rico giving himself headaches for a while. He handed the cards back, then spoke to the stripper.

"Get lost," he said.

Rico put the cards away. He had lost his bluster, and Valentine leaned over and gave him a hard poke in the chest. A big guy, but totally out of shape.

"You're stepping on my toes," Valentine said.

"I am?"

"This is my turf."

"Hey, I didn't—"

"How long you been down here?" Valentine said. "A couple months? And already you've scammed the Micanopy Indians and put a bullet in one of their dealers. Now I hear you're planning to take a bookie for a few million. You've got a lot of fucking nerve, son."

The bartender came over. Valentine ordered a round of sodas. Once the bartender was gone, Valentine continued. "Normally, I'd toss you in the ocean, only my son says you're someone who can be talked to. So, here's the deal. You take us on as partners, or you get lost."

"Partners?" Rico said.

"That's right."

"I don't know what you're talking about."

Valentine gave an exaggerated shake of the head. "You don't?"

"No," Rico said.

Valentine leaned over and lowered his voice. "Nigel Moon, asshole."

Rico acted like he'd been kicked. He drew back in his chair and stared at the floor. Valentine would have given anything to know what Rico's pulse was at that moment. A hundred fifty? Two hundred? He loved making punks sweat, especially lowlifes like this who gave Italians a bad name.

Their sodas came. The bartender could sense the tension, and placed the glasses on the table without a word. Rico picked up his glass and held it a few inches off the table. Valentine and his son did the same. Rico clinked their glasses with his.

"Partners it is," he said.

CHAPTER 27

Climbing into his father's Honda, Gerry said, "Pop, no offense, but your car smells like something died in it. It's time."

Valentine pulled away from Club Hedo's valet stand, got onto Collins Avenue, and headed north in heavy traffic. "For what?"

"A new set of wheels. You've got the dough. What about a Beamer, or a Lexus?"

That was the thing about his son's generation; they assumed that if you had money, you were dying to spend it. Valentine's generation was exactly the opposite. If you had it, you wanted to keep it. "I like this car," he said.

They drove in silence. Then his son popped the question.

"So, are you going to tell me, or what?"

"Tell you what?"

"How you know all that stuff about Rico."

"No," he said.

"At least tell me how you read the backs of those cards."

"You didn't believe what I told him?"

"About throwing your eyes out of focus?" Gerry

pointed at his left eye. "This eye *is* out of focus. There was no writing on the back of those cards."

"So why don't you get glasses?"

"Pop, stop beating around the bush, would you?"

"Why do you care?"

"Because it's important," his son said.

Valentine was missing something. He glanced sideways and saw his son's mouth tighten. "Don't tell me," he said.

Gerry stared through the windshield. "Afraid so."

A few hundred decks of Riverboat playing cards had been sold to small-time hoodlums across New England by enterprising Riverboat employees. Every cop in Atlantic City knew about it, but no one had done anything. It was too damn funny.

"How much did you pay for them?"

"Five hundred bucks," his son said.

The gift shop inside the Fontainebleau's main lobby was empty. Taking a deck of cards off a rack, Valentine dropped it on the counter and took out his wallet. A jolt went through his spine as the cashier rang it up.

Gerry had laid claim to a couch in the lobby. As Valentine unwrapped the deck, his son sat at rapt attention, oblivious to the bevy of half-clad young ladies strolling about.

"Shuffle them," his father said.

Gerry gave the cards a good mix. Valentine took

them back, shuffled them some more, then took the top card and held it between his thumb and first finger.

"King of spades," he announced.

Gerry took the card and turned it over. "Do it again," he said.

Valentine repeated the trick, expecting his son to catch on.

"Come on, Pop. You're killing me."

"It's called the one-ahead principle. When you handed the deck back to me, I spotted the bottom card, which was the king of spades. I shuffled, and brought the king to the top." He did an overhand shuffle, showing his son how easy it was to bring the bottom card to the top. "With me so far?"

Gerry nodded, his eyes never leaving the pack.

"Now, when I take the top card off in my right fingers, I already know what it is. I pretend like I'm reading the back of the card, while I'm actually learning the identity of the new top card of the deck."

"How?"

"It's called the bubble peek. I squeeze the top card of the deck with my left thumb. The front corner of the card hits my left forefinger, which rests along the top of the deck, and the corner bubbles up."

Holding the deck as if for dealing, he exposed the move to his son. "Normally, sitting as close as you are, you'd spot this. The reason you don't is because the card in my right hand hides it from your line of vision. But the card doesn't hide it from mine."

Valentine shifted his arms so Gerry could see the cards from his angle. He did the bubble peek again, and said, "See it?"

"It looks like the four of clubs."

Valentine turned the top card over. "You learn fast," he said.

"I bet you can do that all night long," his son said. "Does it take much practice?"

"Couple of hours in front of a mirror."

"Show me."

Valentine gave him half the deck and walked him through it. Within a few minutes, his son was "reading" the backs of the cards like a pro. They got onto an elevator filled with giggling young girls in bikinis, and Gerry immediately began to flaunt his newfound skill.

"Wow," one of the girls gushed, "you're good!"

Nigel and Candy ate lunch in their bungalow.

Eating the Delano's food every day had gotten Candy spoiled. Fresh seafood and steaks covered in special sauces, potatoes served a dozen different ways, salads with fruits she'd never heard of and couldn't pronounce, homemade desserts to die for. So when Nigel had said, "Let's order a Domino's pizza," she hadn't realized what a letdown it would be, the pie swimming in grease when it arrived, the pudgy pizza boy standing in his goofy uniform in the doorway, staring at the furnishings, then Nigel, then her.

To wash the pizza down, Nigel ordered a bucket of Shiner Bocks from room service. He'd discovered the beer in Texas while touring. After downing four, his drunkenness went to the next level. Soon his eyes were at half-mast, his chin dotted with tomato sauce.

"I want to ask you a question," she said.

He smothered a belch. "By all means."

"What's the deal between you and Rico?"

"We're partners in a business venture."

"He's a scumbag. I don't like you getting involved with him."

"I thought he was your friend."

"You don't need to be hanging out with swindlers. Or pulling scams."

"So he's not your friend anymore."

She reached out and took his hand. "Not as much as you're my friend."

Nigel smiled. "I've been hanging out with crooks my whole life. They're called record producers and concert promoters. And look where it's gotten me."

"Rico is different."

The table they were eating at was covered with dead soldiers and pizza crusts. Nigel killed the last Shiner Bock, and Candy found herself wishing she had waited until he was sober to have this conversation. Sensing her displeasure, he took her hand and kissed it.

"No one's going to get hurt except a bookie," Nigel said.

"Will you show me?"

He said yes, went into the bedroom, and returned with his laptop computer. It was a paper-thin job with a carbon battery and a screen with better resolution than most TVs. Sitting beside her, he clicked on an icon, and Candy found herself staring at an Excel spreadsheet. In the left-hand columns were the names of hundreds of different colleges. In the right-hand columns, projected point spreads.

"You're betting on basketball games," she said.

"That's right," he said.

"You could lose."

"No, I can't."

"Yes, you can. There's no sure thing, unless Rico's fixing the games."

"*Au contraire*," he said. "There is a system, and it has nothing to do with fixing the games. And it always wins. Want to see how it works?"

Candy felt her skin tingle. The stupidest damn things turned her on, like the smell of buttered popcorn and truck drivers with sweaty chests. Guys speaking in French was at the top of the list. Her hand dropped on Nigel's crotch.

"You speak French."

"Yes. I mean, *oui*."

Candy squeezed the little dipper, and his drunken eyes lit up. "More," she purred.

"Of course," he replied. "But first, let me get out of these clothes."

CHAPTER 28

"Never heard of him," Bobby Jewel said.

"You sure?" Rico said.

Bobby Jewel was the biggest bookie in south Florida. He worked out of a newspaper store on the Arthur Godfrey Road, which connected Miami Beach to the rest of the world. His operation was as big as two closets sitting side by side. In the back room, two Cuban guys worked the phones, taking bets. Bobby was the face to the operation and sat at the cash register, his four-hundred-pound body pouring out of a helpless chair. Acting perturbed, he yelled into the back room, "Hey, Jesus!"

A window slid back, and Jesus stuck his head out, his mop of black hair partially obscuring his face. Bobby loved Cubans, and used them in his operation whenever he could. He called them the Jews of the Caribbean.

"Yes, Mr. Jewel."

"You ever hear of some ginzo named Tony Valentine?"

"Ginzo?" Jesus asked.

"A wop. A guinea. You know, an Italian."

Jesus shook his head. From where Rico was sitting, he could have been a shaggy dog. "Ask Pepe," Bobby said. "Will you?"

Jesus quizzed the man sitting next to him. "Pepe doesn't know him, either." Then his phone rang, and he shut the sliding window.

Bobby slurped the Starbucks Mocha Frappuccino Rico had brought him. He wasn't very old, maybe thirty-two, but the weight made him look closer to fifty. "Satisfied?"

Rico stared into space. An alarm was going off inside his head. Tony Valentine wasn't connected; if he was, one of the men in this little store would know it. So how had he known about the murder at the Micanopy casino and that Rico was planning to scam Bobby? Valentine hadn't heard it over a wiretap because Rico spoke in code whenever he talked business over the phone. Rico took a long, deep breath. Someone had fucking told him.

"Earth to Rico," Bobby said.

Rico blinked awake. "Sorry."

"Something the matter?"

Coming out of Bobby's mouth, the line sounded comical. Rico straightened up in his chair and dropped his voice. "I got this deal I can't stop thinking about."

Bobby crushed the empty plastic cup in his massive hand, the sound like a bridge collapsing. "Yeah?"

Rico said, "Nigel Moon, the rock star, came into

my club a week ago. We played golf, guy thinks he's my friend. He's a real pig, but he's got money coming out of his ass, so you gotta love him, you know?"

"I'm with you so far."

"So Nigel and I get drunk. He says, 'I want to show you something.' So I let him. It's a software program on his laptop. Says he paid twenty grand for it."

Unwrapping a candy bar, Bobby bit off an end. "What's it do?"

"This is sweet. The program analyzes point spreads on college basketball games. Moon bought it from some scammer in Las Vegas. This scammer convinced Moon that each week, there are one or two games where the point spread is wrong. Some statistical-error mumbo jumbo."

Bobby laughed so hard that he started to choke. Reaching into a cooler, he extracted a bottle of Pepsi and unscrewed the top with his teeth. Everyone had heard about scams out in Las Vegas where con artists sold devices that predicted the outcome of sporting events. The devices were always junk. The scam worked by predicting games that had already been played, then convincing the sucker otherwise. Rico watched the soda in Bobby's bottle disappear. He wished Bobby would offer him a drink, but Bobby wasn't like that. He hadn't reached four hundred pounds by sharing his food.

"What a sucker," Bobby said.

"Here's the good part. Nigel told me this computer program has given him an incredible tip, and he wants to place a big bet."

"How big?"

"Two hundred grand."

"You're shitting me. On which game?"

"Miami College against Duke. He thinks Miami has a chance."

"Of beating the spread?"

"No, of winning."

Bobby slapped the counter and roared with laughter. The exertion caused him to belch, the sound so loud that it hurt Rico's ears. He was easily the most disgusting human being that Rico had ever known, and Rico was looking forward to taking him to the cleaners.

"Is that what his computer program tells him? That stinky Miami College is going to beat the number three team in the nation? I can cover that two hundred grand. What's your take?"

Rico smiled to himself. It had gone exactly the way Victor had said it would.

"Twenty percent," he said.

"Deal," the bookie replied.

Taking the Chinese leftovers out of the minibar, Valentine and Gerry ate out of the white cartons. Mealtime had been a no-nonsense affair in their house, and silence ruled. When the food was gone, Gerry said, "I need to talk to you about something."

Valentine arched his eyebrows. "What's that?"

"The bar."

Gerry's bar in Brooklyn had been a constant source of friction. Valentine had put up the seed money, and the liquor license was in his name. The problem was the office in back, where Gerry ran his bookmaking operation.

"What about it?"

"I'm thinking of selling it."

There was a rap on the door. Valentine got up and stuck his eye to the peephole. It was Gladys Soft Wings. He glanced at his son, who was in his Jockeys, and said, "Company," then cracked the door, and said, "Good morning."

"I got the tribal police to search the dealers' lockers." She held up several typed sheets of paper. "Here's what they found."

"Come on in." He heard his son scoot into the bathroom, then opened the door fully. Gladys walked in and tossed her handbag on the bed. Valentine took the typed sheets out of her hand and scanned the list, paying careful attention to the items owned by Karl Blackhorn. Being the most inexperienced member of the gang, he was the most likely candidate to have left something incriminating in his locker.

Fifteen items were listed beneath Blackhorn's name. Most of it was ordinary stuff like aftershave and hairbrushes. There was an envelope from an Eckerd drug store, and in parentheses it said *Pictures*. He pointed at the word, and said, "Did the tribal police let you see what the pictures were?"

"Yes," she said. "They were taken at a restaurant, and showed some men sitting at a table, pigging out on barbecue."

"Know any of them?"

"Oh, sure," she said after a few seconds. "Karl, Smooth Stone, and the other three dealers we arrested. And there's a dealer who left the casino."

"Who's that?"

"Jack Lightfoot."

It made all the sense in the world, and Valentine was surprised he hadn't seen it sooner. Jack Lightfoot had come to the Micanopy reservation to do a job for Bill Higgins. But because he was a criminal, he had immediately taken up with other criminals and taught them his special method of cheating at blackjack. Gerry emerged from the bathroom, smelling like a barber shop. Valentine introduced him to the Indian lawyer.

"The apple didn't fall far from the tree, did it," Gladys said.

"I'll take that as a compliment," his son said.

Valentine again looked at the list of Blackhorn's things. The second-to-last item was a bottle of Bayer aspirin, and in parentheses it said *Expired*. He said, "Did anyone look inside the aspirin bottle?"

Gladys shook her head. "I didn't think—"

"Was it plastic or see-through?"

"Plastic. Should I call the tribal police and ask them?"

"You bet."

She called on her cell phone. It took five minutes for the captain on duty to get the items out of storage, find the aspirin bottle, and unscrew the childproof lid.

"Huh," Gladys said. "The chief found a tiny square of paper. He says it's no bigger than a quarter."

"Ask him if it's sandpaper."

She did. "He wants to know how you knew that."

Valentine felt the burn of calling it right. One piece of the puzzle had been solved. "Practice," he said.

CHAPTER 29

Billy Tiger had given airboat tours in the Everglades since he was a teenager, and had met no resistance when he'd asked the man who managed the marina to lend him a boat for the afternoon.

The man had tried to give him a powerboat with a fan engine, thinking Tiger wanted to raise hell for a few hours, but Tiger had taken a johnboat instead. The fan boats could be heard for miles, while the electric johnboats were not heard at all.

The Micanopys had inhabited Florida for three hundred years, but only since the early 1900s had the tribe lived in the Everglades. This shift had been caused by a pair of ruthless robber barons named J. P. Morgan and Henry Flagler, who had descended upon the state and laid claim to the Micanopy tribal lands—all of it beachfront—then hired soldiers and policemen to drive the Micanopys out.

Tiger piloted the johnboat down a brackish waterway choked by mangroves and rotting willows. His ancestors had done a smart thing coming here. There was so much swamp—over five thousand square miles—that a man could get lost whenever he chose, and stay lost for as long as it suited him.

A small body of land loomed ahead. It was bright green and covered in dahoon holly. Tiger slowed the engine, and the johnboat bumped the ragged shoreline. He splashed his hand in the water to dispel any water moccasins, then cautiously stepped out of the vessel.

His feet began to sink. He was standing on a tree island. The Everglades were home to hundreds of such islands. He heard a sarcastic quacking and glanced at a flock of roseate spoonbills nesting in a tree, their pink plumage and clownish faces a sharp contrast to the swamp's greens and browns. Pollution from sugar plantations had nearly wiped out the spoonbills, and only recently had politicians attempted to correct the problem.

He took Harry Smooth Stone's instructions from his pocket and read them again. Then he checked the time. Four o'clock.

To kill time, he counted the spoonbills. A dozen filled the trees, half of them babies. A few years ago, there had been less than five hundred in all of Florida. Seeing such a big family made Tiger happy in a way that he could not put into words.

He sprayed himself with Cutter. It was the strongest insect repellent on the market, yet he was still getting chewed alive. Finally he got in the johnboat and pushed himself away from the shore. With swamp people, there was no accounting for missed appointments. Sometimes they showed up, and sometimes they didn't.

He headed back the way he'd come. Flies hopscotched across the water, only to disappear beneath the surface. He considered dropping a line, then imagined Smooth Stone sitting in his cell, wondering what the hell had happened to him.

A two-foot bass sprang out of the water. *Forgive me, Harry*, Tiger thought. Killing the engine, he removed a fishing line from his slicker, then looked over the boat's edge. Tiny shiners lurked below. Plucking one from the water, he kissed it for luck, then impaled it on the hook and threw it in. The water exploded beside the boat.

Tiger nearly jumped overboard, believing a hungry gator had snuck up on him. Only, what came out of the water was human, but no less dangerous. He watched the familiar figure climb aboard and flop down across from him.

"You scared me, man. What if I had a gun?"

"Then I would have had to take it away from you."

"Like hell you would," Tiger said.

His name was Joe Deerslayer, but everyone called him Slash. In and out of trouble his whole life, he'd hidden in the swamps rather than go to prison for robbing a 7-Eleven and shooting the owner in the face. He wore nothing but ratty underwear, his body covered in red sores.

"I've got a job for you," Tiger said.

"Not interested."

"Smooth Stone sent me."

Slash helped himself to Tiger's water bottle. "What's he want me to do?"

"Pressure a guy."

A powerfully bad smell was coming off Slash's body. He shook out his stringy black hair, which fell well past his shoulders, and said, "Who?"

"Name's Tony Valentine. There's a woman who works for him. She's old. Smooth Stone wants you to scare this old woman and make Valentine go home."

"Where's that?"

"Palm Harbor. It's on the west coat, near St. Petersburg."

"I know where it is. What's Smooth Stone paying?"

Tiger reached under his seat and removed a bundle of bills wrapped in Saran Wrap. He tossed the bundle to Slash. "Thirty-five hundred. There's a red Chevy Impala waiting for you in the casino parking lot. The keys are under the mat. In the trunk there are clothes and a map to Valentine's house. The old woman works there."

"Make it five," Slash said.

"Come on. It's an easy job."

"Old women bite as hard as anyone else. It's gonna cost you five."

Tiger swallowed hard. Five grand was what it cost to have someone killed. He'd seen it in the newspaper a hundred times. Irate spouses or jealous girlfriends would hire hit men to kill their mates. The hit men always charged five grand.

"Harry just wants you to scare her."

"Don't tell me what to fucking do," Slash said.

The swamp grew deathly still, and Tiger heard the sound of his own breathing.

"Put the rest of the money in the trunk of the car," Slash said, as if the matter were already settled.

"I'll . . . have to ask Smooth Stone."

"And a gun. Something small and light."

"Right."

"With ammo."

"Right . . ."

"And give Smooth Stone a message for me."

"What's that?"

"Tell him next time, don't send a boy to do a man's job."

Tiger did not know what stung more, the mosquito chewing his face, or the insult. He watched Slash dive over the side of the johnboat and disappear in the brown-black water, then started up the engine and headed back toward civilization.

The town clown's name was Russell Popjoy. He was a sergeant with the Broward County police, assigned to the Davie area. A week ago, he had paid Ray Hicks a visit and shaken him down for forty-two hundred dollars so Hicks could run his carnival without fear of being harassed or shut down.

Hicks had not expected him to show up at the hospital. But Popjoy had, walking into Mr. Beauregard's room Saturday night, right as visiting hours were ending. He was an inch shy of being a giant, with bulging weight-lifter muscles and red freckled skin. He stared at Mr. Beauregard strapped to the hospital bed, then at the monitor taking his heartbeat. Then he'd shaken his head.

"Is he—"

"Going to be okay," Hicks said.

Mr. Beauregard had passed the critical stage the night before. He'd lost a lot of blood, but chimps could do that and still survive, their hearts big and strong.

"I saw him once in Louisiana," Popjoy said. "I'm from there. Saw him in a pet shop. I was a kid." The sergeant rotated his hat in his hands, holding back, then said it anyway. "The owner was a crazy old coot. He said, 'Gimme a dollar and he'll play a song for you.' So I gave him a dollar. Then I walked over to his cage."

Mr. Beauregard's eyelids fluttered, and he made a gurgling sound. Hicks found the water bottle with the flexible straw and stuck it into his mouth. The chimp took a short drink and fell back asleep.

"He looks just like a kid," Popjoy said. "But I guess you know that."

Hicks put the bottle on the table and said that he did.

"Where was I?" Popjoy asked. "Oh, yeah. It was the strangest thing. I stood in front of his cage, and he picked up a ukulele and played an old Cajun song. *How Come My Dog Don't Bark (When You Come Around)*. I mean, I didn't say a damn thing."

"You like this song?"

"It's my favorite," Popjoy said. "It was like he read my mind."

Many people had said this about Mr. Beauregard, and Hicks guessed it was because they weren't used to being around an animal as smart as them. A nurse appeared and told Popjoy he had to leave.

Hicks walked his visitor into the hall. The sergeant took a notepad from his hip pocket and flipped it open. "I have a lead on the person who shot him. A young boy sitting on the Ferris wheel saw a black limousine pull up to your trailer. A man got out and went inside. When he came out, the boy thought he saw an object in his hand that looked like a gun."

"A black limousine?"

Popjoy nodded. "The boy didn't make out the plate, but I was wondering if you might know who owned the vehicle."

Hicks sure did. It was the punk from New York who'd paid him to rig the games so a drunk Englishman and his hooker could have an hour of fun. He'd kept the punk's business card, which now resided in his wallet.

And what would Popjoy do with such a piece of information? They couldn't arrest the punk—not enough evidence. But they could pay him a call and shake him down. Which was why Popjoy had come calling.

"Sorry," Hicks said.

Popjoy looked disappointed. He shut his notebook and put it away. Then put his hand on Ray Hicks's shoulder and left it there longer than Hicks would have liked.

"I'm here to help. I want you to remember that."

"Go to hell," Hicks said when he was gone.

CHAPTER 30

Bill Higgins had stayed in his car Saturday night casing Saul Hyman's condo. Once or twice he'd dozed, but for the most part, he'd stayed awake. And now he was paying for it. Sunday, seven A.M., and he felt like he'd been run over by a Mack truck. An old guy doing a young guy's work.

It had been a dull night. At three A.M. he'd called Saul's private line, having gotten the number from a Miami-Dade cop he knew. As Saul picked up, Higgins hung up. He was willing to bet Saul hadn't slept since.

Which was why Higgins hadn't gone anywhere. Let Saul look out his window and see the guy who'd run him out of Las Vegas sitting there, pining for him. That would be enough to make his defibrillator go off.

He played with the radio, trying to find a news station that wasn't Hispanic. He considered calling Tony, just to see if he'd gotten anywhere, but decided against it. If Tony wanted to tell him something, he'd call. Otherwise, it was best to stay out of his way.

They'd met in Atlantic City in 1978. Higgins was there to give testimony against a blackjack dealer who'd ripped off a casino in Reno a few years earlier. Atlantic City had been overrun by cheaters at the time—what hustlers called a candy store—and Higgins had offered to help the local police learn how to spot problem players. The police had agreed. Tony, then a detective, had been one of his students.

Over time, a friendship had developed, and Higgins had immediately realized that Tony was no ordinary cop. He had great instincts and was damn smart, characteristics that were rare in law enforcement. He also had a huge chip on his shoulder and was not someone you wanted to cross. In that way, he was like most cops, including himself. Higgins's chip had come from spending his formative years at the Haskell Institute. Where Tony's had come from, he had no idea.

A Hispanic kid on a flashy bike had braked next to Higgins's rental. Higgins rolled down his window.

"You Bill Higgins?" the kid asked.

"Who's asking?"

The kid took a brown envelope from his basket. Higgins's name was written on it in Magic Marker. He watched the kid pedal away, then tore the envelope open.

Inside was a page taken from the *Wall Street Journal*, dated last Friday, with a yellow Post-it.

Thought you'd like to see this, it read. Higgins scanned the page.

Hackers Scam Internet Casino for $2 Million (Reuters)

100 gamblers got very lucky last Sunday afternoon.

Or did they?

Yesterday, CyberGamble, a Nevada software company that hosts online casino games, revealed that a hacker cracked one of the firm's servers last Sunday and corrupted the site's craps, video slots, and poker games so that players couldn't lose. For a period of approximately two hours, 100 gamblers across the country racked up winnings in excess of $2 million.

Higgins realized he was gritting his teeth. He'd been opposed to Internet gambling for years. Players routinely got screwed by unscrupulous Web sites, while legitimate Web sites routinely got screwed by hackers. But the bad thing was that anyone could play, including kids, and Gamblers Anonymous was reporting hundreds of cases of eight- and nine-year-old addicts. His eyes returned to the page.

CyberGamble, a publicly traded company, is liable for $500,000 of the stolen money, while a $1.5 million insurance claim with

Lloyd's of London will cover the rest. The 100 winners are being allowed to keep their winnings, as there is no proof they were involved in the scam.

He had a good laugh. How stupid were these folks? Of course the hundred winners were involved. Maybe not all of them, but certainly the majority. They were the takeoff men. Hustlers used takeoff men all the time. They were usually upright John Q. Citizens who appeared beyond reproach. Their cut was generally 25 percent.

A car horn's beep shattered his concentration. Looking up, he saw a rattling Toyota Corolla sitting next to his car, headed in the opposite direction. Behind the wheel sat a grinning Saul Hyman.

Saul's eyes were dancing. Then Higgins understood. Saul had hired the kid on the bike and written the note. He'd seen the article and realized it would hold Higgins's interest long enough for him to pull his car onto the street.

Higgins shrugged his shoulders indifferently. He'd already admitted to himself that he was too old for this kind of work, and this proved it.

"That's it?" Saul said indignantly.

"What do you want, a medal?"

"I outwitted you, flatfoot."

"You look cute in a dress," Higgins told him.

Saul gave him a Bronx cheer, then sped away.

★   ★   ★

"Put some clothes on," Nigel said. "We're going out."

Candy was lying naked in bed, sipping coffee and reading the *Miami Herald*. She'd woken up expecting Nigel to be angry at her. She'd questioned him the night before. For a lot of guys, that was enough to get rid of a woman.

Only her prince hadn't said a word about it. They'd made love, and then breakfast had arrived at their door along with a dozen red roses, just like the day before, and the day before that. Nothing had changed.

"Fancy or casual?" she'd asked.

He gave it some thought. "How about Madonna in heat?"

Candy went through her clothes. She had a leather miniskirt with a slit up its side that was supposed to be worn with leggings. She slipped it on, then tried on several blouses, finally settling on a red job that looked like a three-alarm fire. Nigel hung in the doorway.

"Lovely," he said.

At eleven-thirty, an executive from Polyester Records appeared at the bungalow's door. Polyester had signed Nigel's band, One-Eyed Pig, to do a greatest-hits collection, and Candy had seen the contracts and reams of legal bullshit lying around. The executive's name was Rod Silver. He was about thirty and talked like a pitchman on the Home Shopping Network. He shoved a promotional poster in Nigel's hand.

"So what do you think? Beautiful, you ask me. The colors are outstanding."

Candy peeked over Nigel's shoulder. The poster was a group shot of One-Eyed Pig taken twenty years ago. Wild-eyed, Nigel sat chained to his drum kit. The other members hovered around him, holding their instruments protectively in front of their bodies, like they were afraid of what Nigel might do if he got loose.

"Great," Nigel said.

Silver kept talking all the way to the stretch limousine parked in front of the hotel. The limo was pink, as was the driver's uniform, a Miami Beach fashion statement if there ever was one. The driver was a mean-looking black man with a shaved head.

Candy got in, her bare legs sticking to the leather seat. She felt cheap, but Nigel seemed to be having a good time, and that was all she cared about. Silver sat opposite them and glanced discreetly out the window as Candy got comfortable.

"Where are we going?" Candy asked.

"The Virgin record store," Silver said. "Nigel's going to sign autographs."

"You mean the Virgin store on Collins?"

Silver nodded enthusiastically. "There's already a huge crowd. This baby's going to go platinum in six weeks. Mark my words. Six weeks."

Candy looked at Nigel. They had gone shopping in the Virgin store three nights ago. It was two blocks from the hotel. Sensing her confusion, he explained. "I can't just show up, my dear. My fans would not tolerate it. I must appear in an impossibly expensive car being driven by a menacing-looking fellow who may or may not be a homicidal maniac."

"It's in the contract," Silver explained.

Candy looked at the driver, then at Nigel. "Is he?"

"Is he what?"

"A homicidal maniac?"

"He's an actor," Silver said. "We hired him because he fits the bill."

Candy fell back in her seat.

"Oh, wow" was all she could think to say.

The line outside the Virgin store stretched around the block, the faithful done up in leather and chains and motorcycle boots. They would have looked real tough if not for the gray hair and potbellies. The driver got out and opened their door.

"It's show time," Silver declared.

He walked Nigel and Candy to the front door, where they were greeted by the gushing store manager and a handful of employees. Introductions were made. Nigel shook everyone's hand while clutching Candy to his side. Candy played along, smiling and giggling and showing plenty of leg.

"I saw you at Shea Stadium in 1980," the store manager said. His name tag said Trip. A forty-year-old hippie who looked like he smoked his breakfast. "Greatest concert I've ever seen.

You went through three drum kits and two cases of beer."

"I was sick that night," Nigel said.

"You were?"

Nigel nodded. "Had to take it easy."

Trip laughed. So did Silver and the driver. Candy didn't get it but laughed anyway, because that was what you did around a celebrity.

The store was a high-ceilinged monster with the personality of an airplane hangar. Trip escorted them to the back. A large area had been cleared. Sitting on a table were stacks of CDs and DVDs. Hanging behind the table, a giant poster of Nigel's famous *Rolling Stone* cover, his naked upper torso swathed in rusty chains, his eyes gleaming like a maniac's. Candy had always thought it was the ugliest picture she'd ever seen.

"Ohhh," she purred into Nigel's ear.

"Does it turn you on?" he said.

"Uh-huh."

A devilish gleam spread across his face. He got behind the table and took the chair. A pen was produced. He took it in his right fist, poised for the onslaught.

"Ready?" Trip said.

"Bring on the mob," Nigel replied.

Trip clapped his hands like a dance instructor, and the employees opened up the store. The crowd came in a little faster than Candy would have liked, and she got behind Nigel and stayed there as he chatted and signed autographs. She'd seen her share of celebrities, and Nigel was a class act. He was friendly and didn't mind pumping the flesh.

Soon the store was mobbed. No one was leaving, and Candy found herself staring at a big white sheet on the other side of the room. It was covering something fairly large, and at first she thought it was a car. Only, it was too small to be a car.

A voice came over the store's PA. Nigel lifted his head. Trip was standing by the sheet, mike in hand.

"Folks, we have a real treat for you this afternoon. Through the generosity of Polyester Records and the Rock and Roll Hall of Fame in beautiful Cleveland, Ohio, we have flown in one of the most famous musical instruments in the world." Grasping the sheet with his free hand, Trip whisked it away to reveal a gleaming drum kit, the initials NM written in block letters on the face of the base. "Used in the famous East End recording sessions for One-Eyed Pig's first album, *Baby, You Need It Bad*, here they are, Nigel Moon's own drums!"

The crowd hooted and hollered. Someone started to chant "Nigel, Nigel" until it became a chorus. Nigel got out of his chair and wrapped his arm around Candy's waist.

Candy could feel his heart beating wildly.

"Are you all right?"

"Of course," he said.

They walked over to where Trip stood, and Nigel took the mike. "*Monster, Monster,*" the crowd chanted, that being the name of the band's most famous song. Nigel tried to speak. The crowd would not stop.

"Would you?" Trip asked, holding up a pair of sticks.

Nigel stared at them, then him.

"Where's your bathroom?"

Trip pointed across the room. Nigel handed him the mike, then bowed to the crowd. Still chanting, they parted and let him through.

He was moving quickly, like he really had to go, and Candy saw him pick up speed as he reached the front of the store. Instead of veering to his left—in the bathroom's direction—he went straight instead.

His body hit the front doors hard.

CHAPTER 31

"You look like a bag of wet doughnuts," Victor Marks said.

"It's been a long week," Rico admitted.

"Appearances are important," Victor said, his tone scolding. "In this racket, they're the most important thing you've got."

They were sitting at the Seafood Bar in Victor's favorite hangout, the Breakers in Palm Beach. The bar was an aquarium, and Victor identified the fish as they swam past. "The orange and white one is a clown fish. That one's a purple damsel. And that big guy is a spotted eel. Every day, the eel eats one of the other fish. It costs the hotel a lot of money to keep replacing them. Know why they leave the eel in the aquarium?"

"No," Rico said.

"Appearances." Victor motioned for the bartender. "Two more," he said, pointing at their glasses. When the bartender was gone, he said, "How's the basketball scam going?"

"It's going to be tough to pull off."

"Of course it's going to be tough to pull off. If pulling cons was easy, every blowhard from here to Cincinnati would be in the racket. You've got to play the part."

"I'm trying."

Victor touched Rico's sleeve. "Look at me."

"Okay."

"What do you see?"

What Rico saw was the best-dressed guy in the hotel, an eighty-year-old with a perfect haircut and capped teeth and tailored clothes. He saw a guy he'd like to be one day.

"A guy on top of the world," Rico said.

"That's right. And I'm working a job, right now."

"Here?"

"Yup. Surprised?"

"Yeah . . ."

"It's called the confidence game, kid. You've got to exude confidence, otherwise you won't fool a blind man."

"What you got going?"

Victor dropped his voice. "I come here three or four times a year, and I always leave with a bag of money. Twenty grand, sometimes more. Pays for my vacation and the broad on my arm."

Rico felt his spirits pick up. Victor did that to him. Victor was the epitome of what a criminal was supposed to be, the master of a universe of his own creating. Every pearl he passed along, Rico knew would bring him closer to his own dream.

"Come on. Tell me."

"It's the Titanic Thompson/Arnold Rothstein con."

"What's that?"

"You didn't read the book I gave you?"

Rico lowered his head in shame. He hadn't read a book in twenty years.

"No."

Victor looked out the window as two well-kept women walked by. He spoke in a normal voice, no longer caring who heard. "I give you a book, you're supposed to read it. Titanic Thompson was the greatest con man of the twentieth century. Arnold Rothstein was one of the greatest gamblers of the twentieth century. He fixed the 1919 World Series."

"The Black Sox scandal," Rico said.

"Go to the head of the class. One night in New York, Rothstein got into a poker game at the Roosevelt Hotel with a bunch of heavy hitters, one of whom was Thompson. Rothstein ends up losing half a million bucks. We're talking 1927 here, which might make this the biggest pot ever."

"Was Thompson cheating?"

"Of course he was cheating!"

Rico slumped in his bar chair. "How?"

"That's the good part. Thompson had been watching Rothstein for years. He'd noticed that whenever Rothstein played poker, he always bought the cards himself. That way, the cards were always clean. So Thompson loaded marked decks in every gift shop and stationery store within a two-block radius of the hotel. When Rothstein showed up to the game and took two brand-new decks out of his pocket, Thompson knew they were his."

Rico beamed. "Is that what you're doing here, using marked cards?"

Their drinks came. Victor sipped his soda water, savoring the moment. "The hotel has its own decks of cards. I went to the plant and bribed them into changing the plates."

"You mean *all* the decks in this joint are marked?"

"Heh, heh, heh," Victor said.

Victor's scam was a lot like Tony Valentine's marked-deck scam. A real sweet deal. That was the thing about the old guys, Rico thought. They knew how to make money without getting their fingernails dirty.

Thinking about it reminded Rico why he'd asked Victor for a meeting, and he lowered his voice. "Victor, I have a problem."

Victor was watching broads. A pair was standing outside, smiling and waving through the glass. Victor blew one of them a kiss. "I took her husband for ten grand, and she's been flirting with me ever since. God, I love rich people."

"A real problem."

Victor turned in his chair. "What's that?"

"A guy named Tony Valentine is putting the muscle on me."

"Tony Valentine?"

"You know him?"

"He was a dick in Atlantic City. Made life

miserable for me and my crew." The fun had gone out of Victor's voice. "What does he want?"

"A cut."

"What for?"

"He knows about the scam I pulled at the Micanopy casino, and about Bobby Jewel."

"How does he know that?"

"Dunno. I haven't told the details to anybody but you, Victor."

Victor's eyes grew narrow. "Bull."

"What do you mean?"

"You probably told the last broad who showed you her titties."

"You think so."

"Yeah. You've got a big mouth."

Victor was talking to him like he was a punk, showing no respect. Rico didn't like it. "The only person I told the details to was *you*, Victor."

Victor took out his wallet and threw down his resort charge card, money not allowed on the property. The bartender said, "On the house, Mr. Marks," and Victor put the resort card away. Under his breath he said, "Are you accusing me of ratting you out?"

"You're the only one who knows."

"You came to *me* six months ago, asked me to teach you the ropes. Said you wanted to screw a bookie out of a few million. So I taught you the rackets. And this is my reward?"

Rico grabbed the older man's sleeve. "I didn't tell *nobody* else."

Victor slapped his hand on the bar so hard that a school of tiny fish disappeared. The bartender hurried toward them, a worried look on his face. Victor waved him off. Shaking free of Rico's grasp, he said, "Go back to New York, kid. You're out of your league down here." Then he straightened his jacket and walked away.

Rico got out of the Breakers, but just barely. Two mean-faced security guards appeared within moments of Victor's departure. They followed Rico to the valet stand and watched him get into his limo and drive off, the one in shades scribbling down his license number. Staring at them in his side mirror, Rico let out a stream of obscenities.

He drove through Palm Beach, drawing stares from other limo drivers, who wore hats and neckties. He needed another driver, someone to play the part, so he could play *his* part. Victor was right. Appearances were everything.

He drove west until he saw signs for the Florida's Turnpike. There was no doubt in his mind that Victor had told someone. And that someone had told Valentine. It could have been anyone—a mutual friend, even a barber—but Rico had to find out who it was, before he told someone else.

He got on the turnpike and headed south. He needed to put the screws to Valentine and make him talk. Which was what he probably should have done in the first place.

Fishing out his wallet, he removed the napkin that Gerry Valentine had scribbled his phone number on, and dialed it on his cell phone.

"Fontainebleau hotel," an operator answered.

This was going to be too easy, he thought.

CHAPTER 32

The scene at the Virgin store got ugly fast.

Nigel's turn on the drums had been advertised in the newspaper and on the radio. The crowd had come to get a taste of the old-time mayhem that only he could produce, his wild-eyed, manic intensity one of the few lasting images of the cocaine- and booze-injected rock and roll of the early eighties.

The record promoter tried to defuse the situation by grabbing the mike and telling a few bad jokes. Someone in the crowd threatened to kick his bonded teeth down his throat. Candy ducked out the back door and circled the building. The pink limo was parked out front, but she was not sure she wanted to be associated with it.

Instead, she started walking to the Delano and immediately regretted it. She was dressed like a streetwalker, and cars did the slow crawl down the street, a few male drivers waving handfuls of bills, trying to entice her to jump in.

Candy cursed them, and Nigel for reducing her to this. It was one thing to be a whore. It was something else entirely when the man you loved made you feel like one.

Her stilettos left puncture wounds on the Delano's wood floors. The Rose Bar sat off the lobby, an unfriendly space with muted lighting.

"Where is he?" she demanded of the bartender, knowing that it was to the bottle that her lover had surely run.

Polishing a highball glass, the bartender pointed in the direction of the bungalows. Candy stormed out.

She had to pass through the patio restaurant to reach the bungalows, and a couple she'd chatted with in the pool now avoided making eye contact. Why had she let Nigel talk her into wearing these horrible clothes? It made her so angry, she wanted to kill someone.

The bungalow was empty. Nigel's clothes sat in a pile on the bathroom floor, his bathing suit gone. She changed into a bikini, then searched for something sharp to plunge into her lover's heart when she found him.

A few minutes later she did. He was sitting on the shore a hundred yards from the hotel, a bucket of Shiner Bocks by his side, the incoming tide splashing on the soles of his feet. His body was big and milky white, his back covered with curls of graying hair. Shielding his eyes from the sun, he stared up at her.

"With that?" he said.

Candy looked down at the hotel corkscrew clutched in her hand.

"You're going to kill me with that?"

No one was around. Yes, that was exactly what she was going to do.

Her lover shook his head. "Be serious, my dear."

She halved the distance between them, wondering how he'd look with the corkscrew sticking out of his ear. Oblivious to the danger he was in, Nigel patted the blanket.

"Sit," he said.

"Fuck yourself."

"Please."

"You think I wouldn't do it?" she said through clenched teeth.

"Not if you thought you were going to get caught."

She looked up and down the empty beach. "Caught how?"

"There's a young fellow from the hotel sitting in the bushes, smoking a joint. When I'm finished with these beers, he'll take the bucket to the hotel bar and get a refill. It's called the deluxe service. I pay for it."

The intoxicating smell of reefer floated above the salty air. She threw the corkscrew against Nigel's back, then marched over to the palmetto bushes and saw the employee sitting in the sand, having a little fun. He was jet-black, from one of the islands, and Candy stuck her hand out.

"Give me that," she said.

He obeyed, and she took a monster hit, then handed it back to him. "Thanks." Then she walked back to where Nigel sat.

"Feel better?" her lover asked.

Candy helped him polish off the remaining Shiner Bocks. The tide was coming in, and their suits quickly filled with sand. A fresh bucket of beer appeared. Nigel opened two.

"I'm from Middlesbrough," he said. "It's a factory town in the north of England, known for its mills. I used to work in one, dying white lace. I learned from my father, who learned from his father, who didn't graduate the sixth grade. My father was a little better: He made it through high school."

He clinked his bottle against hers, his eyes swimming. "So did I. And vocational school. But I still went to work in the mill. One of those stupid family traditions, I suppose. Not that it was a bad life. Just horribly dull. On weekends, I got drunk in the pub."

Candy was on her third beer. The sun was hot; tomorrow she'd be as pink as a lobster. She looked into Nigel's face. She was still mad at him. "So?"

"I'm getting to the good part," he said, wiping his mouth on his wrist. "I knew these blokes who had a band. They called themselves One-Eyed Pig. I would go to gigs with them, help them set up. They paid me in beer." He smiled, the bottle inches from his lips. "One day, the lead singer, Troy, calls me up, says he has a problem. The band's drummer quit. Troy offers me the job."

"And a star was born," she said sarcastically.

His eyes narrowed. "Not really. I don't play the drums."

"Very funny."

"I'm not a musician. Troy wanted me to fake it for a gig in the next town. I would pretend, and they would play a tape."

"How do you pretend to play the drums?"

"The drumsticks were made of Styrofoam. No sound."

A big wave came in and knocked her back a few inches. Nigel, a hundred pounds heavier, was unaffected. She scampered back to her position.

"The gig was in this huge dance hall," he went on. "At first, I was scared, but then I realized that this was the only time I was going to get a taste of being famous, so I jumped around and did crazy things with the sticks and made a complete horse's ass of myself. The crowd was mostly dopey kids. They loved it.

"There was a record producer there. Bloke named Flash Summers. Liked to wear outrageous designer clothes and have an underage girl hanging on each arm. He signed us up on the spot."

"But you don't play."

"It didn't matter. Flash loved me. Said I was the greatest natural showman he'd ever seen. He wrapped his arms around me, said he was going to make me famous."

Another wave came in. Nigel held Candy's hand so she was not dragged backwards. They were big hands, yet also soft and gentle. "The band was born that night," he said. "Flash knew it, the crowd knew it, and we knew it. We cut our first album the next week."

"Who played the drums?"

"A studio musician they hired."

Candy stared out at the endless stretch of blue. She had seen Nigel play, remembered it as clearly as what she'd had for breakfast. The AIDS concert in New York's Central Park. She'd watched it on TV, Nigel's maniacal solo piercing the still night air. That couldn't have been a recording.

"But I saw you play," she insisted.

"Where?"

"On television, from New York."

He took the empty beer bottle from her hand, replaced it with a fresh one. "Another hoax, I'm afraid. After the album went platinum, we were expected to tour. Flash knew we couldn't do concerts with a tape and survive, so he put this drummer in a hollowed-out amplifier directly behind me. He would play, and I'd fake it."

"In an amplifier?"

"He was a dwarf. Flash found him in the Tom Thumb circus."

Candy put her hand over her mouth. "Cut it out."

"I'm serious," he said. "Guy could play any instrument. Sing, too. He's out in Vegas now."

"Doing what?"

"A mean Elvis Presley impersonation. He wears one of those white leather outfits with all the lace. Calls himself Elfis."

Candy didn't see the monster wave roll in. As laughter poured out of her mouth, it hit her in the face, and she went under.

"I want to ask you something," she said after they burned up the sheets with their lovemaking.

"No," he mumbled, his face buried in the pillows.

She shoved him playfully. "Come on."

He rolled over on his side. "What?"

"Why do you hang out with guys like Rico? What is it going to get you, except in trouble?"

He thought about it for a while, his finger tracing a heart in her bare midsection.

"Do you know what it's like to have everything handed to you, and you didn't do anything to deserve it?"

Candy shook her head no.

"It *sounds* great," he said. "And in the beginning, it is. Like one of those great Charles Dickens tales about a young boy being mistaken for a prince and given the run of the castle. It's fun, but then it starts to wear thin. You're not the person people think you are. The person you really are, you can never go back to being. It's like dying, and waking up in someone else's bloody body."

He touched her chin, then managed a faint smile. "I hang out with guys like Rico for the same reason that I gamble. It makes me feel alive."

CHAPTER 33

Valentine and his son spent the afternoon in their hotel room watching the surveillance tape of Jack Lightfoot.

Valentine had enjoyed the company. Normally, Gerry would have been poolside, talking a pretty girl into slathering tanning lotion on his back. Only, he seemed more interested in figuring out how Lightfoot was cheating, and asking lots of questions.

Valentine's cell phone rang. He retrieved it from the night table and glanced at the caller ID. It was Mabel, calling from his house.

"You shouldn't be working on a Sunday," he said by way of greeting.

"Don't worry, I'm putting in for overtime," she replied. "I called to see if you got my fax."

"What fax?"

"The one I sent to your hotel. It was an E-mail from a person named mathwizard. I think he figured out your blackjack scam."

"You sent it to the hotel's main desk?"

"Yes. Yesterday morning. When I didn't hear from you, I figured I'd better call."

267

"Thanks for the heads-up."

He said good-bye, then called the front desk on the house phone. Two minutes later an apologetic bellman was standing at the door with his fax. Valentine gave him a buck and slipped his bifocals on.

Mathwizard was the alias of a prominent southern California college professor, and one of the top blackjack cheaters in the world. With his son looking over his shoulder, Valentine read the E-mail several times, then found himself staring at the passage at the bottom of the page.

> The strategy, which I call Big Rock/Little Rock, has an enormous impact on the game's outcome. When a dealer chooses to expose a Big Rock (any ten, jack, queen, king, or ace), instead of a Little Rock (deuce through seven), he'll win most of the time.

Valentine put the E-mail down, then thought back to the piece of sandpaper in the aspirin bottle in Karl Blackhorn's locker. And then it hit him. This was something *new*.

His skin tingled. In all his years policing Atlantic City's casinos, he'd uncovered only a handful of new ways to cheat the house—things that had never been done before—and each time, he'd walked on air for a few days. It was a unique feeling, and he'd had to consult a thesaurus to find a word that accurately described it.

Only one had. Aggrandizement.

He called Gladys Soft Wings. "How soon can you get the Micanopy elders together?"

His son said, "You nailed it?"

Valentine nodded that he had.

"Way to go!"

"How about tomorrow morning?" Gladys suggested.

"How about right now?" he replied.

Mabel hung up the phone and glanced at her watch. The movie started at three. If she hurried, she'd still get a good seat. She heard the computer on Tony's desk make a doorbell sound, indicating new E-mail had arrived. She hesitated, then let her curiosity get the better of her.

It was from Jacques, informing her that he'd been fired from his job. Too many cheaters had been caught in the past few days for management to have any faith in him. So they'd sacked him.

Mabel erased the message and pushed herself out of her chair. That was the thing that people never understood about cheaters: They often cost security people and pit bosses and dealers their jobs. When the losses were really bad, whole shifts were often fired.

Someone was knocking at the front door. It was a loud, impatient sound. Annoyed, she hurried down the hall into the living room. Through the front window she spied a young man standing on the stoop. His right hand held a padded envelope.

He was lean and darkly tanned, his long hair tucked beneath a baseball cap. Mabel didn't like the looks of him, but she didn't like the looks of most young people. She cracked the door an inch.

"Yes?"

"Special delivery for Tony Valentine."

It was not uncommon for Tony to get Sunday deliveries. "Who's the sender?"

"Caesars Palace, Las Vegas."

Caesars was a good client and kept Tony on a monthly retainer. She unchained the door and took the envelope out of his hand.

"Do you have a pen?" he asked. "I left mine at my last stop."

"Wait here," she said.

Mabel turned to go into the kitchen, then noticed that the envelope was from Federal Express. They delivered packages almost every day, and Tony had put his signature on file with the company. The drivers knew to leave packages in the mailbox. Even the subs.

She suddenly felt light in the head. The fear that every girl knew from the time she was old enough to walk swept over her. She had allowed a strange man to gain her trust.

She heard the front door shut and the sound of footsteps behind her. She opened her mouth to scream and felt the driver's powerful hands around her throat.

As Valentine stepped out of the hotel elevator

270

with Gerry, he spotted Saul Hyman standing by the house phones, talking to an operator. Valentine heard him say, "No, that's all right," and watched him put the phone down. Then Saul walked toward them.

"This must be your son," Saul said.

"No, we just look alike," Valentine said.

Saul glanced over his shoulder, as if fearful he was being tailed. "We need to talk. It's about Victor Marks."

Valentine glanced at his watch. He'd promised Gladys Soft Wings that he'd meet her at the reservation by three. She'd asked the elders for a hearing this afternoon and wanted to review his testimony before he gave it. If he hung with Saul, he'd be late, only he wanted to hear what the elderly con man had to say. He pointed at the hotel coffee shop. "Want to go in there?"

Saul did, and they went in. It was crowded, and the hostess had to seat them in smoking. Someone in the next booth was puffing away, and Valentine wondered if it was going to drive him crazy. Saul took out a pack of his own.

"Don't," Valentine said.

Saul put them away, then nervously drummed his fingertips on the table. A waiter came over, and they ordered coffee. Valentine looked around the coffee shop. Wasn't Bill supposed to be tailing Saul?

Saul reached into his jacket and removed a thick envelope. It ended up in Valentine's hands. "Victor called me in a panic. He met with that punk Rico Blanco this morning. Rico knows something's up. I told Victor that Rico would end up murdering him if he got mad enough. Victor didn't like that."

Valentine peeked inside the envelope. It contained photographs taken off a television set, and he recognized Farley Bancroft, the dapper game show host of *Who Wants to Be Rich?* Opening the envelope a little more, he saw pages of handwritten notes.

"It's all there," Saul said in a whisper. "How to scam a TV game show."

Gerry was looking, as well. "You're kidding me. You really did that?"

Saul looked at Valentine. "Is he square?"

Valentine laid the envelope on the table. "Yeah."

Saul said, "You know anything about the rackets, kid?"

"A little," Gerry conceded.

"He's a bookie," Valentine said.

His son winced. "I shut the bookmaking operation down a few weeks ago."

"You did?"

Gerry nodded. "I decided to go legit."

Saul was hunched over his drink like it was a small fire. "This is touching," he said.

"Shut up," Valentine said, staring at his son. He saw Gerry smile and realized that he was telling the truth. *Legit as in what?* he wondered.

"So, how do you scam a game show?" Gerry asked.

A sly grin spread across Saul's face. "It was beautiful. Victor calls me one day and says, 'I just came up with this terrific con.' Then he reads me an article in *TV Guide* about Farley Bancroft. Article says Bancroft owns a piece of *Who Wants to Be Rich?* Guy's worth a hundred million bucks, easy.

"So I say, 'And what does this have to do with the price of eggs?' And Victor reads some more. The *TV Guide* interviewer asked Bancroft about the multiple-choice questions he asks on the show. Bancroft says he doesn't know the answers, so he can be genuinely surprised when the answer is read."

Saul pulled back in his chair, the grin spreading from ear to ear. "Isn't that great?"

Gerry was lost. "What do you mean?"

"Don't you get it?"

"Get what?"

"A guy as powerful as Farley Bancroft is going to know the answers on a show he owns," Saul explained. "He was lying."

"So?"

"Victor hired a voice expert to analyze Bancroft's voice," Saul said as the smoke from the neighboring table created a halo around his head. "When he read the multiple-choice answers, his voice changed on the correct one."

"A tell," Valentine said.

Saul nodded. "The voice expert taught Victor how to read the tell. Only, Victor had a problem.

273

He couldn't get on the show. That's when he teamed up with Rico Blanco."

"Why Rico?" Valentine asked.

"The network that airs the show is union. The union is mob-connected, and gave Rico a list of contestants. Rico worked down the list and found a guy he could work with. Victor taught the guy how to read Bancroft. Guy went on the show and won a million bucks."

"Is that breaking the law?" Gerry asked.

Saul nodded his head vigorously. "The guy signed an agreement not to defraud the network. It's a serious crime."

Valentine thumbed through the envelope's contents. There were names and dates and telephone numbers and copies of E-mail letters and bank account numbers and everything he needed to paint a picture of Rico Blanco as a big-time scam artist. But more importantly, it showed the trail of a crook working solo, and was enough evidence for Valentine to give the newspapers and save the Micanopy casino from being shut down. Bill Higgins was going to be very happy. He slipped the envelope into his jacket pocket, and said, "I really appreciate this, Saul."

"My pleasure," the elderly con man said.

CHAPTER 34

L uck, Rico believed, was a tiny naked chick who looked like Jennifer Lopez and sat on his shoulder whispering advice in his ear.

Luck had been good to him over the years. She'd made sure his voice wasn't taped when John Gotti was causing mischief, and spared Rico from a life in prison. And she'd managed to keep him out of harm's way when a dozen other schemes had gone haywire.

Today was another good example. Driving south from Palm Beach, Rico had decided that after he got Tony Valentine to tell him who the snitch was, he would take Valentine out of the picture. Valentine knew too much and could only hurt him in the long run.

So he'd come up with a plan. He'd drive to the Fontainebleau, tie Valentine to a chair, and shoot him between the eyes. He'd make Gerry watch, then let him go. Word would spread fast as to what he'd done. And wise guys like Valentine would start leaving him alone.

Walking into the Fontainebleau's lobby, he passed the coffee shop. A menu board was outside. Today's special was a BLT on whole wheat.

His favorite meal as a kid.

Eat, the little naked chick on his shoulder said.

So he went in and ordered a BLT. Firing up a cigarette, he'd heard a familiar voice from the next booth. Gerry Valentine's Brooklyn accent was sharp enough to cut bread with, and he'd leaned back and listened.

And heard everything.

More than once, he'd considered shooting all three men right there in the coffee shop. Bang, bang, bang, and leave their brains on the walls. Only, Florida had the death penalty and let condemned men's heads catch on fire in the electric chair.

So he'd swallowed his rage, eaten his sandwich, and waited.

Eventually, the three men left. Throwing money down, Rico slid out of the booth and made a slow advance toward the front of the coffee shop.

Out in the lobby they stood, plotting his doom. Rico's hands began to tremble, wanting to do it right then. The three men went outside. Rico watched their movements through the glass front doors.

The valets brought up their cars. Valentine drove a beat-up Honda, the old man a Toyota Corolla. They drove away, and Rico ran outside.

His limo was parked by the door, too big to fit into a conventional spot. He got his keys from the valet and jumped in.

Then he had to make a decision. The Honda had

turned left, heading toward the causeway, while the Toyota was going north toward Bal Harbour. Who should he follow?

The old man, Rico decided, just to get him out of the way.

Mabel awoke tied to a chair.

She was in Tony's office in the back of the house. The blinds were drawn, and she had no idea how much time had passed since the deliveryman had sent her into dreamland. By now, she imagined he'd taken Tony's big-screen TV and anything else of value and hightailed it back to the hole he'd crawled out of.

A dull, aching throb clouded her vision. The guy had looked like a creep, so why had she let him in? Because she'd wanted to believe he was all right. A character flaw for sure, but one she was not about to give up on. Most people were decent. It was the minority that spoiled things.

She wiggled her chair over to the desk and banged it with the chair arm. The phone, which sat less than a foot away, did not move. Which left what? Yelling at the top of her lungs, she decided.

She was about to do just that when the door banged open.

"Oh, my," Mabel said.

It was her attacker. He wore a pair of dirty blue jeans, no shirt, no shoes, his long, lifeless hair flopping on his shoulders. His upper torso was lean, the skin covered in angry red dots. He pulled up a chair and sat in it backwards. His breath reeked of marijuana.

"Don't scream," he said.

"No, sir."

"You're going to help me," he said.

Mabel found herself staring at his feet. The soles were black, as were all his toes. Tarzan of the swamps, she guessed. "I am?"

"The guy you work for, this Valentine guy, you need to call him, tell him to come home."

"Then what?"

He took a second too long to answer.

"Then I leave."

Mabel glanced at the phone on the desk, then shrugged her shoulders.

"That's easier said than done," she said.

"How's that?"

"He doesn't leave his cell phone on. His number is there on the desk. Call him if you don't believe me."

Her attacker scratched his chin. There was not an ounce of fat on his body, and every time he moved, his muscles redefined themselves.

"I can relate to that," he said.

He went into the kitchen and returned with two sodas that he'd taken from the refrigerator. He untied her arms and gave her one. "Okay, so we wait for him to call. Then you tell him to come home."

"That could be a while," Mabel replied.

"Your boss doesn't care about you, huh?"

The comment caught her by surprise. She'd never looked at Tony's not calling in that light. Tony was a wounded male, walking around the world without his mate of forty-plus years, and as a result now doing stupid things. But he still cared about her. Because if he didn't, she'd stop working for him, plain and simple.

That was, if she lived through this.

"He'll call eventually," she said. "May I ask you a question?"

He took a long swallow of soda. "Sure."

"What's your name?"

"Joe," he said. "My friends call me Slash."

Mabel felt a knot tighten in her chest. What kind of name was that? *You're a goner,* she thought.

"Mine's Mabel," she said.

Tony's study was the largest room in the house and contained his library of gambling books, a weighted roulette wheel, several boxes of marked cards and loaded dice, a rigged poker table from a gambling club in Gardena, California, and other assorted ephemera.

Slash searched the room, looking for money. Finding none, he began examining the equipment.

The Kepplinger holdout caught his eye, and he took it off the shelf, strapped it to his body, and tried to make it work. The device was used by hustlers to secretly hide cards up the sleeve of a jacket. Tony said it took hundreds of hours of practice to properly use it. After five minutes, Slash ripped the device off his body and threw it on the floor.

Then he noticed the painting hanging over Valentine's desk. "This must be worth something," he said, taking it down.

The painting was a reproduction of Caravaggio's *The Card Sharps*. It showed three men playing cards, two of whom were cheating. Caravaggio was famous for his paintings of saints and Bible stories, and a museum curator in Italy had hired Tony to examine the work and determine if Caravaggio knew anything about card cheating.

Tony had spent exactly one minute examining the painting. Based upon the hand positions of the young cheater with the plume in his cap, he had determined that Caravaggio was indeed in the know about his subject matter.

"It's a copy," Mabel said.

Slash put his fist through it. Then he entered the closet and started opening boxes and shaking them out on the floor. Mabel wondered how long it would be before Slash got bored and decided to kill her. Tony had said that violent people could not stay focused on a subject for any length of time, and Slash was proving this to be true. Eventually he'd run out of things to rip apart and would take out his frustrations on her.

"What the hell is this?" he asked.

"You'll have to bring it over here so I can see."

He brought the item over. It was still in its box.

Mabel stared for a moment before realizing what he'd discovered. Then had an idea.

"That's the most amazing cheating device ever made," she said.

"Cheating at what?"

"Blackjack."

Slash pulled up the chair and sat in it backwards.

"Do you play?" Mabel asked.

"Used to," he said.

"Well, the device you're holding is called the David, as in David vs. Goliath. It's a blackjack strategy computer. Have you ever heard of card-counting?"

Slash grunted in the affirmative.

"The David does the counting for you. With it, you can beat any casino in the world for thousands of dollars. I'll take that back. Millions of dollars."

"Is your boss a cheat?"

"He catches cheaters," Mabel said.

Slash emptied the box onto the desk. The David was the size of a deck of cards. With it came a battery pack, connector wires, and a special pair of men's boots with microswitches buried in the toes. There was also a keyboard that was used to "talk" to David while practicing.

"What are the boots for?"

"Each boot has a hidden microswitch," Mabel said. "You input the cards with your toes."

He tried the boots on. They fit. A knowing look spread across his face.

"You know how to work this thing?"

Tony had spent twenty minutes showing her. Mabel didn't think that really constituted knowing. Only, she wasn't going to tell him that.

"Why, yes," she said. "Yes, I do."

CHAPTER 35

Bill Higgins was reading the last section of the Sunday newspaper when Saul Hyman's rattling Toyota pulled up alongside his rental. The passenger window on the Toyota came down, and Saul said, "Don't you ever go home?"

Higgins stared at the elderly con man. He'd stayed outside Saul's condo because he didn't feel like staying in his hotel room. It was a pleasant day, and he'd read the newspaper from cover to cover while listening to a baseball game in Spanish on the radio.

"No," he said.

"Tony asked you to watch me, didn't he?" Saul asked.

"Tony who?"

"Valentine. I just saw him. I gave him enough evidence to put that scumbag Rico Blanco behind bars."

Bill put his newspaper down. Maybe hanging around hadn't been a waste of time. A bus had pulled up behind Saul's car and blared its horn. Saul shook his fist at the driver in his mirror, then said, "Want to come inside for a drink?"

"You're on," Higgins said.

Saul's condo was about what Higgins had expected. Nothing great. He'd known lots of criminals in his life. Few ended up with much when they got old. He stared at the apartment houses across the street that were blocking Saul's view of the ocean. Between them, he could see a tiny slit of blue, but just barely. Saul appeared and handed him a glass of ice tea.

"Salud," he said, clinking glasses.

Higgins took a sip. "Remember when I ran you out of Vegas?"

"Like it was yesterday," Saul said. "You were very nice about it, as I remember."

"Don't think I didn't consider roughing you up," Higgins replied.

Saul acted like no cop had ever laid a hand on him. "Why didn't you?" His guest shrugged, and he said, "Because of my size? I avoided a lot of beatings because I was small."

"That had nothing to do with it," Higgins said.

The phone rang. Saul picked it up, listened, then said, "Who sends packages on a Sunday?" He listened some more. "It's from Tony Valentine? Okay, send the guy up." He hung up, then said, "Indulge an old man. Why didn't you?"

"The guy you ripped off had been caught cheating at poker at one of the casinos," Higgins explained. "The casino looked the other way because he was a high roller. I never liked it, and figured he got his due when you fleeced him."

Saul smiled. "The arm of justice is long, huh?"

"Something like that," Higgins said.

"Would you mind telling me what you're doing in Miami with Tony Valentine?"

"None of your business," Higgins said.

The doorbell buzzed. Saul said, "Excuse me," and left the room.

Higgins raised his glass to his lips. Sunlight flooded the room, exposing the old and faded furniture, and he guessed Saul was living on Social Security, with maybe a little something stashed away. Not a lot, but enough to get by. Higgins would be up for retirement himself in a few years. The thought did not thrill him.

He heard the angry retort of a gun being fired, then Saul's scream. He jumped off the couch, the drink's ice cubes hit the floor, and his hand reached for a pistol that wasn't there. Saul came into the living room with blood pouring down his face.

"Run," he said.

Higgins didn't know which way *to* run. Saul bolted past him, followed by a man with a stocking over his face. He was holding a .45 Smith & Wesson and pointed it at Higgins. The next moment, Higgins was lying on the floor, clutching his thigh.

From the rear of the condo he heard the shattering of glass. Then the stockinged man returned. Kneeling, he went through Higgins's pockets. He rose, holding Higgins's cell phone, and left the condo.

Higgins examined the wound in his leg. Blood was spitting out like a geyser. Taking off his socks, he tied them together, then crawled into the kitchen and found a wooden serving spoon in a drawer. With the socks and the spoon he made a tourniquet, tied it an inch above his wound, and twisted it until the bleeding stopped.

He found the phone and dialed 911. He told the operator he'd been shot, and stumbled with the address.

"Just hang on," the operator reassured him.

He limped through the condo, looking for his host. In the back was a guest bedroom, and Higgins peered through the open doorway. Blood was on the floor and bedspread, and the wind blew stiffly through a busted window. The room began to spin, and he realized he was about to pass out.

He took several deep breaths, then forced himself over to the broken window and looked down. Four floors below, Saul Hyman floated in the condo's rectangular swimming pool, the water clouded with blood.

Laughing, Rico Blanco sped south on I-95. The look on the old man's face as he'd jumped through the window had been a real keeper. Terrified, but also ashamed, like he'd known deep down that this was what happened to rats. They got drowned.

He turned on the radio. The three o'clock news came on. The day was still young. That had been one of John Gotti's favorite expressions. They would steal something—a truckload of furs, or a container out of a plane at Kennedy airport, or something off the docks—and the Teflon Don would say, "The day is still young," and they'd go out and steal something else. A real taskmaster.

His cell phone rang. Rico picked it up, then realized it was the cell phone he'd just stolen. He answered it anyway. The line was filled with static.

"Hey, Bill, it's Tony Valentine," the voice said.

So the guy he'd shot in the leg was also part of this. Rico wished he'd killed him.

"You're a dead man," he told Valentine.

Then he tossed the cell phone out the window and laughed some more.

Five minutes later, his own cell phone rang. Rico looked at the caller ID. It was Jorge. Rico gritted his teeth. Jorge was never supposed to call him, especially on his cell phone where it might be overheard. Soon the ringing stopped. He drove until I-95 ended and became Dixie Highway.

He took Dixie into Coral Gables and drove to an apartment complex. The complex straddled the line between dumpy Little Havana and ultrapricey Coral Gables. That was what you got in south Miami. The haves and the have-nots.

He went to the first building and took the elevator to the fourth floor. Jorge looked surprised when he opened the door and saw Rico. Jorge was dressed in his underwear, his six-foot-six body filling the doorway.

"I told you never to call me," Rico said.

"Yeah, well, I got a problem," Jorge said, ushering him in.

The apartment was trashed, the walls covered with Miami Dolphin cheerleader posters and a naked Pamela Lee stained by food. Jorge's roommate, Lupe, slept on the couch, the TV bathing him in artificial light. He was two inches taller than Jorge, and his legs stuck comically over the edge. They went into the kitchen, and Jorge shut the door.

"It's like this," Jorge said. "I got this girlfriend, and she—"

Rico cut him short. "You need money?"

Jorge looked sheepishly at the floor. He was from Brazil, where men were supposed to act like men and not have to ask for things like money. "Yeah," he whispered.

"You knock her up?"

"Uh-huh."

"How far along is she?"

"Three months. She wants two grand for you-know-what."

Rico hid a smile. Jorge was twenty-four and talked like he was twelve. A boy in a man's body. "You'll have all your money tomorrow."

"All of it?"

"That's right. Once the game is over."

"Who we playing?"

"Duke."

Jorge's eyes lit up. The kitchen door swung in.

Lupe entered, his Frankenstein hair standing on end. God had made him menacing-looking, and he stretched his impossibly long arms as he yawned, then slapped Rico good-naturedly on the shoulder, sending him sideways into the stove.

"You gonna give Jorge heeez money?" he asked.

"Tomorrow," Rico said, clutching his arm. "You'll get all your money tomorrow. Both of you."

"What he talking about?" Lupe asked.

Jorge retrieved a basketball from behind the refrigerator and began dribbling it behind his back. Lupe had no education and relied on Jorge to fill in the blanks. They were both dumb as paint, and getting them accepted into Miami College had cost Rico a small fortune.

Jorge stopped dribbling the basketball and tossed it across the room. Missing Rico's nose by inches, it landed with a loud *fhap*! in one of Lupe's enormous palms.

"Tomorrow we play for real," Jorge said.

CHAPTER 36

Driving to the Micanopy casino with Gerry, Valentine called Bill Higgins's cell phone and got a frantic busy signal. He didn't like it when people threatened him, but his son said, "Pop, it was probably just a crossed connection. Happens all the time with cell phones."

"The guy called me a dead man."

"Welcome to south Florida."

They found Gladys Soft Wings waiting for them inside the casino's lobby. She wore her emotions on her sleeve and looked mad as hell. Tapping her wristwatch, she said. "Where have you been? The elders have been waiting a half hour. This is unacceptable."

Valentine nearly told her to take a hike. He didn't have to be doing this. He had his case against Rico. Running Bear's problems no longer figured into the equation.

"You want us to leave?" he asked.

She glared at him. "You're kidding, right?"

"Not at all. I don't need you, or your crummy attitude. And I don't need your tribe's money, which, by the way, I still haven't accepted a nickel of." Valentine thought he saw steam coming out of her ears. He ducked around the corner into the men's room. When he returned, she looked better, and he said, "Do we understand each other now?"

"Yes," she said.

"Then let's go."

She escorted them through the back doors and across the parking lot to a trailer that was serving as a courthouse until a real one was built. Inside, they found the tribe's elders sitting behind two long tables. To their left sat a shackled Running Bear. To their right, Harry Smooth Stone and the three accused dealers, also in shackles, and their lawyer. Behind them, the same six tribal policemen, still armed with Mossberg shotguns.

In the center of the room were the props Valentine had told Gladys to bring: a blackjack table, an easel with drawing paper, and Magic Markers.

"Entertain them for a few minutes," Valentine said.

She shot him a furtive glance. "What do you mean?"

"Start talking."

She did, and he picked up a Magic Marker and began writing on the easel. When he gave lectures for casino executives, he would write while someone timed him with a stopwatch. The exercise never took more than five minutes.

Four minutes later he capped the marker and glanced at Running Bear. The chief was going to be a free man soon and would go back to helping his people build a better life for themselves. It was payment enough, he decided. Gladys picked up the cue.

"Mr. Valentine is now going to explain how our blackjack dealers have been cheating our customers. Mr. Valentine has informed me that this method of cheating—which he calls Big Rock / Little Rock—is something new, which I guess means that Harry and his gang are not just your average run-of-the-mill cheats."

"Objection!" the accused's lawyer said, jumping to his feet.

"Sit down," the lead elder said.

"But—"

"Save it. Mr. Valentine, the floor is yours."

Valentine walked over to the easel and pointed at his handiwork. "Before I start, let me ask you a question. Are any of you familiar with this chart?"

The five elders put their glasses on and stared at the easel.

The elders mumbled among themselves. Finally their leader said, "No."

Valentine blew out his lungs. There were three hundred Indian casinos in the United States, and the majority of them didn't understand the basic rules of their own games.

"Okay," he said, "here's the deal. Back in 1962, a mathematician named Edward Thorp wrote a book called *Beat the Dealer: A Winning Strategy for the Game of Twenty-one*. In the book, Thorp explained how to count cards at blackjack. I'm sure you're familiar with card-counting?"

The elders nodded in unison.

"Good. Thorp also explained something called Basic Strategy. Basic Strategy is the best possible way to play blackjack. The rules of Basic Strategy differ, depending on the number of decks of cards in use. This chart is based upon the number of decks you're using in your casino." He paused as the elders stared at the chart. "This making sense?"

Again, the elders nodded.

Basic Strategy/Micanopy Two Deck Game

PLAYERS HAND	DEALER'S UP CARD									
	2	3	4	5	6	7	8	9	10	Ace
17	S	S	S	S	S	S	S	S	S	S
16	S	S	S	S	S	H	H	H	H	H
15	S	S	S	S	S	H	H	H	H	H
14	S	S	S	S	S	H	H	H	H	H
13	S	S	S	S	S	H	H	H	H	H
12	H	H	S	S	S	H	H	H	H	H
11	DD	DD	DD	DD	DD	DD	DD	DD	DD	H
10	DD	DD	DD	DD	DD	DD	DD	DD	H	H
9	H	DD	DD	DD	DD	H	H	H	H	H
8	H	H	H	H	H	H	H	H	H	H
Ace, 8	S	S	S	S	S	S	S	S	S	S
Ace, 7	S	S	DD	DD	DD	DD	S	S	H	H
Ace, 6	H	H	DD	DD	DD	DD	H	H	H	H
Ace, 5	H	H	H	DD	DD	DD	H	H	H	H
Ace, 4	H	H	H	DD	DD	DD	H	H	H	H
Ace, 3	H	H	H	H	DD	DD	H	H	H	H
Ace, 2	H	H	H	H	DD	DD	H	H	H	H
Ace, Ace	SP	SP	SP	SP	SP	SP	SP	SP	SP	SP
Ten, Ten	S	S	S	S	S	S	S	S	S	S

9,9	SP	SP	SP	SP	SP	S	SP	SP	SP	SP
8,8	SP	SP	SP	SP	SP	SP	SP	SP	SP	SP
7,7	SP	SP	SP	SP	SP	SP	H	H	H	H
6,6	H	SP	SP	SP	SP	H	H	H	H	H
5,5	DD	DD	DD	DD	DD	DD	DD	DD	DD	DD
4,4	H	H	H	H	H	H	H	H	H	H
3,3	H	H	SP	SP	SP	SP	H	H	H	H
2,2	H	H	SP	SP	SP	SP	H	H	H	H

KEY
S = STAND
H = HIT
DD = DOUBLE-DOWN
SP = SPLIT YOUR HAND

"Now, Basic Strategy is known by most black-jack players. And by *all* dealers and pit bosses. Most casinos sell laminated cards with Basic Strategy printed on them in their gift shops. Players are invited to use them at the tables."

One of the elders mumbled under his breath. Now they really felt stupid, Valentine thought.

"What this means is simply this: Basic Strategy is how the game is played. So much so, that if a player doesn't use Basic Strategy, another player will spell it out to them. Or the dealer will."

"Huh," one of the elders said.

Valentine went to the blackjack table. Taking a deck of the casino's cards out of its box, he shuffled them. The cards had been canceled, the edges cut short so they could not later be introduced into a game. He dealt three hands, two for the players, one for himself.

For the players, he dealt the cards faceup. His own hand he dealt one card faceup, the other facedown. His faceup card was a six. He pointed at it.

"To play Basic Strategy, you assume the dealer's hidden card is a ten. That's because there are more tens in the deck than any other cards. Since I have a six showing, my cards probably total sixteen, which is a weak hand. Make sense?"

"Yes," the lead elder said.

Valentine pointed at the first player's hand. It was a pair of sevens. To the elder sitting at the far end of the table, he said, "Sir, let's pretend these sevens are yours. How would you play the hand?"

The elder stared at the chart. "I'd split my cards."

"Very good." He pointed at the second hand, an eight and a two. To the same elder he said, "How would you play this hand?"

The elder again looked at the chart. "I'd double-down my bet."

"Correct. Now, both of these bets are risky. When you split pairs, you double your wager. The same thing occurs when you double-down. But according to Basic Strategy, it's a good time to do this, because the dealer is probably going to lose. Make sense?"

The elders said yes. Valentine glanced at Harry Smooth Stone and the three accused dealers. Pancakes of sweat were showing through their clothes, their lives about to be changed forever.

Picking up his hand, Valentine flipped his cards. His second card was a ten. He dropped the cards on the table so the ten was showing, the six now hidden.

"Let's pretend I just dealt the cards, only this time, instead of having a six as my faceup card, I have a ten." He pointed at the first player's sevens. To the elder on the far end of the table he said, "How would you play these cards now?"

The elder looked at the chart. "I'd take a card."

"You wouldn't split them?"

"No," the elder said.

Pointing at the eight and two, he said, "What about this hand?"

"I'd also take a card," the elder said.

"Not double-down?"

The elder shook his head.

"Why?"

"Because that's what Basic Strategy says you should do," the elder said.

Holding his two cards, Valentine walked forward. He flipped the six faceup and held it in his right hand. In his left, he held the faceup ten.

"Think of the six as a little rock, the ten as a big rock. These cards force the players into making certain decisions. The little rock hurts the dealer, while the big rock helps the dealer. Everyone with me?"

The elders nodded. So did Gladys and his son.

"So, here's how the scam works. Your dealers

296

have a tiny piece of sandpaper hidden on their clothing."

"Objection," the defendants' attorney said. "There's no evidence."

Gladys Soft Wings rose and asked that the bag of evidence found in Karl Blackhorn's locker be introduced. A tribal policeman brought the bag forward. The expired aspirin bottle was removed. The policeman opened it and displayed the piece of sandpaper.

"Oh," the attorney said.

Valentine continued. "Your dealers are sanding the edges of the cards in their games. They sand one edge if the card is a big rock, another edge if the card is a little rock. That way, they know the cards by feel.

"The cheating happens during the deal. When the dealer deals his first card to himself, he feels what it is. When the second card comes out, he feels that, as well. Then he flips the *higher* of the two cards faceup. The big rock gets exposed, and the players are forced into making bad decisions. They have no chance of winning."

"Why didn't this show up in the take?" the lead elder asked.

The take was the amount of money each game was expected to make based upon its average winning percentage. Valentine pointed a finger at Harry Smooth Stone, who had shrunk in his chair. "Harry took care of that. He was skimming the difference and keeping it for himself and his dealers."

"Surely our accountants would have picked up on this."

"Are your accountants part of the tribe?" Valentine asked.

The lead elder bristled; so did everyone else at the table. Valentine decided he'd had enough of being nice, and got up close to the guys making the decisions. "Your accountants are involved. So are several other employees, including Billy Tiger. You can't have this much cheating going on without lots of people knowing. The fact is, gentlemen, you're running a crooked operation. You need to clean up your act, or risk getting exposed and ruining it for all the other Indian casinos around the country.

"You can start by educating yourselves in the games. Then you need to change a few policies. Like hiring ex-convicts to work for you. The fact is, you're all *guilty*, either of stupidity or of not having enough common sense to police yourselves more closely."

He heard Gladys let out a deep sigh. It was obviously not the closing argument she would have chosen. The elders went into a huddle. It lasted a few minutes, then the lead elder told Harry Smooth Stone and the three dealers to rise.

"Do you have anything to say in your defense?"

Smooth Stone stared straight ahead, the others at the floor. The air conditioner made a sound like it was about to blow up. One of the tribal policemen shut it off, and the trailer turned deadly still.

"No," Smooth Stone muttered.

Neither did the others.

"Very well," the lead elder said. "By the power vested in us through the Micanopy nation, this council finds you guilty of cheating the tribe and of the murder of Karl Blackhorn. You will be turned over to the Broward County police along with the evidence presented here today, and tried in the white man's court." He paused, then added, "You are a disgrace to your forefathers. To all of us."

Then the tribal police escorted the guilty men out of the trailer.

Valentine watched them file out. The only evidence presented here today was *him*. Which meant he'd have to hang around for questioning, depositions, and a jury trial. He was going to become part of the system again, whether he liked it or not.

He could not believe how much the thought depressed him.

He went over to the defense table. His son was smiling, and Valentine realized it was the first time Gerry had actually seen what he did for a living. A tribal policeman removed Running Bear's shackles. The chief stuck his hand out, and Valentine shook it.

"Jack Lightfoot taught them this trick, didn't he?" Running Bear said.

Valentine nodded.

"By reversing the process and showing little rock, Lightfoot let the drunk Englishman win eighty-four straight hands."

"Right again," Valentine said. He watched the elders file out. None came over to thank him. He guessed they hadn't liked the scolding.

"Let's go," he said to his son.

"The chief and I would like to take you and Gerry to dinner tonight," Gladys said. "There's a wonderful restaurant on Las Olas that we think you'll like."

Valentine nearly said yes. He'd been wanting a good meal for days. Only, his head wasn't in the right place. He didn't like helping casinos anymore, even ones that helped people. Tomorrow, he might feel different, but that was tomorrow.

"No thanks," he said.

Gladys looked hurt. So did Running Bear. And his son looked as embarrassed as hell.

Valentine walked out of the trailer.

CHAPTER 37

I-95 was the usual madhouse. His son was handling the wheel and kept shooting unhappy glances at his father. Finally he couldn't hold it in, and said, "That was rude, Pop."

"Those people aren't our friends," he said. "We don't owe them anything."

"But you helped them. And they wanted to say thanks."

"I help a lot of people. They can say thanks by paying me."

"That's not my point. You didn't have to be so crummy to them." A car cut them off from the right lane, and Gerry punched his horn. "By the way, why were you so crummy to them?"

Valentine stared out the window. Back home, in his closet, was his yellow suit. In its pocket, an airplane ticket to Memphis. He took a deep breath. "Standing in front of the elders, I was reminded of why I enjoyed being on the road with Kat so much."

"Why's that?"

"Because sometimes, I hate working for casinos."

"Is this one of those times?"

301

"Yeah."

"Are you thinking about getting back together with Kat?"

What he'd been thinking about was flying to Memphis next week and watching her from the audience. Showing his support without stepping foot in the ring.

"Yeah."

"So, what you're saying is, you'd like to get away every now and then, but not shut down the business."

Valentine nodded. "That's exactly what I'm saying."

"Sounds like you need a partner."

Valentine's head snapped. Gerry momentarily took his eyes off the highway, and they stared at each other. Then his son's eyes shifted back.

"You're kidding," Valentine said, "aren't you?"

"Mabel says you have more business than you can handle. I'm going to sell the bar. If I have anything left after I pay you the fifty grand I owe you, I wanted to buy into Grift Sense."

Valentine blinked. Pay him back? Buy into his business? The past three days did not balance out the last twenty-two years, and Gerry did not sit high on his list of potential business partners.

"I figured you could teach me the ropes," his son went on. "It would be fun. And you could see me and Yolanda more, and your grandson."

Valentine blinked again. "You're going to have a boy?"

"Uh-huh. Yolanda got tested."

"You pick out a name?"

"We sure did."

"What is it?"

His son laughed. "Wait until he's born, Pop."

Valentine watched the cars hurtling past them. Gerry was offering to share his family. It sounded great, but was Valentine really ready to be around his son and Yolanda and an infant? It would be like stepping back in time, something he was not sure he wanted to do. His cell phone rang. The caller ID said UNKNOWN. He answered it anyway.

It was Bill Higgins.

"Tony," his friend said. "I've been shot."

The emergency room at Mount Sinai Medical Center was filled with the elderly and frail. Higgins, one of two gunshot victims, was in a room with two patients attached to respirators. Saul Hyman, the other gunshot victim, was down the hall.

Valentine pulled a chair next to Bill's bed. His friend's eyelids were at half-mast. Then they snapped open. "Get my chart, will you?"

Valentine got the clipboard hanging off the bed. Bill said, "Tell me what it says."

Valentine read the description of Bill's wound. The bullet had missed the bone in his leg. From what Valentine could surmise, the doctor expected him to heal without complications.

"Good," Bill said. "I wanted to be sure he wasn't lying to me."

Valentine put the clipboard back. Out in the hallway, a uniformed cop stood guarding the door. North Miami was a haven for the retired, and shootings were not the norm, like they were a few miles west and south.

Bill motioned him closer. "Rico Blanco shot us."

"You sure?"

"He was wearing a stocking, but he said something when Saul opened the door. Saul made his voice. It was that scumbag."

"When did you talk to Saul?"

"In the ambulance. They brought us over together."

"Did Rico steal your cell phone?"

"Yeah. How did you know?"

"I called you earlier. Rico answered, and threatened to kill me."

"Jesus," Bill said. "You have your gun?"

Valentine shook his head. He'd left his Sig Sauer at home.

"Get my jacket," Bill said. "It's hanging in the closet."

Valentine brought Bill's jacket over to the bed, and Bill removed his hotel room key from a pocket. "Room 784. There's a safe in the closet. My piece is in it."

"I'm not going to shoot him, Bill."

"No, you're going to run him in."

"I'm retired, remember?"

"Ex-cops count for something, and you've got

me backing you up. Gather your evidence and take him to the police. You'll be doing everyone a favor."

A doctor in a white gown accompanied by a plainclothes female detective entered the room. Valentine had introduced himself to the detective earlier, and she'd given him the green light to visit Bill. "Time's up," she said. "I need to talk to your friend."

"Combination is 7474," Bill whispered.

Valentine patted him on the shoulder. "Talk to you later."

Saul Hyman's room was at the end of the hall. A uniformed cop sat outside the door, reading a dog-eared copy of *People*. Valentine glanced through the doorway. Saul had a private, and lay on a bed with tubes running up his nose and pumping fluids into his body. He was unconscious, his arms and legs in casts, a step closer to the great beyond.

"What's the prognosis?"

"He should live."

"The guy who shot him might try again," Valentine said.

The cop stood up. "Please identify yourself."

Valentine gave him his card, then said, "He was helping me on a case."

The cop put the card in his pocket. "Can you give me a description?"

Valentine gave him Rico's description right down to the color of his mustache. Normally, he didn't care what happened to crooks, but this was different. Saul had helped him and, in doing so, nearly gotten killed. Valentine owed him.

"Don't worry," the cop said, "we'll get this guy."

Not if I get him first, Valentine thought.

CHAPTER 38

Slash shook Mabel awake early Monday morning. He let her use the bathroom, then tied her legs back to the chair. She was hungry, but that didn't concern him. He wanted to learn how to use the David card-counting computer.

The David was strapped to his waist, with two wires going down to his crotch, where they were separated by a Y-connector, with separate wires running down each pants leg to the special boots. Inside each boot were two switches, one mounted above and one below the big toe. The switches corresponded to the switches on the practice keyboard, which Mabel held in her lap.

"Show me again," he said.

Mabel stiffly nodded her head. She'd awakened feeling numb, like someone on a lifeboat who's discovered they've run out of water. She was going to die; it was just a matter of when. She removed a legal pad off the desk and pointed at the chart she'd drawn the night before.

"The David will calculate the best way to play blackjack, based upon the cards dealt. The

307

information that the computer requires is input through numerical codes.

"There are fifteen codes. Each of the switches in your boots represents one of four numbers—eight, four, two, and one. By tripping the switches separately, or in combination, you can input any number from one to fifteen. With me so far?"

Slash made a face. "Don't lecture me. How does the rest of it work?"

"I'm getting to that," Mabel said.

"Do it with the cards," he said.

Mabel looked around the study for the cards. Slash had held them last, and now they were gone. He misplaced things constantly, then lost his temper. In exasperation she said, "I don't know where you put them. We'll have to use a fresh deck."

Slash rifled the drawers in Tony's desk. In the bottom one, he found several unopened decks of cards. A pack landed in her lap.

"There," he said.

Mabel unwrapped the cards while staring at the desk. In a middle drawer she saw the open box that contained Tony's Sig Sauer semiautomatic handgun. He'd shown her the gun the first day she'd come to work for him. Did the empty box mean Tony had taken it with him? Or was it someplace in the house?

"Hurry," Slash said.

Mabel shuffled the cards. Tony spent most of his time here, so it was logical that the Sig Sauer was also here. Only, Slash had searched the room last night, and no gun had turned up.

"Come on," he said.

Mabel dealt two cards onto the desk. The first was a nine, the second a two. Slash stared at them for several seconds. Then he studied Mabel's chart.

"Fuck," he said.

"First you input a twelve to tell the computer that it's a new deal. Then input one to tell the computer how many decks are in use."

Slash wiggled his toes in the boots. "Okay," he said, still sounding unsure.

"Now input eleven to indicate the combined value of the two cards."

"Okay," he said.

Mabel dealt two cards to herself, one faceup, the other facedown. Her faceup card was a six. Slash input its value without being told. Then grinned. The David communicated in a Morse-code-type signal that was felt against the skin, and she guessed the computer was talking to him and telling him how to play his hand.

He said, "It just buzzed me twice. What does that mean?"

"Were the buzzes long or short?"

"Long."

"It means you should double-down your bet," Mabel said.

"I'm going to win the hand?"

"That's what the David is saying."

"Okay, so I double my bet. Deal me another card."

Mabel dealt him a third card. It was a ten, giving Slash twenty-one, the most desirable outcome possible. She turned her facedown card over. A ten, giving her a sixteen. The rules called for her to deal a third card for herself. It was a seven. She had busted.

"You win," she said.

Slash looked perplexed, and Mabel realized he still hadn't grasped how the David worked.

Thank God, she thought.

His Honda drew a glare from the Loews valet.

Valentine had spent the morning talking to Gerry about becoming his partner. Typical with his son, he had not thought things out—like where he planned to live, or what money he'd use to buy a car for Yolanda and the baby—and Valentine was having second thoughts when he pulled up to the hotel. As he handed over his keys, he remembered something. Gerry planned to pay him back after he sold the bar, which meant Valentine would have fifty grand to play with. Looking at the valet, he said, "Time for a new car, don't you think?"

Bill's room was on the seventh floor. Valentine opened the door with Bill's key, stuck his head in, and said, "Anyone home?" then went in.

Fresh flowers were on the night table, and a mint creased the pillow. His son pilfered it. Valentine said, "Put it back."

310

"But, Pop, you said he wasn't coming back here."

"Doesn't matter. You didn't pay for it."

Gerry put the mint back. Opening the closet, Valentine spotted the safe above the clothes rack. From his wallet he removed the slip of paper with the combination Bill had given him. He punched it in and heard the safe make a whirring sound. Inside he found a .45 Glock and a spare clip.

"So, what do you think?" his son said.

The gun felt good and solid in his hand, and he slipped it into his jacket pocket. He knew what his son was asking. *Make a commitment, Pop. Say yes right now.*

"Something's bugging me," Valentine said.

"What?"

"Why this sudden urge to go legit?"

His son didn't flinch.

"I don't want my kid knowing I was a criminal."

It was the right answer, only Valentine wasn't sold. This was Gerry he was talking to.

"One thing at a time," he said.

"What do you mean?"

"First you sell your bar, pay me back, then you relocate, then you start working for me." He paused and looked Gerry square in the eye. "As in, I'm the boss. Understood?"

His son dutifully nodded his head.

"Understood," he replied.

CHAPTER 39

Club Hedo was located on a narrow street in South Beach, the windows papered with eight-by-ten glossies of naked lovelies. TOP-LESS, BOTTOMLESS, TWO-DRINK MINIMUM. A mean-looking bouncer sat on a stool outside the door.

Ray Hicks found a parking spot at the block's end. Mr. Beauregard sat beside him, listening to the radio. Leaving the hospital, Mr. Beauregard had managed to snatch a green surgeon's hat off a passing tray, which he now wore comically on his head.

Hicks stared at his friend. Mr. Beauregard's previous owner had neutered him, but Hicks had long suspected that the surgeon's knife had not cut deep enough, and a vestige of manhood still remained. Mr. Beauregard loved women. He loved to stare at their pictures, or when they walked into Hick's trailer. The fact that he'd never acted on these impulses meant nothing. He had them, and that was the problem.

Hicks shut the radio off. Mr. Beauregard flapped his gums disapprovingly.

"We are going across the street," Hicks said. "There will be women inside. Naked women. You must not touch them. Is that understood? *You must not touch them.*"

The look on Mr. Beauregard's face was forlorn. Hicks had once found a *Playboy* in his cage. All the naked pictures had been pawed until the colors had faded. The chimp let out a sigh.

"Thank you," Hicks said.

They crossed the street, looking no stranger than any of the dozens of bizarre couples Hicks had spotted driving through South Beach. The bouncer leapt off his stool.

"You can't come in here!"

"Deal with him, Mr. Beauregard."

Even in his weakened state, Mr. Beauregard was more powerful than any man, and the bouncer sailed over the hood of a parked car and hit the pavement with a dull thud. Mr. Beauregard thumped his chest triumphantly.

The club was cavelike, the patrons bathed in fruity-colored strobe lights. Hicks walked through the beaded entrance. Up onstage, three naked women were dancing. Mr. Beauregard let out a primal yell.

It was a frightening sound, and the patrons dived under tables or into the johns or out the front door. From behind the bar, a man in a ruffled tuxedo shirt ran out, swinging a baseball bat. Mr. Beauregard took it from him, then whacked him.

"Give me that, Mr. Beauregard."

The chimp tossed him the bat. Hicks crossed the room. A smoky mirror hung on the back wall, and he hit it with the bat. Glass rained down, exposing an office on the other side. Hicks and Mr. Beauregard entered through the door.

At a desk sat a startled Hispanic with his pants off. Beneath the desk hid a naked girl.

"Where is Rico Balnco?" Hicks said.

"Get that fucking ape away from me! I'm just the DJ."

The naked girl was crying. Hicks pointed the bat in the DJ's face.

"Answer me," Hicks said.

"He'll be at the basketball game tonight," the DJ said.

"What time?"

"Seven, seven-thirty."

"Where?"

"American Airlines Arena."

"Is that nearby?"

"Up the road."

"Will he be driving his limousine?"

"It's the only wheels he's got."

"I would suggest that you avoid calling him," Hicks said.

The DJ was shaking. Mr. Beauregard had seen the girl and was drooling.

"Get him away from me!"

"Do you know what a chimp's greatest sense is?"

"No . . ."

"Smell. I could set him loose on South Beach, and he'd find you in an hour. Maybe less. And do you know what he'll do?"

The DJ didn't want to know. He removed the gold cross that was hanging around his neck, and said, "I swear to God I won't call Rico."

Back in the car, Hicks gave Mr. Beauregard a Snickers bar as a reward for not touching the girl. The chimp tossed it out the window. Seeing so much flesh had set his heart on fire, and Hicks watched him pick up his ukulele. The song that came out was instantly familiar, and one that Hicks had not heard in years.

Layla.

CHAPTER 40

The phone in Nigel's bungalow rang at four o'clock.

They were taking a nap. Candy's eyes opened first, and she stroked her lover's hair. Yesterday, she'd wanted to kill him; now she loved him more than ever. Her mother had always said that if you could love a man, then hate him, then love him again, things would usually work out. On the tenth ring, Nigel reached over her and picked up the receiver.

It was Rico.

Nigel slid out of bed and sat on the edge with the receiver pressed to his ear. "Half hour it is," he said.

Hanging up, he slapped Candy playfully on the buttocks. "Get dressed. We're going to a basketball game."

"Is this the game you're betting two hundred thousand dollars on?"

"Yes."

"I still think this is a mistake," she said, her head buried in goose down.

"What the hell," he said. "It's only money."

He went into the bathroom and shut the door. Candy slipped out of bed and pulled Tony Valentine's business card from her purse. She punched in his cell phone number. Valentine answered on the second ring.

"How would you like to put the screws to Rico Blanco?" she said.

Celebrities did not show up anywhere on time, and Rico was pacing when they met up in the lobby forty-five minutes later.

Nigel went to the front desk, and the hotel manager was summoned. The four of them went into a back room where the safe-deposit boxes were housed. Nigel produced a key and opened a box, then began removing stacks of hundred-dollar bills and dropping them into Candy's leather bag. At twenty he quit.

Rico lugged the bag to his limo. It stayed in the backseat with Candy and Nigel as Rico drove.

The demarcation line between the trendy and hip and the rest of Miami Beach happened at 26th Street, and the sidewalks were filled with garishly dressed retirees. Reaching the Arthur Godfrey Road, Rico put his indicator on.

"Don't be turned off by Bobby Jewel's store," he said as he parked. "It's a toilet, but that's how Bobby likes it."

Calling the store a toilet was being kind, Candy thought as they entered. Small and unbearably hot, the store reeked of body odor. Behind the counter

317

sat an enormous man who resembled Jabba the Hutt. Rico did the introductions.

"Nice to meet you," the bookie said.

A Cuban man came out from the back and counted the money in Candy's bag. Candy had heard that Bobby worked for a syndicate that could cover any bet. The Cuban said something and returned to the back room.

"You want to bet it all on Miami College?" Bobby said.

Nigel grunted. "Think you can handle it?"

"Sure I can handle it. Don't you want to know the spread?"

The newspaper store grew deathly still. Gamblers *always* wanted to know the spread. Bobby was wise to them, Candy realized. Nigel frowned at the bookie.

"I would assume it's a large one," he said.

"Twenty-to-one."

"Can you cover it, or should I take my action elsewhere?"

A bag of potato chips was on the counter, which Bobby kept sticking his hand into. Stuffing some into his mouth, he said, "You're on!"

Bobby explained the rules. On bets over five grand, his syndicate sent a guy over, who took the money to a hidden location, where it was counted and checked to be certain it wasn't counterfeit. Only then was the bet accepted.

Nigel agreed to the terms, and Bobby wrote him a chit.

Back in the limo, it was all Rico could do to not kiss Nigel.

"That was beautiful," he said.

The basketball game was scheduled to start at seven-thirty. Rico drove them back to the Delano, then joined Nigel in the bungalow for a drink. Candy said she wanted to take a walk on the beach. Instead, she went to the Rose Bar. It was packed.

"Over here," a voice said.

Tony Valentine sat in a corner booth, blending in with the dark wood. Candy slipped into the seat across from him.

"How did it go?"

"Bobby Jewel took the bet," she said.

A waitress came and took their drink order. Valentine stared at her. She looked different from the other day on the balcony, less harsh. Shedding her whore skin, he guessed. "Who is Miami College playing tonight?" he asked.

"Duke."

Duke was one of the best basketball teams in the nation, and a Final Four favorite. Even their benchwarmers could whip Miami College's starters. Any money on Miami College was a sucker bet.

"Doesn't Nigel suspect something is up?"

"Nigel has this computer program that says Miami is going to win."

"Did Rico give it to him?"

She smiled. "Yeah. How did you know?"

"The game is fixed, but Rico doesn't want anyone to know that. So he conned Nigel with one story, Bobby Jewel with another. If he gets caught, the police won't know which story to believe."

Their drinks came. Valentine sipped his coffee. In Candy's face he saw a struggle going on. She stared at the carbonated bubbles in her soda.

"How do I protect Nigel from getting hurt?"

"Tell him everything, including your relationship with Rico."

"He already knows I'm a hooker."

"You told him?"

"Last night. I think he'd already figured it out. I told him I'd quit for him."

"What did he say?"

"He kissed me."

They finished their drinks. Valentine wanted to tell her to get out before she got hurt. Instead, he took out his wallet and paid the tab.

"So what's going to happen?" she said.

"I'm going to go to the game tonight and figure out what Rico's doing. Then I'm going to Bobby Jewel's store. You and Nigel shouldn't come in with Rico when he comes to collect the money."

"Okay."

"I'm going to grab Rico when he comes in. Then, I'm going to take him to the police and have him arrested. I won't bring up your name or Nigel's."

"What if Rico gets violent?"

"I'll deal with it."

She reached across the table and squeezed his hand.

"A man of his word. I like that."

Valentine slipped out of the booth. "See you at the game."

CHAPTER 41

"What the hell is this?" Slash said angrily. Mabel stared at the letter in her abductor's outstretched hand. Normally, she needed her glasses to read, only the type was so large, it wasn't necessary. Slash was holding Tony's latest piece of hate mail.

"It's from U. R. Dead," she replied.

"I know. I can read some. Who sent it?"

"A person my boss put in jail."

The phone on the desk rang. It was within reach, and she imagined picking up the receiver and yelling "Help" at the top of her lungs. Slash had the same thought, and put his hand around her throat.

"Pick it up, say hello. If it's your boss, get off the line."

"I thought you wanted me to tell him to come home."

"I changed my mind."

He loosened his grip, and Mabel picked up the receiver. It was Tony.

"I'm on the other line," she said. "Call you right back."

She hung up, and Slash shook the threatening letter in her face.

"Your boss is a cop."

"He's retired."

"Cops don't fucking retire," he said contemptuously. "Someone threatens him, he's going to be prepared. It's called survival."

She watched Slash tear through Tony's study, pulling out drawers and turning them upside down, as well as boxes of gaffed gambling equipment. Soon, half of Tony's things were lying on the floor, the room a total shambles.

Slash had dropped the U. R. Dead letter in her lap, and Mabel stared at it long and hard before she made the connection. Slash had figured out that there was a gun in the house, probably in this very room. And he didn't know where it was.

Taking 595 west into the Everglades, Gerry felt the skin on his arms start to tingle. He'd grown up in Atlantic City, later moved to Brooklyn, and was not accustomed to seeing alligators sunning themselves by the roadside. The locals called them gators. Up north, *gators* was slang for pimp shoes, and cost a thousand bucks a pair.

He pulled into the casino's parking lot. It was full, the poor getting poorer. Driving around back, he parked his rental near the trailers. After the trial, he'd seen Running Bear walk into one of these trailers, ready to go back to work, not holding a grudge against the elders or anything like that. Gerry had been impressed as hell.

He knocked on Running Bear's door, then stepped back. The chief emerged a moment later, his long shadow touching the hood of Gerry's car.

"It's Gerry, isn't it?" the chief said.

"That's right."

"What can I do for you, Gerry?"

"Something has come up."

"What's that?"

"My father wants to bust the guy who killed Jack Lightfoot. He'd like you and me there backing him up."

Running Bear considered the request, then went into the trailer. When he came out, he was wearing his hat. "Let's go," he said.

Valentine had grown up loving college basketball. Then one day, five star players at Seton Hall University in New Jersey had gotten caught shaving points. Overnight, the college had become known as Cheating Hall, and his love affair with the game had ended.

Miami College played their games at American Airlines Arena, the same auditorium used by the city's pro team. Tonight's game against Duke was sold out, and he begrudgingly approached a scalper standing outside the front doors.

"Need a ticket?" the man squawked.

Fifty bucks got him first row, second section. At the door, a security guard made him open the paper bag he was carrying. Valentine showed him the binoculars he'd just bought and was let inside.

The arena was packed, the crowd drinking beer and having a good time. Duke was on an eleven-game winning streak, and many fans were wearing their blue and white colors. Valentine settled into his seat and removed the binoculars. The two teams came out onto the court and began shooting warm-ups.

He scoured the faces at courtside. Candy's red hair stuck out like a flag. She was sitting directly beneath the basket. To her left sat Nigel. To his left, Rico. The arena was warm, yet Rico was wearing a sports coat. Packing heat, he guessed.

The national anthem was played, and then the game got under way.

Years ago, he'd gotten his hands on a New Jersey Casino Control Commission report on sports betting. At the time, New Jersey's governor wanted to legalize sports books and compete with Nevada in this lucrative market.

The commission had painted an ugly picture of the business. Through a variety of unsavory sources, they'd learned of an NFL playoff game being fixed, a semifinal match at Wimbledon that was thrown, point-shaving in both college basketball and the pros, scores of rigged boxing matches, and a dozen racetracks where it was common for jockeys to allow a rider having a bad streak to win a race.

What all of these events had in common was that

money was being wagered on them—several billion dollars a year—and the commission had concluded that New Jersey's casinos would be putting themselves at risk by entering the business.

By halftime, Duke was up by four.

It was an ugly game, with Duke having a difficult time getting off their shots. The players looked frustrated, and so did their coach. He was a black guy with a trigger temper, and he screamed at his team as they ran off the court.

Valentine went to a concession stand. Five bucks bought a program and a soda. Walking back to his seat, he read the team players' biographies while slurping his drink. All of Duke's players came from the Midwest. Miami College's players hailed from Florida, except for two—Jorge Esteban from Brazil, and Lupe Pinto from the Dominican Republic. Both were freshmen, and both were starters.

The teams were back on the court, taking warmups. Reclaiming his seat, Valentine removed his binoculars and searched the court until he found the two foreign players. Both had shaved heads, making it hard to tell how old they were. As they hit basket after basket from different spots on the court, a thin smile creased his face.

CHAPTER 42

Mr. Beauregard's ukulele had gone silent. Hicks was driving through Miami searching for American Airlines Arena and saw the chimp rub his stomach. On average, he consumed eight pounds of food a day, and Hicks guessed he was starving.

"Hamburgers, Mr. Beauregard?"

Mr. Beauregard clapped his hands excitedly. He loved hamburgers. Downtown Miami was fast-food heaven, and soon Hicks was sitting in the drive-through at a Burger King. At the squawk box, he was greeted by a sultry Latino voice.

"Welcome to Burger King. Would you like to try today's special?"

"What is that?"

"Two quarter-pound bacon cheeseburgers covered in special sauce for a dollar ninety-nine."

Mr. Beauregard jumped up and down in his seat. He loved the special sauce.

"Give me ten," Hicks said. "And a small fries."

They ate in the car. Mr. Beauregard was not keen on bread products and tossed the buns out the window. Soon a security guard came out of the restaurant. He was a Cuban macho man and glanced menacingly at them, then pointed at the buns lying on the ground. "They teach you this at home?"

Mr. Beauregard stuck his head out the window and snarled. The guard recoiled in fear. Hicks jumped out of the car, fearful he might call the police.

"Please excuse my friend."

"Your friend?"

"I am the owner of a carnival."

"Is he . . . dangerous?"

"My friend, this is the world's smartest chimpanzee. Do you like music?"

"Well . . . yeah," the guard said.

"Mr. Beauregard, play for the gentleman."

Mr. Beauregard took his ukulele off the floor, and the music that came out was Spanish-sounding, like calypso. "Holy shit," the guard said.

"He's good, isn't he?" Hicks said.

"It's my favorite song," the guard replied.

In the fourth quarter, the game heated up.

Miami College began to play like they were possessed, and with five minutes left in the game, the score was even.

Since the half, Valentine had watched Jorge and Lupe exclusively with his binoculars. They were an unusual pair of athletes. Jorge was constantly busting up plays and stealing the ball from Duke's forwards. He rarely shot the ball, preferring to pass to one of his teammates and let him get the glory.

Lupe, whose statistics in the program were terrible, was playing like he was possessed. He passed, he stole, he dunked, and he had more rebounds than anyone on the court. Two of Duke's players were trying to cover him, leaving a Miami College player wide open.

With two minutes left in the game, Miami College took the lead for the first time. The crowd rose, screaming like it was the greatest thing they'd ever seen. Valentine knew better. Miami College could have easily been ahead by ten points. Jorge and Lupe were playing below speed, a pool hustler's term for playing just slightly better than your opponent.

They were pros.

"Your father hurt Gladys Soft Wings's feelings," Running Bear said.

Gerry gripped the wheel. He'd read somewhere that I-95 ran over eighteen hundred miles and that the Miami stretch, which was less than ten of those miles, was the most dangerous. When they were free of the madness, he said, "Please apologize to her for me."

"Your father needs to do that himself," the chief said.

"I wouldn't hold my breath."

"Why?" the chief said. "Is your father above apologizing?"

Gerry pulled the car into a no-parking zone a hundred yards from the entrance to American Airlines Arena and threw it into park. Turning, he looked the chief in the eye.

"It's like this. My father's father was an abusive drunk who beat up my grandmother. When my father got old enough, he threw his father out of the house. Then he spent the next twenty years trying to make up to him for doing it."

"Did he?"

"No," Gerry said.

"So he carries around a lot of guilt."

"Yes," Gerry said.

Running Bear was about to say something, but then the front doors to the arena burst open, and a crowd of maniacal fans came pouring out.

Duke self-destructed in the final two minutes and lost by seven points. At the buzzer, screaming Miami College students stormed the court, cut down the nets, and carried their team out of the arena on their shoulders.

Through his binoculars, Valentine watched Rico, Nigel, and Candy leave. He hurried to the lobby and through the front doors, saw them standing in the VIP parking area.

He walked outside, and a car parked across the street flashed its brights. It was Gerry, with Running Bear in the passenger seat. He crossed and got in.

Rico's limousine pulled out of VIP parking a

minute later. His son threw his rental into drive and cut into traffic.

"You figure out what Rico's doing?" his son said.

"Yeah. He brought in two pros, enrolled them in Miami College, and paid them to play like bums until this afternoon."

Gerry nearly rear-ended the SUV filled with fans in front of them. "Miami College won? Do you know what the odds were on that happening?"

"Twenty-to-one," Valentine said.

Gerry slapped the wheel. "You knew this was going down, didn't you?"

"I knew the game was fixed, if that's what you're asking me."

"Why didn't you tell me?"

Valentine leaned forward so he was hanging between the seats. He shot a glance at Running Bear, who seemed amused by this exchange. He looked at his son, who wasn't.

"Just drive," he said. "Okay?"

Ray Hicks had parked in the municipal lot two blocks away from the center. Leaving Mr. Beauregard in the car with the Ultimate Rhythm and Blues Cruise on the jazz station, he'd walked to American Airlines Arena and waited for the crowd to come out. Rico Blanco and his two friends were among the last people to emerge. Rico looked happy. He wouldn't look that way for long.

Hicks ran back to his car. Mr. Beauregard had

jacked up the radio and was clapping his hands to an old Sam Cooke song. Hicks pulled out of the lot, handed the attendant his ticket, then waited impatiently while the attendant figured how much he owed.

"Just keep it," he said, throwing the attendant a twenty.

Hicks raced down the street. Rico's black limousine whisked past his car, going in the opposite direction. In his mirror, Hicks saw the limo hang a left at the light.

There was no place to turn around. Pulling into an alley, Hicks waited as dozens of cars whizzed past on the street. Mr. Beauregard grew agitated and played hurry-up music on his ukulele like in the old Westerns.

Hicks tapped his fingers on the wheel. There were times when his friend did not amuse him, and this was one of them.

CHAPTER 43

Arthur Godfrey was a famous 1950s radio show host. One day, out of the blue, he fired his longtime sidekick on the air. Candy's mother had told her about it, and Candy had hated Arthur Godfrey ever since, even though she knew nothing else about him.

Rico parked in front of Bobby Jewel's newspaper store on the Arthur Godfrey Road. It was a beautiful night, the sidewalks teeming with blue-hairs. Candy put her hand on her stomach and groaned. Nigel glanced her way.

"Are you all right, my dear?"

"I . . . feel sick."

"There's ginger ale in the cooler," Rico said from the front. "My mother always said carbonated bubbles were good for a bellyache."

Candy feigned discomfort, then shut her eyes. Nigel petted her arm.

"You can stay in the car," he said.

"Only if you stay with me," she said.

"Of course," Nigel said.

Candy slit her eyes just enough to see Rico's reflection in the mirror. He was glaring at her, his teeth clenched. He wanted all three of them to go in, so Bobby Jewel wouldn't be suspicious.

"Up to you," Rico said.

Candy heard him get out of the car, and opened her eyes. Rico stood in front of the newspaper store, banging on the glass. Bobby Jewel appeared, scowling, and let him in. Candy heard a loud tap on the window on Nigel's side of the car. Her boyfriend jumped an inch off the seat.

Tony Valentine stood outside. He had a no-nonsense look on his face.

"Is that the man who saved your life?" Nigel asked.

"Yes."

"He looks rather mean."

Candy didn't think he looked mean at all. Just a man who knew what he wanted. She watched Valentine walk down a narrow alleyway next to the newspaper store. Then she got out of the limo and held out a hand to her boyfriend.

"Better hurry," she said.

Bobby looked like he'd been run over by a truck. His hair stuck straight up, and his shirt was drenched with sweat. He flopped onto his stool behind the counter.

"Some game, huh," Rico said.

"Missed it."

"Duke lost!"

The bookie picked up a towel and wiped his face. "I've got some bad news for you."

"You do?"

"Yeah."

Rico found himself looking around the store. The place was trashed. Then he saw something on the door to the back room that made his heart stand still.

Blood.

He edged closer. The stain was elephant-shaped. He placed the tip of his shoe against the door and pressed in. On the other side, one of Bobby's Cubans lay on the floor, the back of his head removed by a bullet. His co-worker was slumped over a bank of telephones. Rico let the door slowly close.

"All of us got hit," Bobby said. "The store in West Palm, Pompano, and me. I was across the street getting a pastrami sandwich when it happened." He stared at the door and shook his head. "I loved those two guys, you know?"

"You call anyone?" Rico asked.

"Guys I work for are sending a cleanup crew over."

"I'm really sorry."

"Thanks."

Rico pointed outside. "I've got Nigel Moon with me. He wants to know when he can pick up his money."

"Tell him he'll get his two hundred grand tomorrow."

"*His what?*"

"You heard me. The guys that ripped me off stole everything."

"But we made a bet."

"I called it off. Didn't you get my messages?"

Rico took his cell phone from his pocket. He'd put the phone on mute at the basketball game. It said he'd gotten three messages. He hit retrieve and heard Bobby say, "It's Bobby. I just got robbed. The bet is off. Call me."

The cell phone hit the counter.

"But we made a bet."

Bobby shrugged. "So make another one."

Six months of planning down the toilet, Rico thought. *Six months of my life.* He reached into his jacket and drew his beloved .45 Smith & Wesson. "Get up."

Bobby swallowed hard. "You fixed the game, didn't you?"

"Move the legs, fatso."

"I called you, man . . ."

"I trusted my future to you."

Bobby got off his stool. He walked over to the bloodstained door and stopped.

"Don't make me go in there."

Rico pumped two bullets into him, thinking of Jorge and Lupe and Jorge's pregnant girlfriend and the rent on the bar and all the other payments he was going to miss, and shot Bobby twice more for good measure. Bobby lurched forward, taking down the door.

"Ahhh," someone groaned.

Rico dragged Bobby away, then lifted the door. A dazed Tony Valentine lay beneath, clutching a

Glock. Rico took his gun away. Then it hit him what had happened.

"You did this," he said.

Gerry stood on the sidewalk with Running Bear, ten steps away from Bobby Jewel's place. The sidewalks were teeming with retirees, the cool night air bringing them out from their airconditioned dwellings. He checked the time. A minute had passed since his father had gone around back. His father had said if he didn't come out in two minutes with Rico, that Gerry and Running Bear should go in.

"You hear that?" the chief said.

"No. What?"

"Sounded like a gun."

Gerry hesitated. What should he do? What would his father do? Go in, he thought. He started to, then saw his father stagger out of the store with Rico behind him. His father's hands were tied behind his back, and he looked dazed. Seeing them, Rico raised his gun.

"Back off," he said.

Gerry started to move, and Running Bear stopped him.

"He'll kill him," the chief said.

Twenty people were on the sidewalk, yet no one was paying attention. They were seeing it, but not seeing it. Gerry backed up and watched Rico open the back door of the limo and shove his father inside. People kept walking right by.

"He's going to kill him anyway," Gerry said.

Running Bear pulled him backwards. "Get in the car," he said.

They jumped in. The Honda was facing east; so was Rico's limo. Rico pulled out of his spot. Gerry followed him, the traffic heavy.

At the light, Rico did a crazy U-turn in the intersection, his tires screeching. The limo had a wide turning radius, and he hit a newspaper machine and sent it through a plate glass window. Gerry made his own U-turn and spun out the Honda.

Running Bear jumped out and ran after Rico's limo, which had gone a hundred yards, only to become stuck in traffic. The chief's strides were long and easy, and as he got close to the limo, he went airborne.

His body made a loud *bang* as he landed on the limo's roof. Traffic started to move. Rico tried to shake him by driving all over the street. Running Bear punched out the driver's window, then drew a knife from his belt and plunged it into Rico's arm.

Rico let out a scream that could have raised the dead, and finally—*finally*—the old geezers shuffling down the sidewalks woke up from their comas.

The limo veered drunkenly from left to right. Running Bear hung on for half a block, then was thrown to the ground.

Moments later, Gerry was helping him stand up. The chief had twisted his ankle and had to lean on him to remain upright. Gerry stared at the bloody knife in his hand.

"He won't go far," Running Bear said.

CHAPTER 44

Slash had torn the house apart.

Bound and gagged, Mabel watched him destroy the study, then listened as he moved through the house. Shelves were pulled out, glassware broken, the heirlooms and sentimental bric-a-brac that Tony and Lois had brought from Atlantic City tossed around like so much junk. Seeing him destroy things was hard. Hearing it was somehow worse.

When he returned, he was holding a sandwich. He untied her hands and removed the gag. "You want this?"

"Yes," she said.

"Where did he hide the gun?"

"Tony must have taken it with him."

"You better not be lying."

The sandwich was baloney with mayo and tasted as good as anything she'd ever put into her mouth. Slash pulled up a chair and attached the David to his waist, then fitted the special boots on his feet.

"One more time," he said.

The playing cards were on the desk, and Mabel picked them up. She shuffled, then dealt two hands.

Slash's cards were a six and a three. He wiggled his toes in his boots.

"The David just gave me two clicks," he said.

"That means double-down on your bet," Mabel said.

"Okay. Deal me another."

Mabel dealt him a ten, making his total nineteen. Mabel's hand was a seventeen, which the rules did not allow her to draw on. Slash had won.

They played another round.

"The David gave me a long buzz," he said.

Mabel had written the David's code on the pad. A long buzz meant stand, a short click meant take a hit, a double click meant double-down, and a short buzz meant split your hand. Slash hadn't consulted the pad once, preferring to lean on her.

"Stand," Mabel said.

He won again. He let out a whoop that sent a shiver down Mabel's spine.

"I'm going to be rich," he declared.

Yes, Mabel thought, *you are*. He was going to succeed, not because he was skilled at operating the David, but because he did not fit the profile of the cheaters who did. Those people were usually white males between the ages of thirty and fifty who spoke articulately and dressed well. Slash was none of those things, and would fly right by even the most seasoned surveillance personnel.

Only one thing was standing in his way. Her.

Rico's arm was bleeding all over the seat. He'd

looked at the wound and not seen any bone and decided that was a good thing. Driving north on I-95, he'd settled into the right lane and hit the cruise control, then used his knees to steer while making a makeshift bandage out of some paper napkins and rubber bands he found in the armrest. He glanced in his mirror at Valentine sitting in the backseat.

"Show me your hands," Rico said.

Valentine turned sideways and lifted his arms. His wrists were tied together with twine, his hands clean.

"I'm going to make an example of you," Rico said.

"Why's that?"

"You fucked up the greatest score I've ever had."

"I did?"

"You killed Bobby's Cubans and stole my money."

"Those Cubans were dead when I walked in."

"Don't play stupid with me. You and Gerry ripped off Bobby Jewel. The money you stole was going to net me four million bucks. Think about it when I gouge your eyes out."

"You don't have the guts," his passenger said.

Rico started to draw his .45, and the limo swerved into the left lane. Horns blared and tires screeched. Rico realized that was exactly what Valentine wanted—to draw attention, and get someone to punch 911 on a cell phone. He straightened the wheel, and the exertion sent a burning sensation through his arm that made him want to scream.

"You're history," he said through clenched teeth.

Ray Hicks had given up trying to find Rico's limo.

There was too much traffic on I-95 and not enough horsepower in his engine to race around in the blind hope of spotting him. Better to come back another day and settle this, he decided. He headed north toward Davie.

Crossing the Broward County line, Hicks saw smoke coming off the highway. A quarter mile ahead, a black limo was weaving drunkenly between lanes. Hicks floored his accelerator, and soon passed signs for Hallandale, Pembroke Pines, and Hollywood. Just north of Hollywood, the limo headed west on 595. Mr. Beauregard, who'd been aimlessly plucking chords, broke into the *William Tell Overture*. The music sent an icy chill down Hicks's back.

Soon they were in the last undeveloped area of Broward County and heading toward the Everglades. Hicks saw the limo's indicator come on. Rico was going onto the Micanopy Indian reservation.

Hicks followed him.

Mr. Beauregard continued to play chase music. It made Hicks's heart race, and he had almost convinced himself the chimp was psychic, when he realized how foolish that was. Mr. Beauregard's gift was sensing human emotions—like anger and fear—and picking the appropriate music to accompany those feelings. Had Mr. Beauregard truly been psychic, Hicks would have sold his carnival and put him on television.

CHAPTER 45

Slash had graduated from Mabel's school of blackjack cheating. He had gone through an entire deck of cards without once having to ask Mabel a single question, the codes and computer signals now second nature.

"Well," he said, "I guess that's it."

Mabel felt his eyes burning her face. She was holding the cards in her hands.

"Let's play another round," she suggested.

"I'm done," he said. "You're a good teacher."

Her throat went dry. Slash's face had taken on a visceral quality. She tossed the cards onto Tony's desk. They scattered, and she found herself staring at a book lying next to the phone. Tony was an avid reader—westerns, mysteries, anything by Elmore Leonard—only, she'd never seen him reading *this* book. She stared at the spine. It was Dostoyevsky's *Crime and Punishment*.

She thought about how she was going to do this. Thought about it calmly, because that was what Tony had told her to do in tough situations. She remembered the gang of hustlers he'd caught past-posting at roulette. Mabel had watched the

343

tape several times, but had not seen what the gang was doing until Tony had pointed it out. While two members distracted surveillance by yelling and banging the table, a third member—a petite old lady—had surreptitiously placed a late bet. The scam had flown right by everyone, and all because the old lady had *slowly* put her late bet on the table. So slowly, that no one had noticed.

"And you are a wonderful student," Mabel said.

"You think so?"

"I'd give you an A."

Slash grinned, and Mabel calmly reached across the desk and removed Dostoyevsky's masterpiece from its resting place. Placing the book in her lap, she flipped it open. As she'd expected, it was hollow, and she removed the Sig Sauer resting inside and aimed it at Slash's hairless chest.

Her abductor stared down the gun's barrel. He smiled, exposing two crooked rows of teeth. "You got me," he said.

"Yes, I do," she said.

"You're a cagey old broad."

"Flattery will get you nowhere."

Slash lifted his arms as if to stretch, and Mabel twitched the gun's barrel.

"Don't move," she said.

"Wouldn't dream of it," he said.

Yes, you would, Mabel thought. *I'm a sixty-five-year-old woman with lousy vision. If you jump me—and I'm sure that's exactly what's going through your deranged mind—I might get a round off. Wounded, you'd still be strong enough to strangle the life out of me.*

Mabel aimed the gun directly at her abductor's heart. It took Slash a few seconds to comprehend.

Forgive me, God.

Slash leapt out of his chair. But by then, Mabel had already squeezed the trigger.

As Rico pulled off 595, Valentine had understood.

Like any other predatory creature, murderers often returned to places they believed safe. Rico was taking him to the swamps, to the place where he'd dumped Jack Lightfoot, and where Splinters had tried to shoot Candy.

Rico drove down the unlit road for a few miles, then pulled over. The shoulder was muck, and the wheels sank a few inches before coming to rest. He got out, then flung open Valentine's door. "Move," he barked.

It wasn't easy to walk with his hands tied behind his back, and Valentine stumbled to find his legs, his body still feeling the effects of having the fat guy in the newspaper store pancake him. There was a full moon, and the swamp was alive with animal sounds.

Rico took out a handkerchief and tied it over Valentine's eyes.

"Walk," he said.

Valentine's feet found the path, and he took a few uncertain steps. He felt a gun barrel press against his left ear, then heard a deafening roar.

The pain was white and traveled through his brain like a hot stake. He fell forward, his head wrenched to one side, away from the burning sensation that consumed the left half of his face. Lying on the ground, he thought about Gerry, and how angry his son was going to be when his will was read.

"Get up," Rico barked.

Valentine staggered to his feet and stumbled down the path.

Rico shoved him. "This way."

Valentine went to his right. Soon his feet found a clearing, the swamp sounds more prevalent than before. Rico stuck the .45's barrel into his spine.

"On your knees," he said.

Ray Hicks came around a bend in the road and saw Rico's limo parked on the shoulder. He flashed his brights, then parked behind the limo and shut off the engine. Rolling down his window, he heard a pair of men's voices coming from one of the trails.

Inside the glove compartment was a pearl-handled revolver he'd won in a poker game, and a Walther PPK. He removed the Walther and checked the chamber to ensure it was loaded. He watched Mr. Beauregard lower his window. Something in the swamps was calling the chimp, and Hicks imagined him running away.

"Mr. Beauregard, I am ordering you to stay here."

Mr. Beauregard stared out the window, ignoring him.

"You will stay here."

The chimp sighed. Hicks got out of the car. From the trunk he removed a flashlight, tested it, then cautiously headed down the path.

The swamp was jungle-thick with vegetation, and the flashlight's beam caught elephant ears and tree vines that reminded him of the Louisiana bayous. As a boy, he'd spent countless hours in the low country with his granddaddy, learning to hunt and fish and all the other things it took to become a man. It had been a special time, and thinking about it had a calming influence on him.

He came to a fork in the path. The men's voices had stopped, the swamp deathly still. Which way should he go? He was left-handed, so that was the direction he chose.

He walked a quarter mile, then came to a dead end. He kicked at the ground in frustration, then heard a gunshot pierce the still night air.

Hicks retraced his steps, then went down the other path to a clearing. His flashlight found a figure lying on the ground. It was a man with a bloody hole in his back. Beside him was another man, blindfolded and on his knees.

Hicks got closer. The blindfolded man had been shot, and his arms appeared tied behind his back. Hicks circled him, just to be sure.

"Is someone there?" the blindfolded man said.

347

"Yes," Hicks said.

"Is he dead?" the blindfolded man asked.

Hicks's flashlight found Rico's face. He gave him a good kick. Rico was as dead as a dog lying on the side of the road. Hicks stared at the blindfolded man with blood pouring down his face.

"Yes, he is," Hicks said.

The man started to weep. Hicks considered untying him, then decided not to. For all he knew, the man was a criminal and would try to kill him.

"Please," the man said, "call the police."

Shaking, Hicks got behind the wheel of his car. He dialed 911 on his cell phone, then smelled sulfur. He looked at Mr. Beauregard, then the open glove compartment. Reaching in, he touched the pearl-handled revolver. It was warm.

A police operator came on the line. Hicks struggled to find his voice. He gave the operator his location and said there had been a killing. The operator said a cruiser was on 595 and would be right there.

"Thank you, ma'am," he said.

Hanging up, Hicks tried to make sense of what had happened. If Mr. Beauregard had been following him, he would surely have picked up Hicks's scent and followed his owner. Only he hadn't. He'd gone looking for Rico. Had he somehow known another man's life hung in the balance?

"I wish you could talk," Hicks said.

A police cruiser appeared in his mirror, its bubble

flashing. Digging a handkerchief from his pocket, he wiped down the pearl-handled revolver and replaced Mr. Beauregard's prints with his own. The police would want to know exactly what had happened. *Keep it simple*, he thought. He started to get out.

Mr. Beauregard picked up his ukulele and became lost in his music. Hicks felt his eyes well up with tears, the song instantly familiar.

"I'll be damned," he said.

My Old Kentucky Home. It had been his grand-daddy's favorite.

CHAPTER 46

"Let me guess," Saul Hyman said. "You cut your ear off and sent it to a broad."

It was ten days later, and Valentine stood in the foyer of Saul's condo, glad to see that the old con man was strong enough to be in a wheelchair, the casts on his arms and legs not slowing him down.

"Can I come in?"

A black male nurse rolled the wheelchair backwards. Valentine entered the condo's living room and stared at the sliver of ocean view. He felt bad for Saul; from the vantage point of his chair, he probably couldn't see the water.

He sat on the couch, and the nurse rolled the wheelchair up so Saul was a few feet away. Then the nurse left.

"When I hit eighty, I want one of those," Valentine said.

"Where's your son?"

"Up in New York, selling his bar."

"You going to let him come work for you?"

"One thing at a time," Valentine said.

Saul smirked. "So how bad is the ear? You going to have a plastic surgeon make you a fake one?"

Valentine hadn't come to Saul's condo to talk about the shredded stump on the side of his head. He put a finger on the rubber wheel of Saul's chair and brought the old con man a few inches closer. "Did you ever have an epiphany?"

"I don't think Jews have those," Saul said.

"I did. It happened while I was blindfolded and waiting for Rico to put a bullet in me. I thought I was going to die, and then I had one."

"An epiphany?"

"Uh-huh."

"What was it like?"

"Everything suddenly becomes clear."

"Like Joan of Arc?"

"Did she have them?"

"In the movie, yeah."

"Yeah, like Joan of Arc."

"You going to share it?"

Valentine lowered his voice. The nurse, he guessed, hadn't gone far, and he saw no point in spoiling the relationship. "You're Victor Marks."

Saul laughed like it was the funniest thing he'd ever heard. Valentine placed his hand onto the arm of Saul's wheelchair. "I can't believe I didn't see it sooner. You're in south Florida, so is Victor. All your scams used the mark's money, so did Victor's. And when Rico came here to kill you, you told Bill Higgins that you recognized Rico's voice, even though he was wearing a stocking, and you've never met him before."

The blood drained from Saul's sunken cheeks.

351

He began to look remorseful, and Valentine didn't think it was an act. Almost dying brought out the best in most people.

"Out with it," Valentine said.

Saul lifted his head. "Six months ago, Victor calls from Palm Beach. He tells me he's got colon cancer, maybe two weeks to live. He says, 'I've got a major scam going. I want you to take over.' I said, 'Why not?'"

"Was this the game show scam?"

Saul nodded. "I never made the kind of money Victor did, always got the crumbs. I figured it would be easy. So Victor checks out, and I dye my hair and grow a mustache, and I become him."

"No one noticed the difference?"

"No one knew what Victor looked like, or his voice. And the staff at the Breakers turns over every few months. It was easy."

"So you scammed *Who Wants to Be Rich?* and got hooked up with Rico."

"Biggest mistake of my life," Saul said.

"You didn't know he was a killer."

"No, no. I thought he just wanted to learn the rackets."

"So you taught him."

Saul leaned over and touched Valentine's hand. "This is going to sound stupid."

"What's that?"

"I always wanted a son. A relationship like you have with your boy."

"And Rico was that to you."

"Yes."

Valentine believed him. But it didn't change the words that came out of his mouth.

"There's going to be an investigation, and your name is going to come up. I can't protect you, Saul. I know you've suffered, but the truth still has to come out. Other people's reputations depend upon it."

Saul took a Kleenex from the pocket of his robe and wiped at his eyes. He was crying, and Valentine took the Kleenex out of his hand. No onion inside. He rose from the couch. "My guess is, you've got a week, maybe longer, to hightail it out of the country."

"In my condition?" Saul said belligerently.

"It's up to you."

"What about my condo?" Saul said. "And my clothes, and my car, and all my things? I can't just leave them, can I?"

Valentine shrugged his shoulders.

"Why can't you leave me out of it?" Saul said.

"It doesn't work that way."

"Still a damn cop, aren't you?"

"You've got no one but yourself to blame."

Saul gave him a murderous look. "For what? Giving a guy some advice and passing along a few pearls I learned during my lifetime? Is that a crime?"

Valentine crossed the living room and paused to glance out the window a final time. It wasn't much of a view, the line of blue so small that he couldn't even make out the waves, but it was still there. Waking up to it every day, Saul Hyman, a dirt-poor kid from Coney Island, had probably felt like the king of the world.

Saul had turned awkwardly in his wheelchair and was staring at him. "Tony, please, don't do this to me."

"Have a nice trip," Valentine said.

CHAPTER 47

The bride wore a fantasy ball gown with dangling crystals on the strapless bodice, a silk-organza flair skirt, and a cathedral-length train. She was beautiful in a way that only brides can be, and as she walked down the aisle holding Valentine's arm, the crowd of well-wishers let out a collective *ahhh*.

A smile lit up Valentine's face. At first, the idea of giving Candy away had not thrilled him. What if he slipped around the other guests and said something inappropriate about her past? Only, Candy had begged him.

"You're the perfect person," she'd said.

"I am?" he'd said.

"Yes."

"And why is that?"

"Because I have no secrets from you."

How was he supposed to refuse a request like that? So he'd gone to the rehearsal and let a polite little man fit him for a tuxedo—his first since his own wedding—and gotten his hair done by a stylist so his missing ear wouldn't be too noticeable. And now here he was, leading Candy to her new life and a new beginning.

355

Nigel and the minister waited at the end of the aisle. Valentine had gone to Nigel's bachelor party and tossed away his feelings about egotistical rock-and-roll musicians. Nigel was a square joe. He would make Candy happy. Valentine was sure of it.

The ceremony was just right, the minister's comments heartfelt. Nigel surprised everyone by reciting an English wedding ballad that had been in his family for five hundred years. Then Candy recited a poem about life's choices that had been written by her sister, who'd died in a car accident long ago. Then the minister made everyone stand up.

Nigel said, "I do," and Candy said, "I do," and a dozen waiters standing in the back of the Delano's dining room popped bottles of Moët & Chandon. A toast was made, and a rock-and-roll band hiding behind a curtain broke out in a rousing version of the Rolling Stone's *Satisfaction*.

Valentine crossed the room and found his date. She wore a stunning twin-textured peach gown. He had paid more for it than he'd ever paid for a piece of clothing for his late wife, and he'd felt guilty buying it. But he needed to tell her how he felt, and something expensive was a good way to start.

"Want to dance?"

"Of course."

He found an empty spot on the corner of the dance floor. When he tried to engage her, she said, "I have a question for you."

"What's that?"

"Do you miss her?"

He acknowledged that he did.

"Do you mind telling me how you ended it?"

"Is that important?"

"To me it is," she said.

It hadn't been easy. He'd flown to Memphis and taken her out to dinner, and they'd talked several times on the phone after that. He still liked her, only the chemistry between them had changed. When he'd told her he wouldn't be seeing her again, she hadn't objected.

"I thanked her for helping me get my priorities straight," he said.

"You really said that?"

The band had broken into a slow number. It was too good to pass up, and Valentine and his neighbor glided like a pair of angels across the dance floor.

"I sure did," he said.

ABOUT THE AUTHOR

JAMES SWAIN, a gambling expert, is the author of *Grift Sense* and *Funny Money*. Swain is considered one of the best card handlers in the world. He lives with his wife in Odessa, Florida, where he is currently working on his fourth novel featuring Tony Valentine. Visit his Web site at www.jimswain.com.